EARLY DAWN

EARLY DAWN

A Salt Creek Novel

PHIL LEMAITRE

First Printing, 2021

Cover photography by Phil LeMaitre

ISBN:978-1-7379585-0-5 (Paperback)
ISBN: 978-1-7379585-1-2 (eBook)

Published by Phil LeMaitre
phillemaitreauthor.com

DEDICATED TO EVERYONE WHO HAS LIVED OR IS STILL LIVING WITHIN THE SALT CREEK COMMUNITY AND TO ALL WHO HAVE A HEART FOR SMALL-TOWN LIVING...GO OILERS!

Thursday, January 31, 2013,

Casper, Wyoming

From the vantage point of my desk, I looked longingly at one of the two photographs that adorned a wall in my office. Both were black and white, though the one I focused on was much older and held significant historical importance. It was not the names and dates inscribed along the bottom border that caught my attention. Instead, it was the faces of the boys behind the uniforms.

The antiquated intercom speaker on my desk suddenly sounded with the voice of my assistant, Joanne.

"Sheriff, your nine o'clock interviewer is here."

I reached and depressed the plastic *talk* button. "Great, send her in." I stood up from behind the desk and moved to the middle of the office.

Five seconds later, the office door opened. Upon entry, I watched as Hope Granderson skillfully assessed me with one glance from head to toe that took under a second. Considering that she was a reporter and a professional observer, I expected that she correctly gauged my height at six feet tall and weighing 225 pounds. Then even a casual observer could see that my once brilliant red hair was turning grayer by the moment.

I then saw Hope take a second look, which could only mean one thing: it was my freckles. I have often thought that God must have a sense of humor because I could never blend into a crowd with my prominent pigment dots. Instead, whether I wanted to or not, I always stood out. Hope's then eyes targeted my hands, then my neckline, and then she smiled at me when she looked up at my face.

She also took another microsecond to scan the office used by the previous 12 Sheriffs. Again, it seemed the room remained unchanged since the building's construction in 1925. Dark walnut crown molding adorned the ceiling, floor, and door frames, along with a massive bookshelf and bureau directly behind my desk.

I offered, "hello, I am Sheriff Eddie Crandall. You can call me Sheriff or Eddie, but you can never call me late for dinner."

She appreciated my self-deprecating humor with a slight giggle. "I am Hope Granderson from *The Front Range Dispatch* in Denver, Colorado. First of all, thank you for this interview, Sheriff, and you may call me Hope."

"Well, you are welcome, Hope. But please call me Eddie."

I motioned for her to sit in a chair on the side of my enormous antique oak desk.

Anticipating her impending question, I explained, "I read that it is best to have a chair to the side of the desk instead of in front. Doing so instills a cooperative spirit while also respecting personal space."

"Interesting concept, Sheriff."

"So, Hope, what brings you from Denver to interview a Sheriff in the center of Wyoming?"

"Honestly, Sheriff, I was first intrigued by these two articles."

She removed two newspaper clippings from her briefcase and handed them to me. I immediately recognized them as works from the Casper daily newspaper. The first headline read: *New Sheriff Brings Small-town Values.* The other one announced: *New Sheriff Selects First Minority as Undersheriff in County History.*

"What I want to know, Sheriff, is how you came to break this apparent glass ceiling? As a woman of color, I appreciate it when progressive ideas infiltrate traditional thinking."

I leaned back into his chair, brought up my left leg, and crossed it over my right knee.

"Ah, I see. So you are interested in Undersheriff Jackson. Then perhaps you should interview him; I think you would find both his story and personal testimony intriguing."

Hope shook her head. "I am sorry, I want to know more about you first and then about your selection of Undersheriff Jackson later. You know, a little background excursion."

I smiled. "Okay, what do you want to know?"

Hope reached into her briefcase again and lifted out a yellow legal-sized notepad with pages of notes already scribed. She briefly glanced at the first, second, and third pages and then stated what she knew about me.

"I read that you are originally from Glenrock, where you played football and were a wrestler in high school. I also saw that you first joined the Sheriff's Department in 1983. But this is what intrigues me: you served as the local deputy for eighteen years in a community with less than a thousand people."

Hope paused for effect, which clued me to fill in the information. "Yes, my area of responsibility was in the Midwest-Edgerton area, or as we like to call it, the Salt Creek community. I still live out there today."

"I see; umm, how far are those towns from Casper?"

I stood up and moved the outside wall of my office near the window where a framed county map hung. I pointed with my right index finger and replied, "where you see my finger is where you are now." I moved my finger toward the top of the map, and I continued, "to the north, about 40 minutes away is Midwest and the sister town of Edgerton. They are the last two remnant municipalities within the most productive oil field in all of Wyoming-perhaps even the nation."

"Wow. I have never heard of it before."

"Sure you have," I chided. "Did you ever hear of the Teapot Dome scandal?"

She nodded. "Ya, it sounds familiar. Like something I might have heard in history class."

I smiled. "Well, that whole episode in American history took place just outside of Midwest."

Hope appeared confused. "Wait, I thought Casper bills itself as Oil City? So, are there not oilfields in Casper?"

I smiled again and moved behind my desk and sat down. "In Casper? No. Outside of Casper in Glenrock and Midwest-Edgerton, then, yes. But you have to understand that Casper was responsible for refining the oil and shipping it out."

She nodded. "I detect some animosity there. Do you wish to speak about it?"

I sat forward and placed both of my elbows on the desktop. "Are you a Christian?"

Hope shook her head. "I don't see how that is relevant?"

"I assure you that it is?"

She shrugged her shoulders and then said, "I don't know if I call myself a Christian or not, but my grandmother always took me with her to a Baptist Church."

I nodded. "Good. Then I am sure you remember that in Jesus' time that there was a familiar saying amongst the Israelites that 'nothing good comes from.'"

"Nazareth," she said, cutting me off.

I clapped both hands together to note my appreciation. "Yes, well, the consensus of folks in Casper has always been that nothing good comes from Midwest either."

A brief pause ensued as Hope scribbled some more notes, and then a question came to mind.

I sat back in my chair and crossed my left leg over the right. "After getting elected as Sheriff, why didn't you move into Casper? I mean, I assume there is limited access to anything out there that living in the city could afford you."

I nodded in agreement. "This isn't the first time my duty assignment was in Casper, so I am kind of used to the commute. I wouldn't argue that it would be more convenient to live in Casper or even in Denver as you do, but cities miss one key ingredient that is a must in my household."

"What is that?"

"It is the sense of community. Pick up any newspaper from any large city and go to the local variety pages. You will see stories of people helping one another, protecting one another, and encouraging another. But those are just isolated cases. Community and the sense of belonging together are what people do every day in the Salt Creek area. They do it without thinking about it or even getting credit."

"I see," she said while jotting down more notes. Then Hope thought briefly of how to approach her next question. Meanwhile, I uncrossed his legs and squared myself behind the desk.

"So, Sheriff, what was the strangest case you have ever worked on?"

I rubbed my chin, and then I reached into the bottom drawer of my antique oak desk. I lifted out a large brown file folder and set it on the desktop.

"The strangest would have to be the Savolt disappearance that I have here in front of me. It is my only unresolved case."

Her eyes opened wide when she spotted the tattered file folder. Then she asked, "how long ago did the case open?"

"Late summer, 1984."

I unfolded the details of a popular high school science teacher and assistant football that went missing. The last witness saw Savolt taking water samples from Salt Creek that courses through both towns and the oilfield. I also included information that I had pieced together bit by bit over the years. I even recalled for her the fortunate discovery in a small town in northeastern Colorado that placed the accused murderers in the Midwest when Savolt disappeared.

"Thanks, Sheriff. Do you have another case that also involves Undersheriff Jackson?"

I answered her question with one of my own. "Hope, what kind of time do you have available today?"

"I'm not sure how to answer that, Sheriff?"

"What I mean is this: do you have the entire day to investigate the story, or do you have to return to Denver right away?"

Hope shrugged her shoulders. "I wasn't planning on driving back to Denver until tomorrow, so I guess that I am free all day today. Is that what you are asking?"

"It is."

I then held one finger in the air that instructed Hope to wait. I pressed the antique call button again with my other hand and asked Joanne what my schedule consisted of for the remainder of the day. Joanne relayed that the only thing pressing was the County Commissioner's meeting later that evening.

I turned back to Hope and asked, "as Jesus said, why don't you 'come and see' the community, and I will even treat you to lunch. What do you say?"

Hope looked at her gold-plated Invicta wristwatch and then rose her eyes to meet mine. "Isn't it a little early for lunch?"

I smiled wide. "It is now, but it won't be once we get there."

Hope turned her head as if in disbelief. "Where are you taking me?"

I smiled again and said, "I know a great café in Edgerton. But during the drive, I will tell you about a case that tested the resolve of both Undersheriff Jackson and me."

"What happened, Sheriff?"

"Have you ever heard of the Early Dawn movement?"

Hope shrugged her shoulders and shook her head to say, "No."

"Well, it is an interesting story and worthy of your time, I assure you."

I turned and raised my brown cowboy hat that had sat crown down on the top of a bureau behind my desk. I moved around the oak desk and then gazed upon the photographs that previously occupied my attention. Hope saw my eyes divert to the wall and looked to see what occupied my attention.

"I bet those pictures have stories," she suggested.

I nodded though I kept my attention on the photographs. "The top one commemorates the first high school football game played at night under the lights in all of America."

"You are kidding?"

"Nope. Midwest played Casper on the night of November 19, 1925. We won't mention that Casper won that one, though."

"And the second photo?"

I placed the hat atop my head and then turned to face her. "The second photo is of a group of Midwest High School boys in their football practice gear. These boys all received All-Conference and All-State honors in 1984."

"What happened to the boys? I mean, do they still live out there?"

I nodded. "Yep, some do, but others moved away after graduation." I pointed to the photo again and scrolled over the faces. "That boy is now an assistant district attorney. This boy is an FBI agent, and these two boys became teachers. And this other one completed a 25-year career in the Air Force and then moved back to Midwest to take over as head football coach and social studies teacher.

Then my finger stopped on the face of one particular boy who was a junior at the time.

"This boy has a part of the story that I am about to tell you, or at least, it concerns his daughter and her boyfriend."

I dropped my hand and turned to Hope. "Do you have a tape recorder?"

She smiled. "No, I don't because nobody uses tape anymore." Then she dug into her jacket pocket and produced a digital recorder. "But, I do have this."

I nodded and then said, "Good. I think it best to revisit the case I am about to tell you as if I am telling you a good story."

Hope nodded that she understood. "Okay, let's go."

Minutes later, I inserted the ignition key to my department-assigned and remarkably well-preserved 1991 Chevrolet Blazer. Hope settled into her seat and placed her leather briefcase on the floorboard between her feet. But then I noticed a puzzled look on her face.

"You would think that the citizens of this county could afford to give their duly elected Sheriff a decent vehicle."

I smiled and explained, "I was assigned this vehicle in October 1991, and I have taken care of it as if it were my own. It has 205,000 miles on it with one overhaul of the engine and transmission when it hit 175,000 miles. I convinced the county that this Blazer would require less money to maintain it than to buy a new vehicle."

Hope laughed aloud, and I asked, "what is so funny?"

She looked at me and admitted, "I just had this thought that you might still have a rotary phone."

"Very funny; I just got rid of mine a few years ago."

Hope spun around and grabbed the seat belt, and locked it into place over her lap. She then reached into her briefcase that rested between her feet and pulled out the digital recorder.

She held the device up for me to spot it. "I am ready to start whenever you are, Sheriff."

I cleared his throat, which queued Hope to press the RECORD button.

"The story centered around a high school couple."

Hope interrupted, "I thought this was a story about a particular case?"

"It is, but it began with this particular high school couple and eventually involved me, Undersheriff Jackson, and many others. I assure you that it is a good story."

I took another breath and let it out. "Again, the story starts with a particular teenage girl."

* * *

2

APRIL 15, 2002

OTTEN HOME, 7 MILES WEST OF MIDWEST, WYOMING

Misty Otten looked out the window from her seat inside the school district-owned Chevrolet Suburban. The vehicle served as the school bus for students living west of Interstate 25 in northern Natrona County, Wyoming. The Suburban made its way up the half-mile-long dirt driveway from Misty's house to Smokey Gap Road. The hissing sound inside the Chevy came from the tires as they rolled over the gravel driveway, still saturated from two days of rain.

She scanned the grass flats and clumps of sagebrush in the treeless void that dominated that part of Wyoming. Trees, especially Cotton-woods, were almost always associated with civilization and a source of water. But it wasn't some trees that Misty sought. Instead, she searched for the grouping of Sage Grouse that had adopted her family last year. The birds were already there when her father moved the family onto a 300 acre spread located seven miles west of Midwest.

Misty had just turned sixteen and was near the end of her junior year of high school. Even though she possessed a driver's license, her parents did not allow her to drive to school because they didn't think she was ready for it. She felt her parents were still a little freaked out by the recent tragedies of 9/11 and acted overprotectively. Instead, they had her ride the bus for safety reasons until the end of the school year. So, Misty's routine was simple: she was the last rider to get on the bus in the morning, and if she rode the afternoon bus, she was the first one off since her house was the closest to town.

Without warning, the Suburban struck onto the pavement in a bounce, which marked Smokey Gap Road's end and the beginning of Highway 387. The jolt left Misty feeling a little unhinged. What unnerved her wasn't the chilly or damp weather. Nor was it the sloppy roads that annoyingly delayed her arrival to school. It was a smell.

Typically, on any damp Wyoming morning, the overwhelming and pleasing smell of sagebrush would dominate any set of nostrils. But on that morning, it was the pungent smell of Axe body spray that wafted forward from Lucas Gagnon, who sat behind her.

Lucas had moved to the area three years ago, yet he remained a mystery to everyone. He didn't have any friends save for one. But the other curiosity is that nobody in the area had ever been to where Lucas and his family lived in the wide-open country west of I-25.

At age 17, Lucas possessed high intelligence but was devoid of any social skills.

Misty turned and sneered, "did you take a bath in that stuff?" and then pinched her nose in protest.

Lucas smiled and said, "do you like it? I wore it for you."

"No, I don't like it," Misty said while she pinched her nose with her fingers. "It is something a desperate 7th grader would do?"

Unfazed, he asked, "did you reconsider my prom proposal?"

A small smile parted her lips as she replied, "proposal? You make it sound like a business deal. But, no, I already told you that I am going with Adam."

Her attention then shifted to the Boyer boys, Brandon and Brenton, ages 10 and 12, respectively, who abruptly began making a lot of noise. Like almost everyone in the nation in the months following 9/11, people were suddenly experts in Middle East affairs, terrorism, and military tactics. For that reason, Misty found it hard to watch television. It seemed that every 20 minutes, there was another breaking news alert, and nearly all of the stations mentioned terms like Taliban and Al Qaeda incessantly. The thought that troubled Misty was how the U.S. government could miss all of the warning signs. Even in the center of

Wyoming, the result on the people was becoming hyper-vigilant, even the Boyer boys.

A part of the usual routine was Brenton and Brandon making it their jobs to sentinel the bus route to and from school. That day was not an exception because the boys simultaneously pointed toward something in the distance from the north side of the road.

"Whose pickup truck is that?" Brenton asked?

"What are they doing? Are they messing with something in the oil-field?" Brandon asked?

Misty looked out the window to her left and around the Boyer boys. She immediately spotted the vehicle the boys were alarmed.

"Take it easy, guys. It is a truck from the Mondragon Ranch." Misty assured.

"How would you know?" challenged Brenton.

She took a deep breath and then replied, "Look at the door. It has a 'Rafter-M' brand on it."

"Are you sure?" Brandon asked.

Misty sat back in her seat. "I am sure. For one thing, I worked on the Mondragon Ranch over the summer. And secondly, my dad and Carlos Mondragon have been best friends since high school."

She then looked out the window as the bus drove over Salt Creek just outside Midwest town limits. Then, finally, a thought occurred to her: the Boyer boys were waiting for the next thing to happen like many other people. A few months ago, there was a community-wide alert that Middle Eastern-looking men were photographing critical parts of the oil field infrastructure the week before. However, it turned out that the men were Arabian-Americans but were from Texas. Through their distinctive twangy Texas drawl, the men explained that they were surveying plots for a new natural gas pipeline out of the Salt Creek field.

Meanwhile, large springtime snowflakes hit the windshield of Adam Weiss' car as he headed to school from Edgerton, located one mile east of Midwest. He pulled the knob for his windshield wipers to come on, but nothing happened. Aggravated now, he tried again and again to activate the wipers. Finally, Adam slapped the steering wheel and grumbled that he had found another thing to fix in his car. Over the last ten months, he had made six repairs.

He abruptly pulled his car over in the parking lot of the car wash. Adam then opened his door and kneeled to look under the dashboard and steering wheel. Inside a small plastic box, he located and removed a glass fuse for the wipers. Just as he thought, it was open. Adam deftly inserted a new fuse, replaced the plastic cover, and sat down once again behind the wheel.

Adam's annoyance was not his 27-year-old Toyota Celica car. Instead, it was that he was running late to school. He knew by now that his girlfriend would be anxiously waiting for his arrival.

Every morning during that school year, Adam and Misty had adopted the same routine where he waited for her to arrive on the school bus. Afterward, they would then get to enjoy about 10 minutes together before their first-period classes.

Misty's heart sank when she did not see Adam or his car as the mud-encased four-wheel-drive Suburban entered the school parking lot. After the vehicle came to a stop, she carefully exited her door to keep the mud off her clothes. Then she turned and helped the twin 10-year-old O'Hara girls step down before pushing the seat forward so Lucas could get out. Lastly, Misty held the door open for Stephanie Merrick.

Stephanie was a 15-year-old freshman who rarely spoke to anyone. Instead, she was a recluse and wore hooded sweatshirts almost exclusively. Most of the time, the girl's hood completely covered her head and rarely, if ever, showed her face. Misty had invited the girl over to her house on many occasions, and every time, she declined.

That day was not an exception as Stephanie moved silently by Misty and made her way over the school entrance.

Even in Wyoming, Midwest School was odd because nearly 300 elementary, junior high, and high school students learned under the same roof. Children came from Midwest, Edgerton, and Linch, plus the area ranches to form the school. Oilfield work was the central economic driver of the Salt Creek community, though ranching was another.

Misty quickly walked over to the parking lot entrance. She then looked easterly through the yards of the school faculty homes on Teacher's Row. Since none of the trees had yet to sprout leaves, it only took seconds for her to spy Adam's bright yellow car in the distance as it came to a stop at the crossroads of Highways 387 and 259. Then as he moved forward over the intersection and onto Lewis Street, her heart pounded with anticipation.

"Waiting for Mr. Wonderful again?" asked a voice from behind.

Misty was startled at the boy's voice and quickly turned to him and glared at him.

"Go away, Lucas." Misty snapped. "I am not putting up with any of your stuff this morning?"

"I don't know what you see in him, Misty? I am smarter than him, better looking than him, and I have a future planned out after college. Adam is nothing but a stupid jock and will be lucky to find a job driving a truck out here in the oil patch," Lucas implored.

Misty spun around. "Driving a truck in the oil patch was good enough for my dad, so I suppose it would be good enough for Adam too if he chooses."

Misty raised her hand to block any retort from Lucas. "I told you to leave me alone. For the fiftieth time, I don't want to be your girlfriend! Now, go!"

"I am only trying to save you from a life of constant wanting, which I know I can provide you all you need if you would just give me a chance."

Lucas's words fell onto deaf ears as a yellow car quickly turned into the parking lot and stopped in a parking space near the school library. A tall, dark-haired boy wearing a maroon and white letter jacket emerged from the car within seconds. When Adam turned his head, he immediately recognized Misty's brunette-colored hair and brown eyes. However, his ordinarily pleasant expression turned into a grimace as he focused on something behind her.

"I thought we both told you to leave her alone, Lucas!" Adam thundered.

Lucas held both of his palms out and stammered, "I was just talking to her; that's all."

"If you don't leave her alone, I will...,"

"You will what?" Lucas asked as he cut Adam off. "If you touch me, I will report you to the principal, and you will disqualify yourself from the rest of your track season."

Undeterred, Adam replied, "okay, how about we have that discussion with Dr. Isom. I am sure she will have a little more empathy with me since she's known me my whole life versus you, who just arrived a few years ago."

The first bell of the morning rang loudly on that side of the school, and without any further retort, Lucas spun on his heel and walked toward the library entrance. Simultaneously, Misty stepped forward, threw both of her arms inside Adam's letter jacket, and tightly hugged his torso. She lifted her head and looked into his coal-black eyes and saw her reflection in them. She thought about kissing him, but they stood out for the entire school to see, so she deferred. "Thanks, Adam, you arrived just in time."

"You are welcome," he said while returning the hug and pressing his nose into the top of her head. "How about we get inside before we are late for our first class?"

Misty lifted her head, nodded in agreement, and relinquished her hold on Adam as they made their way to the school entrance.

They made a quick stop at Adam's locker near the east end of the high school hallway, where he hung up his jacket and then grabbed books for his first two classes. Misty, too, grabbed her books, which she sometimes stored in Adam's locker as well.

He grinned at her and then asked, "so, my treat today for lunch. Do you want to eat in the cafeteria or go over to the junction store? It's your choice."

"I don't care about the food, Adam. I just want to be with you."

"Okay, I will meet you here at my locker after the fourth period, then we will walk over there."

* * *

3

Meanwhile, outside the home located on the corner of Navy Row and C Street in Midwest, I stood on my front stoop. The moist sheets of mist didn't bother me one bit. To me, springtime in Wyoming was all about drastic change from one environmental extreme to another. Only in Wyoming could a typical spring day begin sunny and warm with temperatures into the low '80s, only to see the thermometer dip to the freezing mark by late afternoon. I had even seen snow in the Salt Creek community every month except July.

I lifted the cup of coffee to my lips and took a long sip. The word "change" moved through my mind. Then it occurred to me that more than once, I had stood in that very spot and had contemplated the changes I'd seen in the Salt Creek community since arriving in 1983.

I glanced up and down Navy Row to my left. The street was one of two in Midwest owned by the school district to house teachers. On this cold and damp morning, I noted that none of my teacher neighbors lived there when I bought this home from Mrs. Fortney. Back then, the picturesque town park on the other side of the street from my place was nothing more than an empty lot behind the Midwest Town Hall.

I cracked a smile and then finished off the rest of the coffee in my mug. Why I smiled had to do with the fact that I had done this same thing before: waiting for a newly assigned Sheriff's Deputy to arrive at my home office.

I shook my head in disbelief that it had already been ten years since welcoming Deputy Tracy James to the area. I previously thought that Tracy's assignment to the Salt Creek community was a boneheaded idea. But on that today, I offered nothing but praise because Tracy eventually became my wife.

The courtship didn't happen quickly. Instead, it only took three years of working side-by-side and three more years of actual dating before I popped the proverbial question. At this point, we were married for four years, and Tracy was 8-months pregnant with our first child. I was also a newly promoted Lieutenant in the Sheriff's Department.

Remaining preoccupied in reflection, I failed to see or hear the brand-new Sheriff's Department Chevrolet Silverado 4X4 pickup come to a stop in front of our home.

After I heard the door shut, I looked up and waved at the driver. Then I spun around and opened the storm door and shouted inside.

"Hey, hon, he is here!"

Tracy replied, "Okay, I will be right out."

I turned again toward the Deputy, who now walked up to the front sidewalk. To me, the officer looked about my height but much more muscular in his chest and arms. The man also moved like an athlete.

"Lieutenant Crandall?" asked the Deputy.

"Yes, and you must be Cory Jackson."

I thrust out an open hand, and he obliged and gave me a firm grip. I then added, "Why don't you follow me inside."

The Deputy nodded and blurted out, "CJ."

"CJ?"

"Yes, Sir, I preferred to be called CJ over Cory or Jackson."

My face broke into a wide grin. "Okay, CJ, it is."

I held the door open and watched the young Deputy fill the doorframe with discernably broad shoulders. Upon entry, CJ quickly removed his hat as he entered the living room. He stood motionless just inside the threshold until invited otherwise. I took note of CJ's gentlemanly manners and offered him a seat on the couch.

"Do you want a cup of coffee? Or anything else?" I asked.

"Thanks, Sir, I've had my fill already, but a glass of water would be great."

I went into the kitchen, filled a water glass, and topped off my mug with more coffee. As I carried the drinks back to the living room, I stopped and looked down the hallway. The bedroom door was still closed.

"Here you go, CJ," I said while handing him a glass. I then moved over to the recliner that sat directly in front of the new Deputy.

The master bedroom door opened, and both CJ and I turned our heads toward the noise. What we saw was a pregnant woman stepping carefully down the hallway. She, too, wore a Sheriff's Department dark green uniform, albeit a maternity set.

CJ quickly stood up and greeted her, "good morning, Sergeant Crandall."

Tracy blushed and returned the compliment, "oh, thank you, Deputy, but that is not necessary."

Tracy walked around my chair and the coffee table and took a seat on the couch opposite CJ. Both of us watched in amazement as my wife performed a textbook power squat to sit down.

She looked up at CJ and flashed a grin. "Today is the last day I am a Sergeant, so please, call me Tracy."

CJ furrowed his brow while he simultaneously lifted his left hand to pat down a perfectly groomed mustache. Finally, he asked, "what do you mean that today is your last day as a Sergeant? I assumed that you would be training me?"

"Oh, I will, though my husband here will do a lot of it. But don't worry, I will be around," she said.

CJ shook his head from side to side and appeared confused.

Tracy suggested to me, "why don't you take CJ out to breakfast and show him around the community?"

Before I could reply, Tracy stood up and moved over to the coat rack, where she picked up my lightweight Sheriff's Department jacket adorned with a patch on the sleeve. As she handed the coat to me, she smiled at CJ and quipped, "don't let him bore you on the drive around as he did me ten years ago?"

CJ felt a little embarrassed as he was now a part of an apparent inside joke about me. But, instead of a reply, he simply smiled and nodded his head. Then he moved to the already opened storm door and stepped back out onto the porch.

Tracy stood at the large front window and watched me, and the new deputy load up into a 10-year-old Department Chevy Blazer. As soon as I backed out of the carport and moved toward C Street and Navy Row's intersection, she could see my hand pointing toward the houses. She knew that I could not help myself when an opportunity arose to point out the community's historical facts.

She then turned and looked into the small mirror hung outside the little wall next to the front door. Tracy shook her head in disbelief about what was going to happen later on that day. Then she found the word she searched for in her mind: *surreal*. Indeed, only the term *surreal* adequately described the event planned later that day.

* * *

4

If there was one trait about me that everyone could readily see, it was this: I am predictable. I have also heard that I am honest almost to a fault. Plus, they made me aware that my down-home "aww shucks" attitude was dependable.

Back at our home, Tracy smiled at the thought of my characteristics. But, at the same time, she stared at her reflection in the bathroom mirror to put on her makeup's finishing touches. Tracy rarely wore anything other than a mascara hint because most cosmetics did little to compliment her looks. Instead, makeup made her feel like a clown, at times, because she never found the right shades to match her skin tone. So, now she made a habit of going conservative with her appearance.

As she approached the kitchen to make herself a bowl of granola, Tracy thought back to me. She supposed that I and the new Deputy, CJ, were still in Midwest and parked on Ellison Avenue overlooking the football field from atop the cliff. She wondered if I had already mentioned to CJ that Midwest was the first high school football team in the nation to play under a lighted field? Or if I had discussed the infamous Teapot Dome Scandal that took down the Warren G. Harding cabinet?

As Tracy lifted the first spoonful of cereal to her mouth, she stopped and smiled. Tracy mentally tracked my progression through town. She predicted that I showed CJ the Post Office's, then the school entrance, and would soon finish with the Junction store. Only then would we head over to Edgerton's café.

Tracy admitted to me later that if CJ were anything like her, the Deputy might not have an immediate liking to the Salt Creek area. However, Tracy did fall in love with the people and the comforting sense of community that existed. But she also noted the warts of living within an oil field. There were the rusted-out tin-sided garages and the tiny homes in disrepair throughout both townships. It seemed that nothing was new except for the modular homes that went up on Burke Street, just east of the town park. She reminded herself that community counts most and not the shiny new gated communities going up in Casper where people didn't even know their neighbors.

Soon afterward, I parked the same Department Chevy Blazer outside the café. As we exited the vehicle, CJ became amused.

He asked, "Lieutenant, you would think that someone with your seniority would get a newly issued vehicle?"

I looked back at the Blazer with the same pride a father casts upon his child. The unit had been an excellent vehicle for me, and it never crossed my mind to ask for a replacement.

Then I answered the question, "I know what you are thinking, but, no, I don't need a new vehicle. This one has a lot of life left in it."

Then I winked at CJ, "I'll make you a deal; if the Sheriff offers me a new truck this year, I will decline and ask him to give it to you."

Once inside the café, we both heard a small friendly voice that said, "Hey, Eddie! Are you going to have your usual?"

I turned toward the voice and replied, "Hi, Liz. I want you to meet Deputy Cory Jackson. He is the new replacement assigned to the Salt Creek area."

CJ turned and greeted Liz, "pleased to meet you, ma'am."

"You can drop the ma'am stuff, Deputy. When I hear that word, I stop and look for my grandma," she said with a bit of giggle in her voice.

"What should I call you then"?

"Liz. I am Liz Martin and welcome to my place. Since you are new here, you may have any menu item on the house. It is my welcome gift to you."

Momentarily stunned by the hospitality, CJ offered, "Thank you, Liz, and you may call me CJ. Also, I will have whatever Lieutenant Crandall is having."

"Perfect, I will have two orders of pancakes and bacon out to both of you in a jiffy," with that, Liz spun around and walked through the batwing doors and into the kitchen.

CJ and I found two empty swivel top chairs that outlined a U-sharped counter in the middle of the café. I capitalized on the moment to explain that Liz had bought the café a few years back. I also informed CJ that Liz owned over a dozen or so rental properties in the community if he considered living and working locally.

When our food arrived, I asked, "so, what do you think of our little community, CJ."

CJ continued to spread the whipped butter over his pancakes since, in reality, he didn't know how to respond to the question.

Instead, he offered, "well, I don't know. I just got here."

I continued, "according to your file, I see that you served on the police force in Boulder, Colorado. I was most surprised, however, to find out that you are a Wyoming native."

CJ remained silent while he lifted a forkful of pancakes to his mouth.

I persisted on, "But then I remembered a pretty good running back from Green River that dominated the newspaper a few years back. That was you, wasn't it?"

CJ smiled and nodded his head. "Yes, that was me. I was born and raised in Green River, and then I went to the University of Wyoming on a football scholarship."

"I read that too. So, what happened to your playing career? Because I honestly don't remember hearing your name much after your sophomore year."

CJ's face hardened considerably from his natural jovial self. Finally, he dryly replied, "I dislocated my kneecap during summer camp between my sophomore and junior years. It took four surgeries to smooth out all cartilage damage, but it took away my ability to play. Not to mention that I lost my scholarship for my final two years."

"So, what did you do then?"

CJ set his fork down on the plate and took a long swig of coffee. Then he continued, "I enlisted into the Army in 1991, and during those four years, I finished up my bachelor's degree in Criminal Justice."

CJ took another sip from his coffee cup and then looked up to my eyes as if he tried to discern something about me

He asked, "so, is that all you want to know, or is there another question you want to ask?"

I blinked once and bluntly asked, "Okay, CJ, do you think you will fit in around here?"

CJ's muscular shoulders gathered up as if he were about to push himself up off the counter. Instead, he blurted out, "you ask because I am half black and half Mexican, isn't it?"

I didn't take offense. Instead, I diffused the situation by cracking a smile and patting CJ on the shoulder.

"No, that was not why I asked you that question." I picked up my coffee cup and took another sip, and then set it down again. Finally, I asked, "is there a reason why you are so quick to assume that I would have a problem with you being either black or Mexican or purple? To me, it seems like you have a great story to share."

The deputy looked somewhat confused. "What? You want to know about my family?"

I simply nodded and motioned at the Deputy with my hand for him to continue.

"Well, where to start? Umm, my grandfather and grandmother moved to Green River from Chicago in 1949. He was a lifelong railroad man with the Union Pacific, and he wanted to be in a place outside of a large city. So, my dad, Robert, got a job in Riverton as a truck driver after high school. While there, he met my mother, Maria Chavis. She is a Mexican American on her father's side and Scottish on her mother's side.

I smiled and said, "you are pretty mixed up like a lot of other people. Take me, for example; you couldn't tell by looking at me by I am seven sixteenths Native American."

"Funny, I didn't know there was such a thing as the red-haired, freckle-faced tribe," CJ joked.

We finished our breakfasts in relative silence, with each of us seemingly lost within our thoughts. Finally, Liz appeared again and refilled both coffee mugs without request.

Then CJ asked me, "so, are there any families in the area that look like me, or am I the only black person in forty square miles?"

I shook my head. "No, you are not the only black man in the Salt Creek community. We have the Proctor and the Lee families over in Midwest. We also have Joe Proctor's niece, Brianna Marshall, who lived with him during her junior high and high school years. She lives here in Edgerton with her husband. Plus, we have several Latino families in the area, and one of which homesteaded here long before Wyoming was even a State."

"That doesn't sound so ethnically diverse, does it?"

"No, it doesn't, CJ. But it doesn't matter anyway?" Before Deputy Jackson could retort, I explained further, "as I said, it doesn't matter. Once you start working and living out here, people will adopt you into their *OFT* fold."

"What is *OFT*?

"OFT stands for *Oil-Field-Trash.*" When I noticed that the Deputy didn't seem to follow, he explained further. "Yes, oilfield trash. I think it was back in the fall of 1984.... yes, definitely '84 that a few boys nicknamed themselves that in a show of solidarity. Since then, the moniker has become somewhat legendary at the school ever since."

"Oh, that was what that was. I saw a bunch of front yard signs with *OFT* written on them. So, do you mean to say that people call each other *oilfield trash* around here? On purpose?"

I nodded again. "Yes. I know it sounds weird, but people in Casper or even Buffalo to the north of here always have kind of thumbed their noses to folks around here. We always hear the snickering comments behind people's backs about being from a dirty oil patch."

I paused only long enough to take another sip of coffee, then I continued. "High school kids from the area have plenty of stories of going to the Mall in Casper while wearing their letter jackets. Only then to witness store employees following them around. I have experienced the same thing too. I am questioned all the time by people in Casper why I would live in Midwest."

CJ nodded that he understood.

"So, Deputy, do you think you will fit in around here?"

It took a quick second to elapse before CJ answered, which was underwhelming by all rights.

He said, "I think I will. I mean, people seem nice here." Then CJ made an assurance that he was indeed okay with the assignment, "I tend to root for the underdog if you know what I mean?"

"Good, it is settled then."

We exited the café and stepped into the Department Blazer. I backed out of the parking space and turned south onto Second Street to show the Deputy around Edgerton.

Deputy Jackson looked over at me. "So, what will happen later this afternoon with your wife?"

I was momentarily confused by the question, but then I replied, "oh, that. Tracy is leaving the Sheriff's Department today. She starts her new job tomorrow."

"What job is that?"

I tilted his head and replied, "I guess you didn't hear? Tracy will be the new Chief of Police in Midwest."

As we passed by the bowling alley on the passenger side of the road, CJ asked, "so, what happened to the old Chief? Retirement?"

My eyes squinted a little bit. "You could say retired, I guess. The old Chief, as you put it, is my good friend Wyatt Traynor. He is one heck of a cop and was my instructor of sorts when I first came out here in 1983. Anyway, Traynor was injured pretty badly last December during the Christmas blizzard."

I paused long enough to negotiate a right turn onto Center Street that eventually would lead us west out of Edgerton and back onto Highway 387. I picked up my story by recounting how Traynor helped the Highway Patrol rescue stranded drivers on Interstate 25 west of town. Upon his arrival, Traynor found a massive pile of vehicles that plowed into one another because they couldn't stop after driving way too fast for the conditions. It was then that a semi-tractor trailer lost control and hit a car that smashed into Traynor."

"Ouch, that had to hurt."

I nodded, "yes, it did. Traynor found himself pinned between two vehicles for two hours. The scary part was whether or not he would die once they moved the vehicles apart."

"I see that he lived. How bad were his injuries?"

I took a deep breath. "Traynor is in a wheelchair for now, but he may walk unassisted again by next year if he keeps up with the physical therapy. At any rate, his injuries will forever keep him from his duties as a cop."

CJ nodded that he understood, and from experience, he knew that physical therapy was not going to be easy. As he looked to the north of Highway 387, he spotted the community's nine-hole golf course. It amused him to see a red, white, and blue painted pump jack in the middle of one of the fairways.

"Does that pumpjack play as a hazard, or do you get a free drop from a man-made obstruction?" CJ asked.

I smiled. "Do you play much golf?"

CJ shrugged. "I picked it up in college, where I took golf class as an elective. But, yes, I do play."

"Good, I would be happy to introduce you to the league members that meet up every Wednesday beginning in May. But I will need to play one round with you, so you know the course rules."

"What is so special about this course other than the sand greens?"

I held my right hand out and extended my index finger. "For one, you need to bring a .22 rifle or a small handgun that will fit into your bag."

"Why?"

I chuckled. "Well, unlike the municipal track or the country club in Casper, this course will sometimes have rattlesnakes curled up next to the tee boxes."

We rode in silence while crossing over the junction once again. Then a thought hit CJ. What seemed to bother him was the changes happening in his life and career. He secretly wondered if his assignment to the Salt Creek community was as optimistic as I had sold him. But then again, CJ told himself, ""*What choice do I have.*"

* * *

5

By midday, the gloominess of the morning rain had lifted. Left behind was a solid blanket of ground-hugging gray clouds. After the lunchtime bell, Misty pushed open the exit door at the school library entrance. A pleasing perfume of fresh grass and wet Cottonwood bark washed over her. Then she saw her boyfriend, Adam, leaning against the brick wall of the library.

"Hello, lover," Misty greeted.

Adam's cheeks immediately flushed pink with embarrassment. It wasn't out of shame, nor was the words that his girlfriend used that bothered him. What caused Adam's reaction was at the same time that Misty greeted him, Mr. Berg, one of the math teachers, had exited the building behind his girlfriend.

Misty saw that Adam's eyes were not on her, so she turned her head and spotted Mr. Berg's disapproving glare at them. Undeterred, she spun back around to face Adam.

"Don't worry about him; he is just doing his job by trying to keep us in line. Now, come on, I am hungry. Let's go eat."

The teens left Adam's car behind and decided to walk to the Junction store for a change. Adam didn't mind walking except that sitting in his vehicle with Misty provided their only non-supervised contact during the whole day.

Before crossing Lewis Street, the couple waited for a maroon and white painted vac truck to drive past them. As it did, mist off the tires fell upon the couple.

Misty then broke their silence. "Did you have any more run-ins with Lucas?"

"No, not really."

"What does that mean, not really?"

"Nothing." Adam looked away from Misty toward the vacant lot behind the houses on teachers' row. Then, after a moment, he took a breath and said, "during the third period, Robbie Lepsis kept referring to me as a loser."

"Wait, he called you a loser? You are an honor roll student and an athlete. I might add that you were All-State in football. How is that a loser, Adam?"

Adam shrugged and said, "Tim Cormack told Lucas the same thing, but do you know what Robbie said next?"

"No, tell me."

"He said if you are the starting quarterback for a team that won 5 games and lost 19 over the last three years, then that makes me a loser."

"What did you do then?"

"What could I do? I just ignored him. But then Robbie's only friend, Lucas, joined in, calling me a loser repeatedly."

"Adam, please promise me that you won't pound either one of them. I know it is tough, but if you do, it will be goodbye to your scholarship."

"I promise," he said sheepishly.

Misty and Adam entered the building that everyone in the community simply referred to as the Junction because Highways 387 and 259 intersected within 200 yards of the structure. The store itself had evolved over the years from a simple convenience store that only sold candy and microwavable burritos aside from gasoline.

The former owner, Clare Olsen, made the most significant changes to the business by bringing in a grocery section and a hot food line. Clare's nephew, Trevor, now owned it. He felt obligated to provide a community store of sorts without price gouging for the convenience of not having to drive to Casper or Buffalo for groceries.

Fried chicken strips were always the Monday special, so Adam and Misty ate here instead of the school cafeteria. While waiting for their order, they overheard two longtime oil field workers, Hank Gorman and Roger Sands, locked in a fiery debate.

Roger panned, "I am telling you that a witness saw the girl getting into a late 1970's dark green Ford F-150. Doesn't that sound familiar?"

Hank nodded and said, "it does, but it could be a coincidence."

"That is what you think! They never found the teacher's body, and they only got one of the perps. That means the other guy is still running loose," Roger explained.

"I know all of that, but it is a huge stretch to think that the same guy is now grabbing teenage girls," Hank pleaded.

Adam overheard the entire conversation. His mother raised him to respect adults and not interrupt them while they talked to one another. He learned this habit at his grandparents' house in Kadoka, South Dakota. After dinner, his mom and uncles played pinochle at the kitchen table. However, no child was allowed to speak to a parent during the game until acknowledgment.

After a brief pause ensued, only then did Adam ask, "Mr. Gorman, what was that about a girl and a dark green Ford?"

"Oh, hey, Adam. I didn't see you standing there. But, yes, I heard this morning that a teenaged girl went missing two weeks ago in Kaycee. A witness said that a dark green 70's model Ford F150 stopped and picked her up."

"What is the deal with the pickup truck?" Adam asked.

Misty turned to Adam and said, "oh, that is right. You didn't move here until the sixth grade. Me, on the other hand, grew up with this story."

Hank and Roger both took turns retelling Adam about the former teacher and football coach named Tim Savolt. They regaled the popular theory that a pair of strangers murdered Savolt. Yet, around the same time, a mysterious dark green Ford truck made appearances all around the Salt Creek community. The men also credited all of the discoveries in the investigation to some high school boys that included Misty's father. Although one of the suspects was shot and killed, his accomplice had disappeared. Ever since then, the sight of any late-model dark green Ford F150 conjured up the rumor that the collaborator had returned for revenge.

Within a few minutes, their order was ready. Misty and Adam shared a large order of chicken strips with fries along with two Cokes. Then they discussed their plans for prom that upcoming Saturday and what things still needed to get done.

Their challenge was similar to all other small-town high school students throughout Wyoming. However, it was a vastly different experience than for those who lived in the city. For one thing, Adam and Misty would not have a dinner date before the dance because they lived 40 miles away from formal dining in Casper. Instead, each year the Salt Creek community residents came together to decorate the church on Navy Row. Then they hosted a late-night meal for Prom attendees. Once more, they made it affordable too for a low price of $7 each. Another burden was not having the convenience of running around town to pick up things for the event. Instead, teens at Midwest High had to schedule a specific time to trek into Casper during the week of prom.

At this point, Adam still needed to pick up his rental tuxedo. Likewise, Misty needed to retrieve her dress from the seamstress. Additionally, both teens had to go by the florist to collect each other's corsage and boutonniere.

The last obstacle was that Adam and Misty would compete in a track meet in Douglas on Saturday. Since they didn't know when the team would arrive on the team bus, the teens might have to scramble to arrive on time for pictures at the dance.

"So, when are you going to get your tux?" Misty asked.

Adam paused between bites of food and said, "I'm planning on going Thursday right after practice. How about you?"

"Umm, I think my mom is taking me into town on Wednesday night."

"We could go together if you want?"

"Oh, Adam, you know my dad won't go for that. I mean, he is just barely okay with you picking me up for the Prom."

Adam slumped in his seat. "I wish your dad liked me. It would be a lot easier if he did."

Misty shook her head. Then she explained, "my dad doesn't hate you. He just hasn't gotten to the point of trusting you yet."

"Why doesn't he trust me? I haven't done anything that goes against his trust?"

"I know, and I asked him that myself. My dad said that he was once a high school boy too, and he knows what goes through your mind."

Adam didn't offer a retort because he didn't want to argue. It just stung to hear Misty's words that he was still outside with her family in the trust factor.

An hour later, across town and inside the Midwest Town Hall on Peake Street, Deputy Jackson sat in the front row of a mass of folding chairs next to me. The small meeting room filled with 40 people for the occasion of Chief of Police Wyatt Traynor's retirement.

Within the last few minutes, the Chief had entered the room in his wheelchair. The freak accident left him bound to the device for the foreseeable future. Traynor made it known to everyone that he hated being placated too and demanded that he not be treated in his words as a "cripple."

Bill Crooks, the high school civics teacher, and I were two of Traynor's closest friends. The notion of his retirement was partly due to our advice since it would take many more months before he could walk. What was still unknown was how much he would regain following therapy.

At 1 p.m., the Mayor of Midwest, Wendy Wilkins, entered the room to start the ceremony with a brief speech. Then came a flow of residents who stepped forward to say a few parting words of thanks. The speakers included me, Bill Crooks, and concluded with Tracy. My wife regaled the story of how Bill Crooks and Wyatt saved our lives in a bold rescue in the middle of a blizzard. For that, Tracy vowed her eternal gratitude to Traynor.

Finally, Wyatt rolled himself up next to the podium. Before he spoke, he took a moment to clear both his throat and his thoughts. For the last month, the Chief had dreaded this very moment. Instead, Traynor always thought he would leave his post well into his 60s and walk into retirement. Finally, today, he rolled into his exit. The only palatable thing about the situation was the town council accepting his proposal to hire Tracy as a replacement even though she was pregnant.

His words were brief, precise, and poignant. As he finished, Traynor reached up to his badge above his left breast pocket and removed it. He then held the shield for Tracy to grab it. When she reached her hand to accept the badge, Traynor pulled it back playfully.

He winked at her and then motioned for her to lean forward. When she did, he whispered into her ear, "I am always available if you need any help."

Tracy smiled back and nodded her agreement. Then, without another word spoken, Wyatt handed her the badge and wheeled himself to the door, where his wife Lois helped him exit.

When the door closed, one of the board members, Cami Saenz, came forward. She gladly announced to the crowd and the Star-Tribune reporter in the back of the room, "I am pleased to announce the newest Chief of Police, Tracy Crandall."

While the audience clapped politely, Tracy walked up behind the podium and delicately placed her new badge onto her uniform. She spoke even more curtly than Wyatt Traynor but managed to pledge her best to follow in his footsteps.

By 2 p.m., Tracy sat in her new two-room office that constituted the Midwest Police Station. Located behind the Midwest Town Hall, the office was conveniently located directly across from her house. The space was completely different from the home office that Tracy shared with me, but it was a welcomed change.

Meanwhile, I went home, unplugged Tracy's computer, and managed to carry the monitor over to the new office. CJ helped top as he carried the box that contained the computer tower, miscellaneous cords, keyboard, and a mouse.

"Here is your computer, Chief!" I teased.

"Thank you both for bringing that over." Tracy paused while a thought occurred to her. "CJ, how would you like to use the extra office here instead of heading back to Casper all the time?"

I nodded. "That is not a bad idea, hon." I then turned to CJ and said, "I think I can get it approved with the Sheriff and have the extra phone line from my home office transferred here as well."

CJ nodded that he understood. But, up to that moment, the thought of an office had escaped him.

"Okay, I will bring some stuff tomorrow. Thanks, both of you," CJ remarked.

* * *

January 31, 2013

9:55 a.m.

Up to that point, Hope Granderson listened intently. We had just entered Interstate 25 northbound to take us to the Salt Creek communities of Midwest and Edgerton. I sensed her movement out of my peripheral vision and saw her press the STOP button on the digital recorder. When I turned my head to look at her, it was apparent that a question had come to mind.

"Maybe I should interview your wife? I mean, it seems early on in this story that she will turn out as a positive influence on Undersheriff Jackson.

I nodded in agreement. "I suppose that Tracy was just as responsible for mentoring CJ as I am. You will see all of that throughout this story."

Hope thought for a second and then asked, "is the former Midwest Chief of Police still living out there, and is he part of this story?"

I grinned and took a drink out of my travel mug. "Yes, Wyatt Traynor is alive and well and still lives in Midwest. But no, he is not a central figure."

I turned my gaze toward Hope and motioned toward her digital recorder with his right hand. "How about I continue the story."

On cue, Hope pressed the RECORD button.

I cleared my throat and picked back up in the story. "Where we left off was still on April 15, 2002.

* * *

6

On that Monday afternoon after school, Misty sat on the football field's grass and pretended to stretch her legs before practicing the hurdles. Instead, she kept looking up toward the school for any sight of her boyfriend, Adam. Misty thought it was unlike Adam to be late for practice or anything else as she leaned over to stretch her left leg. For one thing, he was a teacher's aide in his last class of the day, Physical Education, which meant he was pretty much already dressed out for track. Usually, Adam would meet her in the small gym to walk down to the field together.

Another thing, being late, was against Adam's nature. Once, over last summer, the boy arrived at Misty's house for dinner 45 minutes earlier than scheduled. He was so early that nobody, except her dad, Steve, was dressed and ready.

While Misty still mused about Adam, Jessica Norman startled her by abruptly sitting down, making her jump. "Gosh, Jess, you scared me!"

"I'm sorry, I thought you saw me. So, what's up?"

"Nothing, I was just thinking about Adam. You haven't seen him have you?"

"I did, and that is what I wanted to tell you about."

"Okay, Jess, go on."

"I was running late since I had to stay after school to get extra help in science. So, as I passed by the school office on my way to the locker room, I saw Adam and Coach Dodson heading into the principal's office."

Momentarily shocked, Misty began running scenarios in her head as to what could be going on.

Jessica interrupted her thoughts. "Don't worry, Misty, Adam probably didn't do anything wrong. You know that he is not one of the bad boys."

Misty narrowed her eyes and asked, "what do you mean by that? Not one of the bad boys?"

Jessica flipped her hair back with her left hand and looked directly into Misty's eyes. The stare lasted long enough for Misty to break it off.

Jessica then asked, "Adam hasn't tried anything with you, has he?"

"What do you mean, Jess?"

"You know what I mean. Do I have to spell it out for you? S-E-X."

Misty refused to reply because anything that she said would be too much information. She also didn't want the reputation of being easy or a prude. So staying silent was her only option.

Jessica noted Misty's silence and added, "You don't have to say anything. Adam is one of the good guys, you know, the type you can say 'No' to, and they still want to be around you? You are lucky to have him."

Before Misty could reply, Jessica stood up and jogged over to the other end of the field to meet with Coach Mercy, who handled the distance runners. Misty turned her head and looked back up toward the school, and once again, no Adam.

An hour into practice, Adam trotted down the dirt path from the back door to the small gym down to the football field. When he reached the bottom, he opened the rusted steel gate, stepped inside, and closed it in a slam behind him.

While settling into the starting blocks, Misty heard the gate yawn a loud squeak when it opened, and the crash closed again behind her. She peeked through her arms behind her and saw Adam walking in her direction. But, instead of jumping up and greeting him, she went back to what she was doing.

Misty wiggled her feet into the starting block pads, and then she said aloud to herself, "*SET.*" Then lifted her hips while placing her weight forward onto outstretched arms. Then Misty said to herself, *"BANG!"* to imitate a track meet starter. She immediately exploded out of the blocks and flew over five consecutive hurdles with relative ease and grace. On most days, she practiced starting her main event, the 100-meter hurdles. Additionally, Misty ran the 200-meter hurdles and the 4X100 meter relay.

As Misty came to a stop and turned around, Adam was only a few feet behind her.

"What took you so long to get to practice?" Misty enquired.

Adam shook his head and said, "I don't want to talk about it. It is just something stupid, that's all."

"I heard that you were in the principal's office. Are you in trouble or something?"

"No, I am not in trouble."

"What, then? Come on, Adam! No secrets. That is what we promised each other."

Adam sighed. "Okay, here is what happened. When I went to my gym locker after PE class, I noticed that someone had scratched the word *LOSER* into the paint on the door."

"You are kidding?"

"I wish that I was."

Misty furtively looked beyond Adam to the top of the cliff that over-looked the field from Ellison Street. She spotted that her dad's pickup sat in its usual spot during practice. Misty also located her dad sitting on the metal railing. Feeling momentarily embarrassed, Misty motioned Adam to follow her while they walked back to the starting line.

Then Misty asked, "so, when do you think it happened?"

Adam scratched his chin and shook his head. "I don't know, but I didn't see anything on my locker door when I dressed out for class. So that only means that it happened during the sixth period today."

"What is the principal going to do about it?" Misty asked.

"I think she is going to talk to every boy in my PE class."

Misty's eyes suddenly opened wide. Then she said, "Lucas and Robbie called you a loser today, didn't they? And isn't Lucas in the same PE class?"

Adam nodded his head affirmatively and then offered, "true, but Lucas wasn't in PE class today. I told Coach that too. But I found out that Lucas checked out after the fifth period."

"But those boys called you a loser today. So, it has to be either one of them," Misty implored.

Adam shrugged to convey his usual "I don't know" type of response. By now, they had walked back to Misty's starting blocks. They both quickly moved out of the path of the group of distance runners who were rounding the corner. Well out in front of the group, Jessica set the pace. But as she passed by the couple, she waved at Adam and Misty. To which Adam gave a friendly wave in return.

Then Misty looked at Adam and told him that he had better go and get in his workout.

Adam smiled. "Okay, but I am just doing some quarter-mile repeats today. But please wait for me to walk back up to the school with you."

Misty rolled her eyes. "Fine. Go do your thing."

From above, on the cliff, Steve watched his daughter. To him, Misty looked more and more like her mother every day. He liked watching Misty during practice so he could offer her some tips over supper. But, for whatever reason, seeing his daughter on the track today reminded him of the first time he met Rhonda during a track meet in Sheridan during their junior year. Then Steve looked over to Adam and knew why those feelings came up.

His future wife ran both hurdle events for the Kaycee Buckaroos. On the fateful day that they met, Steve happened to be standing behind the starting blocks holding two sets of sweat suits for his Oiler teammates. Rhonda asked Steve to hold onto her sweats because the track was wet, and there were no other Kaycee teammates around. From that day on, the two were inseparable.

Steve Otten was a third-generation Salt Creek resident. His great grandfather, Gerrit, immigrated from Holland and arrived in the United States with nothing in his pockets but a pair of working hands. Gerrit found work on the railroad and eventually settled in Omaha, Nebraska. Gerrit's oldest son, Bram, moved to the Salt Creek area to work for a Dutch oil company. Bram met and married a young woman from Home Camp (Midwest) and settled in Dutch Camp. Later, Steve's father also worked the oil field and bought a house in Edgerton, where Steve grew up.

Steve and Rhonda both graduated from high school in 1986, and by August, they wed. In September of that same year, they were surprised that Rhonda was already three months pregnant. Then on February 22, 1987, Misty was born nearly a month premature but was extremely healthy by weighing over six pounds.

Reflecting, Steve was proud that he and his wife had beaten the odds of staying together, but it wasn't their doing. It was God's. Rhonda first brought Steve to church with her while they were still dating. Now, they served as deacons at the Community Church alongside Walt Merino, who had been there for decades.

During high school and after graduation, Steve worked for various oil field service companies in the area. He even worked two jobs at times to support his young family. His lucky break came in early spring 1991 when Steve purchased a used backhoe and a trailer at auction. Over that summer, Steve hired himself out for contract work, and by fall, he bought a used winch truck to expand his capabilities. Through the next few years, he collected other equipment, and in 1994, Otten Services employed four people.

Steve again looked back down at the track and mused over Misty's final run for the day. What worried him was Adam. Since Misty was a sophomore that year and Adam was a senior, the boy would go off to college in the fall. That meant a long-distance relationship that would become hard to maintain due to the distance. The last thing Steve wanted for his daughter was a broken heart.

But living where they did, Steve and Rhonda had a distinct advantage over teenagers' parents in the city. That advantage was this: they all knew one another. It was easy to get to know each other within the Midwest-Edgerton-Linch towns comprising the Salt Creek community. But not just on the surface but at a generation level too.

Like Steve, several families traced their lineage to the workers who arrived in the oil boom era of the early 20th century. Therefore, when a boy asked a girl out on a date, in most cases, the girl's parents knew the boy's family tree to his grandparents.

Likewise, Steve knew Adam and liked him. He knew all about the boy and his mother. As to Adam's father, Steve had only met him a couple of times. But that was before he left Edgerton to become a long-haul truck driver. As far as Steve knew, Adam's dad rarely, if ever, returned home.

Steve also respected that the boy was not a slacker. Adam worked as a roustabout on weekends and in the café three evenings a week. An added plus was Adam attended the same church.

Then Steve asked himself, *"can I trust the boy?"* The answer he sought came immediately. He chuckled aloud. Then he said aloud to himself, "no boy is good enough for my daughter, not even a Pastor's son."

As Steve climbed into his pickup truck, he vividly remembered his private talk with Adam. Steve told the boy to refrain from saying anything or even thinking about anything impure about his daughter. Steve also warned that if Adam violated any condition, he would have a visit with the boy. Steve's talk must have worked since neither he nor Rhonda had anything to grieve about Adam.

Later that evening, Misty sat on the garage doorstep while she talked to Adam on the phone. She hated that her parents would not allow her to take the cordless phone into her room to talk. So instead, Misty used the old avocado green wall-mounted phone in the kitchen with its customary 25-foot cord. Unfortunately, that meant that the only privacy

Misty had was to step into the garage and partially close the door behind her.

Adam still seemed a little off to Misty, and perhaps the whole graffiti incident still upset him. However, when she asked him about it, Adam deferred away from talking about it.

Instead, they mostly talked about the Prom that was quickly approaching later that week. For one thing, they both looked forward to Adam being allowed to drive Misty from her home to the school, then to the post-Prom dinner, and then back home. Even though it was common knowledge that Misty occasionally rode in Adam's car from the school to the Junction for lunch, it didn't necessarily count in her parent's eyes. Contrarily, like the homecoming dance, their dates consisted of Misty's mom or dad driving her and then picking her up at the end. Similarly, when Misty had gone to the movies with Adam a half dozen times in Casper, her parents drove them.

Then Misty and Adam discussed their future and the realities of Adam's post-graduation life in a few months. Adam reported that he received a packet of material in the mail from the University of Wyoming for the upcoming fall semester. Since Adam expected to become the Valedictorian of his class, he would also receive a full academic scholarship to Wyoming.

"When do your classes start at UW again?" Misty asked.

"Hold on," Adam scanned the paper until he found his answer, "it says here that the first day of classes starts on September 9. But it also says that I have to be there on September 5 and 6 for Freshman orientation and dorm assignments."

"I wish you could go closer to me, like Casper College or something. Laramie just seems like another world away to me."

"You know I can't do that because of my scholarship. If I don't have it, I won't be able to go to college since I couldn't afford it."

"Couldn't you ask your mom for the money?"

"Misty, we have already been over this. So no, I cannot ask my mom. You know that she is barely able to pay the bills as it is, plus I would never ask her on principle."

"What about your dad?"

"What about him? He hasn't come around in four years. So, I wouldn't even know how to find him?"

Misty gasped. "You are kidding. How can you not know where your dad is?"

Adam remained silent since it was the truth. His father became a long-haul truck driver after being laid off in the oil field. It was hard for folks in the Salt Creek community when Midwest-Edgerton Resource Production (MERP) sold out its holdings. It was sad in a way, too, since MERP had to relinquish the Federal leases that they had managed for nearly a century. Yet, in the transition between oil field management companies, the people came together to ensure every impacted family had enough to eat while also lowering rent payments.

Suddenly, a small audible "click" sounded on the line that mimicked a connection problem. The sound brought Adam out of his inner thinking and back to the conversation.

He finally replied, "I honestly don't know, Misty. My dad lives out of his truck, and I don't know if he has a cellphone? If he does, I don't have the number."

"I'm sorry, I didn't mean to pick a painful scab."

Adam cut her off. "You didn't. I do miss him, and I don't understand why my dad left us behind. But I have to forgive him."

"How could you forgive that? I mean, your dad abandoned his family."

Adam nodded and conceded that Misty did make a good point, but it was not good enough. He then explained the precise thing that motivated him.

"Misty, what is the verse that immediately follows the Lord's Prayer in Matthew 6: 9-13?"

"Umm, I would have to look that up," she stammered.

"I'll save you the time. Matthew 6:14 says that I must forgive the person who hurt me, or my heavenly Father won't forgive me. I know it seems impossible, but when I get these bad feelings about my dad, I say to myself, *I forgive you* and move on."

"I understand, Adam, but I also feel sorry for your mom."

"Don't feel sorry. My mom is the one that pointed out that scripture to me."

Just then, the voice of Misty's mom, Rhonda, came over the phone and intruded on the conversation. "Misty, you are over your allotted time on the phone. But I forgive you," she said.

Misty fumed, "MOM! How long have you been listening?"

Rhonda replied, "Long enough, now say goodnight," and then she hung up.

Misty told Adam, "Bye, I will talk to you tomorrow."

Likewise, Adam said goodbye and hung up the phone.

* * *

7

TUESDAY, APRIL 16, 2002

OTTEN HOME, SEVEN MILES WEST OF MIDWEST,
WYOMING

It felt like a repeat of the day before when Misty looked out of the kitchen window. She watched the school Chevy Suburban turn onto her half-mile-long driveway. Misty had overslept a little that morning and had yet to eat something for breakfast. Instead, she grabbed a packet of pop tarts to eat on the way to school.

Misty called out to her mom, "bye, I will see you when I get home."

From downstairs in the basement, she heard, "okay, honey, have a good day."

She stepped through the front door and walked across the redwood deck and down the steps. Simultaneously, the small bus came to a stop. Misty opened the door and acknowledged the driver with the usual nod of her head.

The driver, Naomi Wright, was a natural introvert and often spoke only in whispering tones. She lived in Gas Plant with her husband, Kirk, and her two adolescent boys. Naomi took the job because it provided a little bit more income for the family. The position also brought her a little excitement to her day since she had to drive into the vast pristine and undeveloped part of Wyoming.

Only the best roads had any gravel, though most were nothing more than glorified dirt trails with the bumps occasionally graded out every year or so. Although Naomi's vehicle had 4-wheel drive, drifting snow was always a concern because of the ranches' remoteness. But every day, she made a game of looking whether it was a typical Pronghorn or a Mule Deer. At other times, she spotted elk, typically in the springtime. One time, Naomi saw a Moose cow and calf walking down a gravel road.

Naomi liked the Otten place because it was most accessible and close to town, but where she picked up Lucas was way back into the hills. Come to think of it; she had yet to see where Lucas lived because the boy drove a small John Deere Gator all-terrain vehicle. Every morning the boy would be sitting in the ATV next to Razorback Reservoir. Then every afternoon, she dropped him off at the exact location.

After that, Naomi picked up Stephanie Merrick, the O'Hara girls, and the Boyer boys off Long Canyon Road. So far, she had managed the route well though it took her a little over 2 hours from the school to drive the entire loop.

Misty was greatly relieved that Lucas Gagnon was not sitting behind her. He was such a daily pest that even his absences were even more noticeable.

"Ms. Wright, you didn't see Lucas this morning?" Misty asked the driver.

Naomi turned her head 45 degrees and spoke, but Misty failed to hear what she had to say.

"I'm sorry, Ms. Wright, I can't hear you over the Boyer boys." Then Misty turned to Brandon and Brenton and hissed, "hush, you two!"

Once again, Naomi said, "no, I didn't see him where I usually pick him up. There was a man there who said that he worked for Lucas' father. Anyway, the guy said that Lucas got a ride to school this morning."

"What did the guy look like?" Once again, Misty glared at the Boyer boys while she lifted her finger to her lips that told the boys to *hush*.

Naomi fidgeted in her seat as if it were a nervous tick. While she thought, she inadvertently slowed down to almost a walking pace. When she stopped at the end of the Otten driveway, she turned around to address Misty.

"He was a big guy with jet black Elvis-like hair, but that wasn't the weird thing."

"What was it?"

"I dunno, it was what he wore that was weird."

Misty gestured with her hand for Naomi to continue.

Naomi continued, "he wore knee-high rubber boots and a rubber apron over his jeans and flannel shirt. He looked more like a lobster fisherman in Maine than a hired hand in the middle of cow country." The driver then spun around and turned the Suburban toward Midwest.

To Misty, there were two other things from what the driver had said was odd. First, it seemed weird that Lucas did not have a driver's license at 17 years old when they lived in an area most teenagers learned to drive at a much earlier age. Secondly, this was the first time Misty had heard of a hired hand working for Lucas' father. But then again, Lucas rarely offered any information about his family. Nor did he talk about anything else in his life.

Meanwhile, back in Midwest, I had just left home for my daily drive into Casper. The recent promotion and the Sheriff's decision to rescind the requirement for two deputies in that part of Natrona County put me at a crossroads. Yet, up until that year, I had managed to remain working within the Salt Creek community.

My district began in the county's northeast corner across the northern border against Johnson County to Buffalo Creek. Then it extended south along 33-mile Road to Thirty-three Mile Reservoir and then east to the Horse Ranch Road/Highway 259 exit off of I-25. But it also extended east of I-25 to the eastern border with Campbell County. In all, the area was the size of Rhode Island, and now, only one deputy was available to patron it.

Instead, the department created a new position for me: Training Superintendent. My job entailed taking recruits through a structured training regime that lasted five months. Ironically, after Bill Crooks' suggestion, I modeled the instruction plan after the US Coast Guard system of Seamen apprenticeship. Like the service component, recruits experienced various department functions and then chose their primary duty area. Recruits took turns working in the County jail, went on patrol, and transferred prisoners to the court. Some new hires went directly into school resource positions or the SWAT team based on their talents. When I pitched the idea to Sheriff Paulson, he immediately liked it. The Sheriff thought that if an employee enjoyed their job, then Department morale would improve ten-fold.

I appreciated Sheriff Paulson immensely. He filled the vacant seat left behind by Sheriff Witten, who took a senior ranking position within the federal Drug Enforcement Agency six years ago. Unlike my former boss, Sheriff Doan, who still resided at the Wyoming State Prison in Rawlins, I give both successors high marks. But then again, even a scarecrow was a step above Sheriff Doan, in my opinion.

After taking office, one of Paulson's best moves was promoting my longtime buddy, Adam Riley, to Undersheriff. Coincidently, Paulson had recently announced that he would not seek re-election in 2004. Many people, like me, thought Riley was the obvious replacement.

As I drove south on Highway 259 toward Casper, I spotted a vehicle turn off the road a few hundred yards ahead. The pickup truck traveled westerly toward Gas Plant. As I drew nearer and could discern the make and model better, my mouth went dry, and my heart started pounding like a bass drum. I later reasoned that it was a minor panic attack.

I pulled over at the Gas Plant turn-off and came to a stop. When I looked west, a dark green 1978 Ford F150 with what looked like a green license plate crested over the hill and then disappeared on the other side toward the Castle Creek basin.

My mind suddenly flooded with memories. I flashed back to the Savolt case and how a truck matching the same description had hunted Josh Anderson and his friends that fall in 1984. I also thought of the men who occupied that vehicle. Marvin Stiles remained on the lamb though his partner, William Pruitt, was killed by law enforcement. The last time I had processed these memories was ten years ago when Tracy and I found William Pruitt's brother, Dan, frozen to death outside of Gas Plant.

I shook my head and decided my mind was playing tricks on me. But, just to be sure, I waited to see if the truck would show itself rise back up away from Castle Creek. After waiting 30 seconds, all I saw was a different pickup emerge with a maroon paint job reminiscent of the former MERP company.

I asked aloud, "why now, after all this time, were the old cases coming up?" Then I looked at himself in the rearview mirror and suggested, "maybe it is just stress from the change of jobs, or maybe it is becoming a father."

Even as I said it, there was something else that stirred deep inside. I loved my wife, Tracy, but I was always worried about being a good enough dad. My father was a poor example, and I wanted only the best for my unborn child. At any rate, I needed to get my mind back on the task at hand and get to work. So as I pulled back onto Highway 259, I made a mental note to discuss what I saw with Tracy over supper that night.

Back in Midwest, Deputy Corey Jackson arrived at the Police Station behind the Midwest Town Hall at precisely 7:30. Earlier, he had waved hello to me as we headed in the opposite directions on Highway 259.

Tracy approached his vehicle as she was walking across the street as CJ pulled up.

"Hey, CJ. Let me open up the office for you."

"Good morning, Chief."

"Come on, CJ, call me Tracy. When you say the word, Chief, I look for Wyatt Traynor. In my mind, he is the only one worthy of that title."

"Okay, Tracy," CJ resigned.

Tracy inserted her key into the lock, and the latch made an audible click sound. Then, she turned the knob and opened the door. While she held the door with the back of her right leg, Tracy managed to remove a spare key from the keyring and then held it out to CJ.

"Here you go, CJ. This one is yours for as long as you use this office."

"Thanks, ma'am."

Tracy cut him off again. "And no calling me, ma'am, either. I used to call my grandmother that, and I don't like the thought of being old enough to be a *ma'am*, so please call me Tracy."

He was flummoxed. Instead of saying anything that could ultimately get himself into further trouble, he nodded his head and said, "yes."

It didn't take CJ long to bring in his computer and a box full of stuff for the desk. First, he placed the monitor on the desktop and the tower underneath it. Then he unloaded his belongings into the drawers include his custom-made Red-colored Swingline stapler. Ever since he had watched the 1999 movie *Office Space,* he wanted the same stapler himself. So, when Swingline released a red-colored stapler like the one in the movie, he ordered one at once.

As soon as CJ set the stapler down on the desktop, Tracy came out of her office to get a cup of coffee from their shared coffee pot. She spotted the stapler and recognized it immediately.

She asked, "is that the same one from that movie, Office something?"

"Yes, *Office Space*," he corrected.

Tracy reached out to grab the stapler, and CJ pulled it back quickly, just like a child who was unwilling to share a toy.

"You don't want me to touch it, do you?" she asked.

He smiled and did his best to imitate Milton, the film's comedic relief character. "That's it. That is the last straw. I will burn this place down."

Tracy guffawed; however, in doing so, she spilled a few drops of coffee onto the tile floor.

CJ shared a laugh too and then volunteered to clean up Tracy's mess instead of allowing her to bend over with a 36-week pregnant belly.

"Thank you, CJ. I am going to head over to the Junction to do some traffic duty. Did you want me to bring you anything from the store?"

"No, I'm good. I think I am going to get caught up on my emails before I do anything else."

"Okay, suit yourself."

Then Tracy had thought of the juxtaposition between CJ and me. I didn't particularly appreciate using a computer and hated carrying a cellphone. CJ, on the other hand, seemed computer and tech-savvy. Perhaps it was due to our age difference.

Across town, the school's Chevy Suburban parked in the High School lot next to the maintenance shop. Misty didn't wait to help the younger kids like she usually did since she saw Adam's yellow Celica near the library. But, as she stepped around the Suburban, Misty almost bumped into Pete LaRoche, one of the maintenance technicians, who was also one of her dad's best friends.

"Whoa there, Misty. A person's likely to get hurt that way," Pete said.

"Oh, hi, Mr. LaRoche. I didn't see you."

"That's okay, darling. I suppose you are looking for Adam, huh?"

"Yes, of course, I am."

Pete pointed to the south entrance next to the school's library. He instructed, "I saw him standing in the hallway outside of the library just a few moments ago."

Misty nodded and then moved by Pete in a rush. When she went through the door, Misty immediately saw Adam and walked up and hugged him.

While still in his embrace, she said, "I'm sorry about last night and my mom listening in on our conversation. It was just so rude of her."

He squeezed her in his arms and assured her, "it's okay. I mean, at least she didn't hear anything bad."

"It's not funny, Adam. It was just rude."

Adam nodded, even though Misty had no way of seeing his agreement. Instead, he asked her, "what would you do if your daughter was talking to a boy on the phone?"

She thought about it for a microsecond and then replied, "I wouldn't do that to my daughter. I would be more gracious and trusting." Then as if she had second thoughts, "at least, that is what I think now."

Adam smiled. "Okay, how about we go to my locker and get our stuff?"

The couple walked up to the locker with the #11 tag, and Adam lifted the latch. Immediately as the door swung open, a loud "BOOM" sounded, and confetti shot out of the locker, across the hallway, and into the lockers on the other side.

While pieces of paper still floated softly to the tiled floor, Mr. Crooks exited his classroom and into the hallway. There, Crooks found Adam with his hand still grasping the latch on his locker door.

"What is going on here, Adam? What was that noise I heard?"

"I don't know, Sir. All I did was open my locker."

"Are you okay?" Crooks inquired.

The boy nodded that he was and then turned to look inside the locker itself. Not only had there been a small explosion, but a vertical banner now hung from the upper shelf. In all, there were five pieces of printer paper taped together, and each page containing a giant letter. The characters then spelled out the word *L-O-S-E-R*.

* * *

8

Adam was still in shock by what had taken place. So, Bill Crooks looked over the boy's face once again to see if he was injured. He then placed his massive hand on Adam's and slowly pulled the boy away from the locker. As Adam stepped backward, Crooks barked out a command that ordered all the converging students to take a step back and go around because the hallway was now closed.

"It is okay, Adam. Calm down," the teacher said. Then he looked at Misty and instructed her, "stay with him while you take him down to the office. I want him to stay put there. Do you understand?"

Misty nodded her head and let out a curt, "Yes, Sir," and she took Adam by the arm and led him down the hall through a mob of students. Other students asked what happened as they walked, though neither Adam nor Misty knew what to say.

Meanwhile, Dr. Shannon Isom, the Midwest School Principal, arrived at Adam's locker. She had been in the library when she heard the *BOOM*.

"What is going on, Bill?" Isom asked.

"Hey, Doc. I don't know exactly. It looks like someone did a gag on Adam Weiss by arming the opening of his locker with a bundle of seven one and ½ inch diameter, 4-inch-long party poppers."

Dr. Isom stepped forward and inspected the spent party cartridges more closely, and she took a good look at the sign hanging from the upper shelf.

"Bill, that doesn't look like a regular party popper to me because most of them are spring-loaded." The Principal stepped back and looked at Crooks. "I also smell something. Did you catch that too?"

Crooks nodded. "I did. It smells like matches to me. I think whoever did this intended not only to embarrass Adam with the sign and the noise but to hurt him too."

Dr. Isom shook her head in disbelief, but Crooks insisted. "Take a look at the confetti embedded into the wall above the lockers. That would take a heck of a lot of force, Doc."

Dr. Isom noted Crooks' observation and finally resigned, "okay, I will call the police. Do me a favor, Bill. Stand here to keep any of the kids away from the scene."

"No problem, Doc."

Moments later, Tracy's phone rang at her desk. However, when she lifted the receiver off the cradle, Tracy froze because she didn't know what to say. She hadn't yet planned or even thought about how she should answer the phone.

Then Tracy said, "Midwest Police, how may I help you?"

Dr. Isom asked the on the other end of the call, "Tracy? Tracy Crandall? Is that you?"

"Yes, this is Tracy Crandall. How may I help you?"

"Tracy, this is Dr. Isom over at the school. I need you to come over immediately and take a look at something."

"Oh, hey, Doc. What specifically do you want me to do so I know what I need to bring with me?"

Dr. Isom briefly explained the small explosion inside Adam Weiss' locker and how she and Bill Crooks suspect it was more than a gag. Tracy assured the Principal that she would be over and dust the hall locker and the immediate area for fingerprints.

Tracy got up, walked over to the small closet inside her office, and removed the dusting kit that Chief Traynor had left behind. Then she walked into the next room, where she spotted CJ still pouring over emails.

Tracy cleared her throat to get CJ's attention, and when he looked up at her, she asked, "there is an incident over at the school. It seems a prank went too far, which almost seriously hurt one of the students. Do you want to come along?"

CJ shrugged but then asked, "isn't this a Midwest Police jurisdiction since it is at the school?"

"It is, but the victim here, Adam Weiss, lives in Edgerton, which is your jurisdiction. How about you come along just to meet a few people."

CJ shrugged again and stood up. "Fine, let me get my hat."

Five minutes later, Chief Tracy Crandall and Deputy Jackson arrived at the high school parking lot. When Tracy got out of her Midwest Police Ford Explorer, CJ walked up and insisted on carrying the investigation kit since she was pregnant.

It wasn't that Tracy didn't appreciate chivalry; it was that she just didn't see the use of it. During her brief Air Force career, fellow Airman made her feel overtly appeased at times. For instance, when she started working with me, I always went out of my way to do little things like opening doors and getting her coffee. The fact was that Tracy liked being independent, even during her pregnancy.

The law officers walked into the school's main entrance and passed the boys' locker room and the school advisor's office. Then they approached the school's main office countertop; Dr. Isom stepped out of the other room to greet them.

"Thanks, Tracy, for coming so quickly," she said.

"No problem, Doc. Oh, before I forget, this is my replacement with the Sheriff's department; his name is Deputy Cory Jackson."

Before Dr. Isom could speak, the deputy interjected, "Ma'am, you can call me CJ."

"Okay, CJ. I am glad to meet you. Now, the student and his girlfriend are sitting in my office. I have already called their parents, and they should arrive shortly. But the scene is down at locker #11, and you will find your friend, Bill Crooks, keeping the area clear."

"Okay, Doc. We will start at the locker, but we will need to get some statements from the kids. That is after their parents get here and give us permission for the interview."

"Just come on back to my office when you finish then."

As they turned to walk down the hallway, CJ whispered a question to Tracy. "I hate to say anything, but having a teacher so close to the scene could become a contamination threat, don't you think?"

Tracy looked at CJ and furrowed her brow. Then she retorted, "what? Bill Crooks? Don't worry; he is one of us. Don't let me forget to tell you about it later."

When they approached Bill Crooks, Tracy quickly introduced CJ. Crooks went over his observations about the charge's size and how the blast area matched Adam's height.

"Thanks again, Bill, for securing the scene. But don't you have a class to teach?"

Crooks chuckled heartily and admitted, "no, not first period. It is my planning hour."

Tracy went to work quickly, beginning with photographing everything inside and outside the locker. She then took additional pictures of the opposite wall with tiny confetti bits still stuck in the paint. Next, with CJ's help, she donned a pair of latex gloves. Then Tracy slowly removed the bundle of party poppers first. Then she pulled the five pieces of paper which constituted the *LOSER* sign. Only then did Tracy dust the entire locker for fingerprints. She uncovered a slew of them that presumably were Adam's. She made a mental note to obtain his prints for comparison.

Meanwhile, CJ took an interest in the pieces of paper that made up the sign. Specifically, he looked for anything on the paper sheets for unique printer markings. CJ was not a computer or a printer expert, but he had kept up with each upgrade in technology. Unlike his brother, who graduated in 1986, CJ had the luxury of using computers in school and at home since he was in the fourth grade.

What he looked for specifically were any imperfections that most printers inadvertently made on the paper. Surprisingly, CJ didn't find anything along the borders of each page. But each giant letter that spelled out the word *L-O-S-E-R* looked odd. There was a flawed line in the middle of each symbol. Each letter contained a single unprinted line no thicker than human hair precisely in the middle of each page.

"Ah, ha! I think I found something!" CJ exclaimed. Then he motioned for Tracy to come closer. "Take a look at this, Tracy," and CJ took a retractable ballpoint pen out of his pocket to point out his observation. Then he said, "if you look closely, each of these pieces of paper has an identical misprint in the center of the page."

Tracy had difficulty seeing what CJ wanted her to find, even with CJ's pen next to it. But finally, she did see it.

"You mean that skipped line from the printer?" she asked.

"Yes. Printers that have a small flaw like that are just like human fingerprints as no two are identical."

"I see," Tracy said. Then she suggested, "why don't you start with the printers in the library, and we will work around the school from there."

CJ nodded. "You read my mind. I'll see you in a little bit, but I want to be with you when it comes to questioning the teenagers."

"No problem."

While CJ ducked into the library, Bill Crooks reappeared in the hallway. He stood so silently that Tracy didn't know he was there. Though a large man, Crooks was stealthy. Two years before, he drew an Elk tag for the Pine Ridge east of Edgerton. One day during archery season on the Loren Ranch, Crooks sat patiently beside a Ponderosa Pine tree and waited for a bull elk he had seen while scouting. He was so quiet that the bull elk walked within ten yards of him.

Suddenly, a female student walked around the corner from the hallway that connected the high school wing with the junior high wing.

She looked up and said, "hi Mr. Crooks, can I get through? I need to go to the office."

Tracy jumped at the unexpected noise and then gave Crooks a scolding look. Meanwhile, he sidestepped to allow the student to pass.

"If you are going to stand there, put on a pair of gloves and help me seal up these fingerprints I lifted," Tracy ordered Crooks.

Stoically, he followed her instructions, and soon, they had everything wrapped up within the locker. Only then did she offer him a curt, "thanks."

As he took his gloves off, Crooks smiled back at Tracy. "Anytime. So, how about we hit the gun range just as soon as we can after you deliver. I mean, Lois would love to watch the baby."

Tracy smiled. "Thanks, Bill. I would love that. I have craved some good range time."

Not long afterward, CJ appeared from around the corner and informed Tracy and Bill Crooks that he printed test samples. But the pages did not reveal the faulty line in the center. Crooks thought about it for a second and then offered to go around after school to test all the other printers, including the front office. When CJ started to object, Crooks pulled out his wallet.

"It is about time that you know something, Deputy," and Crooks handed CJ his shield.

CJ looked at it and said aloud, "Department of the Interior, Law Enforcement? Who exactly do you work for?"

Crooks grinned. "Bureau of Land Management, to be precise, that is who I work for outside of school hours. Sometimes I lend mutual aid to the local law enforcement around here."

"You are kidding? You govern the BLM lands around here?" CJ inquired.

"Yes, but more importantly to you, I am also the school's Information Technology troubleshooter. That means I can go around the entire school to print test pages from every printer. Plus, if I do it, you will avoid any chain of custody issues that always arise."

Tracy again thanked Crooks, and he promised to call that evening to discuss what he found. CJ then reached down to pick up the investigation kit when Tracy's hand met his.

She mouthed, "I got it," and insisted on picking up the case. Then they walked down the hallway to the office to interview the victims.

A few steps before reaching the office entrance, CJ asked, "so, what is the real story with that, Mr. Crooks? I detect him as a veteran like special operations or a former operator?"

Tracy stopped short of the office entrance and then explained, "yes, you're right, he was in special ops. However, your knowledge of his additional employment is confidential."

"Why?"

"Well, Bill likes people to think that the hundreds of thousands of BLM acres around here are free and open access with little to zero oversight. But, if you ever find yourself in a tight spot, there is nobody I trust my life again than with him."

"What do you mean, again?"

Tracy smiled and replied, "that's another story when I have time to tell it. Now, we need to get in there and speak to Adam and his girlfriend."

Seconds later, Tracy and CJ entered Dr. Isom's office. Already seated next to Adam Weiss was his mother, Bess. Next to Misty Otten was her mother, Rhonda.

"Ah, yes, Chief Crandall and Deputy Jackson. Please come in, won't you," offered Dr. Isom.

"Thanks, Doc. I don't think this will take that long," Tracy said. Then she looked around the room at the parents, who looked a little unnerved at what had happened that morning.

"I just finished lifting a few fingerprints off of Adam's locker. But what I need is to take prints from both Adam and Misty. That way, I can distinguish between their prints and those who may have set up the prank."

Bess Weiss spoke up, "A prank? Is that what you are calling it? From what the kids told me, it sounded more like a definite attempt to hurt my son. Isn't that attempted assault or something?"

"Mrs. Weiss," Tracy started to say but was interrupted.

"Tracy, please call me Bess."

"Okay, Bess. At this point, I don't know if this was not a prank that went bad or if this was intentional. I am opening an investigation, and I hope that by today or tomorrow, Dr. Isom will talk to whoever did this."

"And, what if nobody comes forward?" asked Rhonda Otten.

Tracy turned her head toward Misty and Rhonda. "Then I hope to find a different set of fingerprints that may lead us to who did this inside Adam's locker."

The baby inside Tracy's belly gave a huge kick, which took her breath away for a second. Then Tracy asked if she and CJ could do a quick interview with Adam and Misty alone. Both mothers agreed and stepped out into the waiting area in the main office. However, Dr. Isom remained in her chair.

The interview with Adam only took a few minutes because the facts were so straightforward. He had waited outside the library for Misty to arrive, and then they went to his locker and then a loud BOOM. When Tracy asked him who he thought might do such a thing, he only shrugged. Then Tracy opened the investigation kit and took Adam's fingerprints. When she finished, Adam was allowed to leave.

During Misty's interview, she revealed practically the same narrative as Adam. Likewise, she shrugged when Tracy asked who would do such a thing to Adam. Then Misty was fingerprinted as well.

As Tracy and CJ exited the principal's office, she asked Dr. Isom to call her if anyone came forward with any more information or took ownership of the incident.

Midway to the exit, Tracy stopped in the hallway and asked CJ to bring the investigation kit to her Department Explorer.

When CJ looked like he didn't understand, she said, "please, CJ, take the kit for me. My baby is pushing on my bladder again, and I have to pee."

Flummoxed and somewhat embarrassed, CJ lunged and clumsily took the case from Tracy's hand. He quickly stepped aside as Tracy rushed by him to the restroom on the right side of the hallway.

Instead of sticking around, CJ walked out to the parking lot. Once he arrived at the Midwest Police Explorer, he set the investigation case in the back seat. As he closed the door, his cellphone began to buzz inside the holster on his hip. CJ lifted the phone and pressed the green-colored *TALK* button to answer the call.

"Deputy Jackson, how may I help you?"

"CJ, this is Undersheriff Riley. Did I catch you at a good time?"

"Yes, Sir. It is a good time to talk. How can I help you?"

"Let me cut to the chase, CJ. I named you our departmental representative in a consortium with the counties of Johnson, Sheridan, Campbell, Crook, and Weston Sheriff's Departments. The Governor has asked us to form a committee to investigate a rash of missing teenage girls. In each of the counties, I just listed, there is at least one missing person's case. As you may or not know, we have two cases of our own."

"When and where do I meet, Sir?"

"Tomorrow morning at 9:30 in Gillette. They will meet at the Sheriff Department's main complex. Do you know where that is?"

"I do, Sir. I will be there."

"Thanks again, CJ. I have sent you an email with a lot of other background information. Please take the time to digest it all before you head up there."

"I will, Sir, and I will send a post-meeting report to you."

"That would be perfect, CJ. One more thing, how are you adjusting up there?"

CJ looked up and saw Tracy walking toward him, and then he replied, "I think I will fit in just fine around here."

"That is good to hear. Cool, I will talk to you soon," Riley said and quickly hung up.

Tracy smiled and jokingly teased CJ. "Lover's quarrel?"

He didn't smile. "I wish. Come on, let us go back to the office, and I will tell you about it on the way."

* * *

9

At 6:30 p.m. that night, I pulled into the carport. As I drove down Navy Row, I noticed that my house did not have any lights on, which meant that Tracy was probably still in the Midwest Police Station office across the street. I confirmed as much when I turned around and saw the light shining through the office window. Additionally, Deputy CJ Jackson's department pickup was parked there as well. I then pocketed the keys, walked up the sidewalk, and then onto the redwood porch to the front door.

I called out, "honey, are you home?" which resulted in a silent return. So, I set down my lunchbox on the counter, then turned on the standing lamp next to the front door and walked back outside on the porch. But before crossing C Street, I heard the distinctive rumble of a large block engine. I looked east where I listened to the noise, and my eyes made out the distinctive taillights of a late 70s Ford pickup. Then I looked over at my own 1978 Ford F150 that my father left me in the will. Suddenly, I remembered my experience earlier that morning.

Thirty seconds later, I entered the Police station. The entrance led into a two-room office suite where CJ occupied the first room, while the back office belonged to Tracy. I immediately noticed that CJ had a large paper map of Wyoming affixed to one wall with tape strips when I breached the door. Additionally, the roadmap had different colored push pins in various towns and cities in the State's northeastern portion.

"Whatcha working on, CJ?" I asked.

"Oh, hey, Eddie. I was named to a task force with other Deputies from all of the northeastern counties in the State to figure out a rash of missing teenage girls," CJ explained.

"I heard about that. If you need any help or advice, I am here."

"Thanks, Lieutenant."

At the sound of my voice, Tracy slowly rose from her desk and held her belly as she walked into the other room.

"Hi, honey. How was your day?" she asked.

"It was fine. It looks like both of you had a pretty long day since you are both still here at the office."

Tracy nodded and then sat down in the spare chair across from CJ's desk. She then unfolded about the school's call about a prank in Adam Weiss' locker. CJ added that Tracy had lifted fingerprints, but they were still waiting to see if the papers that made up the *L-O-S-E-R* sign left in Adam's locker came from a school printer. Then, CJ told me about his hunch about the misprint line and how it traced like a fingerprint.

I took it all in and then moved over to the coffee pot and poured myself a cup. I lifted the mug to my lips and immediately tasted the tar-like bitters of years' worth of lousy coffee made in the same pot by Wyatt Traynor. Then I shrugged because even bad coffee is better than no coffee at all.

"Let me look at the photos you took of the locker," I asked.

Tracy nodded. "Okay, but you will have to come to my office because, thanks to CJs help, I downloaded the photos onto my computer."

I shook my head and lamented, "we've come a long way from using a simple Polaroid camera, haven't we? Now, everything is digital."

"Yes, Sir, but this is something that I think you are going to like," CJ said, and then he asked Tracy, "do you mind if I drive your computer?"

"No, by all means, go ahead."

CJ maneuvered himself around the desk and then turned the monitor about 120 degrees so everyone could see the computer screen. Next, the Deputy clicked on a few icons that looked like file folders, which eventually opened up a file with small, pixelated photos. He then opened the first photo.

"So, here is Adam Weiss' locker as we found it. Do you see the bundle of innocent-looking party poppers?" CJ asked.

"I do," I replied.

CJ opened up another photo, but it was a closeup of the confetti stuck on the wall this time. Then he instructed me to watch as he slowly zoomed in on a lone piece of confetti.

"That is stuck into the wall!" I exclaimed. Then I stood erect after bending to see the computer monitor, and I looked at my wife.

"I assume you bagged the party poppers, so can I look at them?" I asked.

Tracy nodded and handed him a large see-through plastic bag that contained the poppers. I peered through the plastic to examine the contents rather than don a pair of gloves and remove them. Then something caught my eye.

"Take a look at the bottom of each of the poopers," I instructed Tracy.

"Why? What did you find?"

"Nope, I want you to find it rather than me pointing it out. Again, look at the bottom, where the string comes out."

Tracy looked again at the poppers while CJ peered over her shoulder. He saw it first and pointed. Then Tracy saw it too.

She looked up at her husband and said, "do you think these were modified?"

I nodded, opened the bag, and took a small sniff of the air trapped inside the bag.

"It smells a little bit like garlic or matches. I can't tell the difference. Anyway, I think this needs to go to the lab in Casper for analysis." I closed the zip lock seal and then suggested, "Hon, I can take anything you need tomorrow morning on my way to work."

"Sure, you can take that bag and the fingerprints into town for me. That would be a big help."

CJ then brought up another photo on the computer screen. Then he pointed out, "look how whoever did this used a thread spool and a coat hanger to make a simple pulley so that when the door opened, it pulled the string to set off the poppers."

Tracy shook her head in disbelief, "how can a teenager come up with that? I mean, that took some thinking, didn't it?"

CJ shrugged and said, "I don't know, but I bet there are instructions on the internet for doing something like this."

I raised my eyebrows and questioned him, "really? One would think that kind of information would be illegal?"

"I know you would think that, wouldn't you? But sadly, the answer is no. We found it perfectly legal for anarchists to share pipe bomb recipes when I worked in Boulder, Colorado. All we can hope now is that the US Congress will pass a law against that stuff following the events of 9/11," CJ explained.

I looked down into my cup, swirled the coffee sludge in the bottom, and took another drink. "Who do you think has enough animosity toward Adam Weiss to do something that could have hurt him badly?" I lifted the cup again and finished the rest of the coffee in a gulp. "I bet Adam didn't rat anyone out, did he?"

Tracy shook her head. "No, but isn't that a little odd, don't you think?"

"No. You see, in situations like these, kids believe it will be worse for them if they finger somebody out. You know, they are afraid of the payback more than the desire to do the right thing."

CJ nodded that he understood. "Interesting, Sir. Did you get that from a college class or something?"

I chuckled. "No, it is something I learned while working within our county prison. I would wager those students and inmates share similar sociological behavior patterns."

"Interesting theory, honey. Maybe I need to follow up with Adam and Misty away from school," Tracy replied.

The sound of the front door opening caught everyone's attention, and then they heard a familiar voice.

"Hello, does anyone work here?"

Tracy was the first to step out of her office, and when she entered the other room, she met Wyatt Traynor coming through the door in his wheelchair with Bill Crooks, who pushed the former Chief from behind.

"Hey, Chief. What are you up to?" Tracy asked.

Wyatt shifted in his seat and said, "I just came by to see how your first full day went?"

"You heard about what happened at school today, didn't you?" she asked.

"I did, but that is not the only reason why I stopped by. Do you know where your husband is by any chance?" Wyatt asked.

"I am here, Chief," I said while carefully moving by my very pregnant wife. CJ also used the opportunity to step out of Tracy's office as well.

Wyatt picked up the brown-colored paper file folder in his lap and handed it to me. Then he explained, "Eddie, this is my copy of the Savolt file. I want you to have it because I think that you will somehow solve this case someday. Don't ask me how I know that you will, but just trust that I have full faith in your ability."

"Thanks, Wyatt. I don't know what to say. Honestly, I haven't thought about that case until this morning as a matter of fact," I admitted.

I then explained how he saw a dark-colored 1970s model Ford F150 that morning and again in the dark when he got home. Wyatt, Bill, and Tracy assured me that perhaps I saw something different, or maybe my imagination got the best of me.

Meanwhile, CJ studied his map and was generally unconcerned about discussing a case dating back to when he was eight years old.

Then Bill Crooks handed Tracy a folder and said, "Tracy, this concerns you, and you too, CJ. Inside this folder are print samples from every printer in the school. But I would pay attention to what I labeled #6."

Tracy opened the folder and skipped to the sixth sample, and CJ reached in and lifted the piece of paper. He held it up into the light and distinctly saw a missing line of ink in the middle of the page, which was just like those in the sign left in Adam's locker.

"So, which room has printer #6 in it?" CJ asked.

Crooks answered dryly, "the science lab." Then Crooks looked at his watch and said, "alright, Wyatt, are you ready to blow this clam bake? We only have another hour before I need to bring you home."

I raised my right eyebrow inquisitively. "Where are you guys going?"

Crooks turned to me and said, "ever since he has been mobile enough after the accident, I have been taking Wyatt out of the house once or twice a week. Tonight, we are going over to the Castle Rock Bar to watch the English professional dart league on TV."

Traynor smiled. "During Vietnam, whenever we came back from the bush, we drank a lot of beer and played a lot of darts. Nowadays, I drink little, play little, but watch a lot of darts."

"Okay, enjoy yourselves," Tracy called out, and just as quickly that the two men arrived, they had departed.

I looked at my watch, which now read *7:26*. Since I didn't feel much like cooking, I suggested that we all go over to the café in Edgerton for supper. CJ initially balked at the idea because he needed to get back home to Casper. But I asserted that CJ could leave from here to attend his meeting in Gillette in the morning. I even offered CJ our spare bedroom for him to stay overnight.

CJ finally agreed but stipulated that he would sleep in his office instead. I then motioned for CJ to follow me across C Street and around the side of my house, and to the storage shed. I removed a sleeping bag and a cot from my hunting supplies and handed them to CJ.

After taking the sleeping bag and the cot over to the office, CJ returned to our house with his Department Silverado pickup, and we climbed inside.

As we drove east on Highway 387 between Midwest and Edgerton, CJ noticed a small light bobbing up and down along the road's side. Suddenly, the pickup's headlights cast upon a man with a headlamp running alongside the road. Incredibly, he wore nothing more than a pair of running shorts and a t-shirt even though the outside temperature was low 40s. Additionally, the mysterious runner had a dark complexion with long hair that danced as he ran.

CJ looked at me in the backseat through the rear-view mirror and asked, "who the heck was that?"

I smiled and said, "oh, that was just Christian Mercy."

"Okay, aside from an odd double entendre for a name, what is his story?"

"How do you know he has a story?" Tracy teased CJ.

CJ shook his head. "All small towns have people with an interesting past. So, I assume that a guy who looks like a Native American running in the dark has to have a story behind him."

I leaned forward close to his ear. "Well, that is a long story, so I will try to sum it up quickly. Christian is an ultra-marathoner and a licensed addictions counselor that kind of adopted us."

"What do you mean about adopting?" CJ asked.

I chuckled. "It is, as I said. Christian has adopted the community and everyone in it as his own. You will see. He is a good man who has found peace in this place we all call home."

CJ slowed the vehicle as they entered the Edgerton town limit. I quickly informed CJ that Christian Mercy was an Arapaho that grew up on the Wyoming Indian Reservation. After high school, Christian went to Kearney State College in Nebraska on a Cross Country running scholarship. After graduation, Christian conducts drug and alcohol interventions from Riverton to Casper and Sheridan.

"So, how did this Christian Mercy arrive here?"

"About eight years ago, he drove from Sheridan to Casper when he took the Midwest exit off I-25. Then by the aid of a topographic map, Christian made his way to Casper through the open country to the west and south."

"Why would that matter?"

CJ could see me smiling at him in the rear-view mirror. Then I asked him, "do you know anything about ultramarathoning?"

"Nope, not a thing."

"Well, Christian is one of the best in the nation." I shifted my body weight off of the wallet in my back pocket. Then I continued, "so, on that fateful day that he drove the backway to Casper, Christian found that all of the oilfield roads and the BLM roads in this area were a great place to train. So, he bought a trailer in Edgerton and trains here, plus he is a volunteer track coach at the school."

Before CJ could respond, I offered one more tidbit of information regarding Christian Mercy. "You should get to know him because other than Bill Crooks, Christian knows every road and trail west of the interstate, so keep that in mind as you patrol that part of your district."

"Thanks, I will."

When we entered the café, there were a dozen or so diners seated at tables and booths. Plus, two other men, who were oil field workers, sat at the counter. Besides, the clumps of gumbo mud underneath their boots gave them away.

Liz Martin came over and greeted us after we found a booth in the large room, and then she took our orders. Remarkably, she did so without writing anything down. But, while we waited for our food to arrive, Adam Weiss came over to the table with a water pitcher in his hand.

Tracy looked up and smiled at the boy. "Hi Adam, I didn't know you worked here?"

Adam blushed, as indicated by a slight hue of red on his cheeks. He then replied, "yes, ma'am. I work here three nights a week, bussing tables and filling drinks. Then I work after church every Sunday breaking down and fixing truck tires for Oscar's Oil Field Service."

Before Tracy or I or even CJ could say anything, Adam revealed something else.

He looked at Tracy and said, "I forgot to tell you, ma'am, that someone called me a loser yesterday, and then someone scratched the same word onto my gym locker.

I leaned forward and asked, "who, Adam?"

Adam shook his head. "I don't want to get anyone in trouble, but after today, I just want this stuff to stop. I mean, after those bits of paper blew past my face, it kind of got to me."

"Adam, who called you a loser?" Tracy prodded.

Adam took a deep breath. "Well, it was two boys. One was Robbie Lepsis, and the other was Lucas Gagnon. But again, I don't want anyone getting into trouble, especially me. I mean, I am trying to finish my senior year out strong because I need the valedictorian scholarship to go to college. So again, I want to be left out of this stuff as much as possible."

"We understand, Adam. I will keep you as far removed as I can," Tracy assured.

Adam blushed again, and he said, "thank you, ma'am. I appreciate it."

Once Adam had moved away from the table to the far side of the café, Tracy then said, "wow." She then took out her notebook from her left breast pocket and made a quick note of the name given by Adam.

CJ asked aloud to nobody in particular, "who is Lucas Gagnon?"

I shrugged and admitted, "I don't know the boy very well, but I could pick him out of a class photo. All I know is that he and his father, Liam, moved here around three to four years ago."

"So, you have met the father?" CJ asked.

"Yes, but come to think of it, I haven't seen Liam in nearly two years."

"How could you miss seeing someone for two years in a place this small?" CJ questioned.

"It is easier than you'd think," Tracy interjected. "The Gagnon's live out west of I-25, but I have no idea the precise location. All I know is that their place is near Razorback Ridge. But what I have always found strange is that there is no mention of a Mrs. Gagnon."

The teenaged girl arrived with their food, which caused a slight hiatus in conversation. Instead, Tracy and I stopped and prayed over our meal. At least momentarily, CJ did not know what to do since it had been years since he prayed before eating. However, he waited patiently, and when we said "Amen," he repeated the same.

Then as if stupefied with a realization, CJ said, "I see that you are both practicing Christians. Though after hearing you both pray, it makes total sense now."

"What makes sense?" Tracy asked.

CJ's wide disarming smile broke across his face. "I've noticed that ever since I have met you two that neither of you curses. Not one time, not one slip up."

I smiled and explained, "well, there are a couple of ways to look at it. First, the author Louis L'Amour never wrote a curse word either. In an interview, he once relayed that he was a good enough writer to articulate his thoughts without using lazy curse words."

"What is the other way you look at it?" CJ asked.

"Well, cursing provides a poor witness. But, as a Christian, I accept the responsibility of sharing the Good News wherever I go. Now, I can't possibly provide a good example if I use expletives to make a biblical point, can I?"

CJ nodded. "I see your point," then turned his focus back to the meal.

A little while later, between bites of his cheeseburger, CJ suddenly asked as if out of the blue, "so who is the other boy, Robbie Lepsis, that Adam spoke about?"

I whipped my mouth with a napkin and replaced it on my lap. "Have you heard of Lepsis Chevrolet?"

"In Casper? Who hasn't?" CJ replied.

I continued, "well, then you know the family. Robbie is the youngest of three siblings, and his father owns the dealership. The boy has been in and out of the juvenile detention center at least three times. Additionally, both Natrona County and Kelly Walsh High Schools have expelled him."

"What were his offenses?" CJ asked.

"Well, he defaced school property, argued with teachers, and threatened students, to name a few of the offenses. So, now, Robbie is on last chance to straighten out here in Midwest."

"I see, but what else do you know about him? I mean, could he have possibly boobie trapped Adam's locker?"

I tilted my head while I thought for a moment. "Perhaps, but according to his Juvenile Probation Officer, the boy got into trouble mainly because he was bored and had few friends. I mean, think about it, Robbie has a car, money, and anything else he could ever want but still ended up sideways with the law."

CJ nodded. "Yep, I have seen the type. I am no psychologist, but my observation is boys like Robbie are simply attention-seeking more than being delinquent." Before taking another bite, CJ had another thought and asked, "what about Robbie's friend, Lucas. Would he have the smarts to pull this off?"

Tracy chimed in, "absolutely, Lucas is brilliant. However, I would question his nerve. I see him as an extreme non-confrontational type."

"Yep, rigging a mini-explosion in a locker is pretty passive-aggressive, wouldn't you agree? But I don't know, maybe it was just a prank gone wrong, and we are making too much about it?" CJ questioned.

Tracy then offered, "maybe I need to have another talk with Dr. Isom in the morning?"

"That would be a good thing, and I will get those evidence bags to the lab. Then, maybe we can find a few things that can start connecting," I assured.

* * *

10

Deputy Cory "CJ" Jackson made a quick stop at the Junction store. There he topped off his gas tank and went inside to purchase a cup of coffee and an egg and sausage biscuit for breakfast. The deputy quickly settled into his department-issued pickup truck and prepared for the hour and a half drive to Gillette. When CJ stopped briefly at the crossroads of Highways 387 and 259, he looked longingly south along Highway 259 that would have taken him home and his comfortable bed.

CJ spent the last night in his new office in the Midwest Police Station on a borrowed cot and a loaned sleeping bag. But reflecting on his night's rest, it wasn't the equipment that prevented him from sleeping well. Instead, his current assignment on the task force kept him awake.

After leaving the café in Edgerton the night before, CJ dropped Tracy and me off at our home adjacent to the Police Station. Then he went back to work. First, he looked up his information on all the teenage girls reported missing in the northeastern part of Wyoming. Next, CJ noted there were two teenagers from Casper. Still, he also noticed that their files were last updated in October of the previous year. Finally, just before 9 p.m., he thought to call the parents on file and explain that he looked further into their daughter's disappearance.

So, CJ picked up the file on Tiffani Wells. On August 14, 2001, Tiffani went missing when she failed to come home after being out with friends at the Central Wyoming Fair. He looked up the parent's phone number and determined it was just within etiquette to call them at that late hour. When Tiffani's mother answered the phone, CJ introduced himself and briefly explained his reason for calling. She told him that her daughter had left town with a carnival worker. Since her daughter was now 18 years old, she wasn't pressing the issue any longer.

Not dissuaded, CJ then took up the file of Tina Singleton. When he spoke to Tina's mother, it turned out that the girl ran away in September to go live with her dad in Phoenix, Arizona. Likewise, the mother wished to stop pursuing the inquiry.

When CJ approached Edgerton, he once again saw a man with long jet-black hair and deeply tanned skin running alongside the road. But then, the runner suddenly darted out into CJ's lane of traffic, forcing CJ to stop. Then he flipped the switch to turn on his wig-wag lights and rolled down his window.

The man walked around the hood of the Silverado and approached CJ. But before the man spoke, CJ preempted him. "You must be Christian?"

Christian nodded. "I heard that your name is Deputy Jackson, but I think I will call you Ke-mo."

He arched his eyebrows in confusion. But before he could retort, Christian continued, "that is short for Ke-mo sah-bee. You know, The Lone Ranger and Tonto."

The deputy's mouth dropped agape, and for a brief moment, he felt dumbfounded about what to say.

"I see you are confused."

CJ nodded.

"Do you know who Bass Reeves was?"

The deputy shook his head.

"He was the famous Federal Marshall that traveled throughout Oklahoma Territory to round up bad guys. He also had a trusty Indian sidekick with him at all times because it was required to enter reservation lands. But Bass Reeves was a black man, like you Ke-mo."

Confused, CJ asked, "but The Lone Ranger was white, wasn't he?"

"On TV, yes, but that is where the black mask comes in."

Christian briefly let the comment sink in. Then he added, "I heard that I should talk to you."

"About what?"

"I hear you live in an apartment off of Wyoming Boulevard and Poplar Street in Casper, right?"

"I do, but I..." his voice trailed off because Christian cut him off again.

"I need a favor. I am starting to train for the Leadville 100-mile race, and I need your place to be a resupply point for water and food."

CJ nodded. "I have heard of that race, though I am not following how my apartment comes into play?"

He checked his side mirror. At that exact moment, a semi-tractor hauling a Caterpillar D9 bulldozer on a flatbed trailer crested over the hill from Midwest. CJ motioned to Christian to move to the side of the road, but the man shook his head. So instead, he turned and flagged the driver to go and around them. It was only after the semi-tractor and two additional pickup trucks passed by them that Christian explained his proposition.

"I need you to store a couple of my water belts for me when I do my long training runs."

CJ nodded again. "So, how long do you run? Or maybe, why don't you tell me about where you intend to go?"

Christian's face remained expressionless. "I start at my trailer, and I run south until I can pick up the old Salt Creek Highway. I like it because one side is gravel, and the other side is pavement in patches."

"Really? Does that old highway still exist? I saw some pictures of it in the Town Hall."

"Yep, after you go over 40-mile Hill, it is there into Casper, though it is mostly over private land. It also just happens to be the first paved road in the State."

"Where do you run after you get to Casper?"

Christian raised his left hand and pointed. "Once in Casper, I go up Poplar Street, and I continue running up Casper Mountain Road over to the other side. Then I turn around and run back home."

Astonished, CJ asked, "how long does that take you?"

Christian replied, "my training run takes me about 24 hours to do 100 miles, but in competition, it takes me around 18."

CJ shook his head in disbelief and couldn't fathom the thought of running for 18 or even 24 hours straight. Still, nonetheless, he was fascinated by the accomplishment. As he ended his discussion with Christian, he assured him that he would be glad to help whenever needed. But, before he left, Christian suggested to CJ that he should probably move to the Salt Creek area soon to save the daily commute. The deputy acknowledged him with a single nod and then watched Christian run off.

On the other side of Edgerton, CJ glanced into his rear-view mirror and observed the small town all but disappear in the reflection. He suddenly realized that the Salt Creek Community was a trove of firsts within Wyoming and perhaps within the nation. He opined to himself that the Salt Creek area was an "interesting place" after all.

Meanwhile, over at the high school, Adam had withstood plenty of teasing about his locker exploding the day before. But, as he passed through the hallways that morning between classes, Adam had enough of the chiding. Even Freshmen snickered "loser" as he walked by them. So naturally, Lucas Gagnon and Robbie Lepsis were incessant in their passive-aggressive attacks on Adam.

The tormenting did not go unnoticed by Bill Crooks, either. During his world history class, the discussion delved into the current state of affairs in the Middle East. Then the topic of religious freedom in the United States came up too. It seemed odd to Crooks that Lucas spoke so callously about Islam, Christianity, and Judaism. Nevertheless, the boy felt that science was his truth.

Then Adam spoke up and defended the first amendment freedoms that US citizens enjoy, only to become shouted down by both Lucas and Robbie. The discussion would have gone entirely off the rails had Crooks not stepped in and stopped it.

At the end of the class period, Crooks waited as Adam and the rest departed the classroom. But, as usual, Lucas was the last child to exit when his giant forearm blocked the boy's path.

"Step away from the door," the teacher instructed Lucas. Then, after the boy stepped back, he closed and locked the door.

"Hey, man, I'm going to be late for class," Lucas protested.

"Well, *man*," Crooks mocked, "I can always write you a pass. But first, I want to know something?"

"Wha-what? What do you want to know?" Lucas asked while he took a few steps backward.

"I want you to fill in some missing data here. That is all. First, what was the name of your last school, and where was it located?"

"Why should I tell you? Isn't that information already in my records?"

"Some things are there, and some things I think are missing. Do you mind filling in the rest?"

"My last school was an American school in the Hunan Province of China."

"China? Why were you there?"

"My father's work brought us there. He did some work for a large laboratory."

"Where did you live before that?"

"Islamabad, Pakistan."

"Why Pakistan?"

"Again, it is where my father had work. So, come on, man, I need to go."

"I will let you go after you answer my second question."

Lucas cut Crooks off, "you mean your fifth question by my count."

"Whatever. So, what is it again that your dad does for a living?"

"He is a scientist. We moved here so he could work without distraction."

"I see. What type of work?"

"Molecular biology, but it would take me too long to explain what he does in terms that you could even possibly begin to understand."

Crooks grinned at the boy, which looked like a grimace through his thick beard. "So, why are you here?"

Lucas sported a massive flash of red on his cheeks that looked more of embarrassment than anger or rage.

The boy turned to his teacher and sneered, "I have no choice. Even though I have completed much more advanced mathematics and science than is offered here, I have to complete other courses like your history class."

Crooks narrowed his eyes into a squint and said, "you are a bright boy. I am sure you could pass the GED."

Without changing his sarcastic facial expression, Lucas spouted, "I can. But I want to go to Stanford. They don't take students with a GED, so I have to stay here to get a high school diploma."

"Well, since you are stuck with us rubes here in the sticks of Wyoming, I suggest you learn to get along with others." He then reached down and unlocked the door.

Lucas quickly stepped through the opening and pushed his way through the dozen or so students who crowded around the opening, waiting to enter the classroom.

Meanwhile, Crooks made a mental note of the conversation and knew there was something more to Lucas' story. Then he spotted a lone piece of paper fall out of Lucas's notebook and land on the floor at his feet. He picked it up, briefly looked at it, folded the page, and put it in his back pocket.

Later that day, and just before noon, the phone rang in Tracy's office in the Midwest Police Station. She reached up to the phone and lifted the receiver with her right hand.

"Midwest Police, this is Chief Crandall; how may I help you?"

"Hey Tracy, this is Carrie Ortiz at the County lab. You remember me, don't you?"

"Yes, of course, Carrie. How are you doing?"

"I am doing well. Look, the reason I called is that I ran the finger-prints that your husband dropped off this morning."

"Great, what did you find?"

"Well, it is a mixed bag, I am afraid. We are still waiting for Tom Sears to analyze the party poppers, but I did make some headway on the fingerprints. First, I was able to match two lifted prints from the two sample cards that you provided. Then when I ran the remaining prints through the State database, I got a hit on one of them."

Tracy reached out for a pen and piece of paper and then asked, "okay, who was that?"

"Unfortunately, those prints are court sealed."

"Hmmm, that has the sound of a juvenile record?"

"Exactly, but then I got something weird."

"Okay, Carrie, what are you not telling me?"

"There were two prints that did not match the others, so I ran them through the Federal database."

"But that is standard procedure. I am having a hard time following."

"Tracy, this is the first time I have ever run prints in the Federal data-base that came back within minutes because, as you know, that can take all day."

"Okay, who do they belong to?"

"I don't know. Both prints must have hit on someone, but instead of a name, I got a message. Let me read it to you; *IDENTITY MASKED UNDER 22 USC 254.*"

Tracy was confused, and she admitted as much when she questioned, "US Code 22? What in the world?"

"I know, I don't even know what that is? Anyway, I wanted to let you know right away."

"Thank you, Carrie, I appreciate it," Tracy said and then hung up the phone. After a few seconds, she lifted the telephone receiver off the cradle and dialed the school office. Her call went directly to Dr. Isom. First, Tracy provided the disappointing news that only validated finger-prints belonged to Adam Weiss and Misty Otten. She then relayed that the other two samples hit on someone, but the names were either sealed or blocked by federal statute.

After the call, she stood up from her desk. It relieved some of her back pain that had progressively gotten worse over the last few months of pregnancy when she did so. Feeling a little bit of relief, Tracy grabbed her jacket, slung it over both arms, and walked out the office door. She thought that a bit of a walk around the Town Hall and the town park might make her feel better.

While walking by the front of the Town Hall that faced Peake Street, she thought about how many changes the structure had gone through and its stories. Once upon a time, it was the only hospital in the region. It then became an oil company's headquarters, and later it became a retirement home. Now, it was just the Town Hall. Additionally, the building directly behind the Town Hall was now the Salt Creek Museum after being used for several other purposes, including a medical clinic.

She then turned to walk up Ellison Avenue, and instantly thought of me. For whatever reason, ever since becoming pregnant, Tracy had strange premonitions of my doom. Admittedly, she was unsure of her occasional prophesy-like feelings, and she indeed never told me about her foreboding thoughts until much later. Instead, she held them back and attributed them to being pregnant. But this one bothered her. For some reason, she felt that I would be alone, cold, and hurt.

When Tracy turned left onto Navy Row, she looked at our home on C Street. It then hit her that this latest fear over me was probably from the memory of what happened to both of us when she had first arrived in the area in January 1992.

Tracy thought back to the phone call with Carrie Ortiz at the crime lab in that moment of clarity. She knew that her next step in the mystery surrounding the prank on Adam Weiss was to interview more students.

Her thoughts were interrupted when she heard the hum of an electric motor operating behind her. When she turned around, former Chief Wyatt Traynor was moving up the sideway.

She smiled and said, "Hey, Chief."

Traynor smiled and offered a curt, "Chief," in return. Then inexplicably, he suggested, "I was just out getting some air. I can't stand sitting at home all day."

"I understand. I don't think I could do that either."

Then a thought his her, and she asked, "Chief, do you have some time to go over something with me? I could use your experience."

Traynor straightened up a little in his electric wheelchair and nodded. Then he said, "sure, I have some time to spare as long as you have some coffee on in the office."

Tracy smiled and replied, "sure, I have coffee, but I have to warn you, it is not as bad as what you used to make."

Traynor chuckled at the joke and then motioned for Tracy to lead the way.

* * *

11

In the early evening, Adam sat in the front passenger seat of Misty's mother's Dodge Ram 2500 extended cab pickup. He looked out the windshield as it made its way west on CY Avenue in Casper. Misty sat between him and her mother, who drove the pickup truck. Rhonda had surprised the teens shortly after track practice by arranging to take both kids into the city to finish collecting everything they needed for the Prom.

They had already picked up Adam's tuxedo on the corner of First and Wolcott Streets and Misty's dress from a Hilltop Plaza shop. So now, all they had to do was stop at the florist just down the street from Natrona County High School. Additionally, Rhonda had offered to stop at Taco John's for supper before heading back home.

Initially, Misty was wary of her mother's generosity. At first, she thought her mom was trying to make up for breaching privacy on the phone a few nights ago. But then Misty thought her mom was still exercising control by driving both her and Adam around. Finally, however, she thought it was nice that her mother was finally warming up to Adam, at least a little bit.

Meanwhile, back in Midwest, Tracy and I had just sat down to eat dinner together in our home. Considering that we had worked side by side for years, it still didn't seem customary for each of us to share our day at the table. But, in the past, we already knew.

Tracy began by filling me in on all the recent developments in the now infamous exploding locker incident. I nodded while listening to my wife while also slowly lifting forked mouthfuls of food.

When Tracy brought up that identity of one set of the fingerprints were blocked under, umm, hold on, let me look at my notes." When Tracy found it, she said, "22 USC 254."

I didn't say anything but did set my fork down on the plate.

"Did you look up the US Code to see what it is?" I asked.

Tracy shook her head and replied, "no, I haven't looked it up. But, frankly, I wouldn't know where to begin?

"Did you try the internet?"

Tracy smiled incredulously and asked, "the internet? Really?"

I nodded affirmatively.

"But how do you do that? Is there some website you have to find first?"

"Nope, all you have to do is type the US Code in the search bar of the search engine, and it will take you to the code. Almost everything by the feds is online now."

Tracy squinted her eyes and looked at me suspiciously. Then she asked, "how is it that my husband, who I begged to remove our rotary phone, knows so much about using a computer?"

I smiled. "I took that class offered by the Department, remember? I am thankful that I did because my new job has me on the computer more and more each day."

I pushed away from the table before Tracy could reply. Then, after setting my dinner plate in the kitchen sink, I waved for Tracy to follow me into our office.

As we entered the room, I grabbed the backrest of Tracy's chair from her desk and rolled it across the carpet to mine.

I sat down in my familiar antique oak desk chair that gave a distinctive creak as my body weight rested upon it. I then reached the top of the desk with my right hand and moved the computer mouse. The darkened monitor screen suddenly flashed to life out of hibernation mode.

I maneuvered the mouse down to the toolbar and selected the search engine, and when it opened, I placed the cursor in the search block.

"What was the number of that code again?"

Tracy looked at her notebook once again. "It is 22 USC 254."

I quickly typed the code into the search field and hit the *ENTER* key on the keyboard. To Tracy's surprise, the search results filled the entire screen.

I traded places with my wife to read the descriptions of each site in the search results. Tracy then opened the link associated with the US State Department and began to read about the statute. Likewise, I followed along from over her shoulder.

Tracy asked, "so, why does someone who has access to our school have diplomatic privileges concerning their identity? Doesn't that strike you odd?"

I nodded and then felt a little silly since she couldn't see me from behind. I finally managed to say, "yes, it does. But you don't have anything until you get a report on the party poppers to see if they were tampered with somehow."

"I know. I said that to Carrie Ortiz when she called with the results of the fingerprints." Tracy suddenly realized that she hadn't told me about the other result, so she offered, "oh, another set matched, but those are court sealed."

I let that sink in and reserved my comment. Tracy didn't take offense either since she had grown accustomed to my silent ruminations. Instead, a small smile started to leak out, as she vividly recalled when they first started working together. Back then, my silence bugged her immensely, but now she was used to it.

My silence continued as we cleared the rest of the table and then cleaned up the kitchen together. Then, suddenly, a knock at our door split the silence in our home. Tracy patted me on the shoulder and asked if I would answer the door while she finished with the dishes.

Upon opening the door, I found Bill Crooks standing on our porch.

"Hey, Bill. Want to come in?"

Crooks turned and, without saying anything, stepped into our house. He immediately looked to the left of the door and into the kitchen and waved at Tracy. Then he fixed his eyes upon me.

"I'm not interrupting dinner, am I."

"No, of course not, Bill. We have already finished." Then I waved Crooks inside the door and over to their couch.

After Crooks sat down, I asked, "so, what can I help you with, Bill?"

Crooks looked at me and then shifted his eyes onto Tracy, who was busy wiping off the countertop no more than 15 feet away. "Thanks, Eddie, but I have something for Tracy, though you can hang around, I guess."

I felt a little slighted, but it occurred to me that my job had changed, and the Salt Creek area was no longer my official concern. So when Tracy heard her name spoken aloud, she put the dishcloth away under the sink, walked into the living room, and took a seat on the couch.

"What's on your mind, Bill?" Tracy asked.

Crooks took a deep breath and slowly exhaled. "Well, I don't know. I have a gut feeling, and I want to vet something with you."

Tracy remained silent but nodded to intimate Crooks to reveal whatever bothered him.

"Okay, here it is. I have a weird feeling about one of my students, Lucas Gagnon."

Tracy nodded and remarked, "I know what you mean. I think he is a little weird myself, but...,"

Crooks cut her off, "yes, the boy is weird. What alerts me is his background."

Furrowing her brow and looking confused, she looked over at me, but I was even more at a loss than she expressed.

"I am not following, Bill."

"I asked the boy about where he used to go to school before his family moved to Midwest a few years ago. It turns out that Lucas attended school in China, Pakistan, and although he didn't tell me, he also spent a year at a school in Syria. At least, that is what I confirmed in his student files."

Tracy shrugged. "Yes, that would be weird that a kid living near Midwest, Wyoming would be such a world traveler."

"Not only that, but these places have been a hotbed of militant activity as of late," Crooks added.

Then an idea hit me suddenly, and I blurted out, "exactly where in China?"

Crooks was a little surprised by my exclamation, and without missing a beat, he turned to me and replied, "he lived in the Hunan Province, to be precise." He saw that I recognized something after he said the name of the area.

"Isn't that where the weird flu was found in chickens last year?" I asked.

Crooks smiled at me. "Yes, it is, Eddie. But I also looked into the other places Lucas lived, and they, too, have had some odd viral breakouts. But the weird thing is that these viruses showed up a year or two after Lucas and his father had moved on. So do the two of you think I am looking into this too much?"

I shrugged my shoulders. "Well, maybe not."

Tracy interjected, "it fits now. You see, Bill, one set of fingerprints on Adam's locker came back with the identity masked by diplomatic immunity. So maybe there is something more here? Perhaps Wyoming is the new Idaho with witness protection programs but of an international version this time."

Crooks shook his head. "No, I think that is a leap too far. But it is a little weird, I would agree." Then another thought occurred to him, "when was the last time that anyone had seen Lucas's father, Liam?"

We looked at each other, and then we simultaneously shrugged our shoulders. When neither of us answered right away, he said, "neither can I. I think the only time I had seen the man was when he came to the school to register Lucas."

Crooks stood up from the couch abruptly. "I'd better get going. I will work on this a little more, but thanks for being a sounding board."

"You are welcome, Bill, anytime," Tracy assured him.

We stood up momentarily while Crooks let himself out of the house. Then I moved over to the front window and watched him climb up into his old Willys Jeep pickup.

Then I turned to face my wife and suggested, "I'm going to give Rob Anderson a call and get his son's phone number."

"That is Josh Anderson from the Savolt case, right? The same boy who is now an FBI agent?" Tracy asked.

"Yes, I will see if Josh can give us some clue why the Gagnon family is here of all places. Maybe, just maybe, Josh could connect a few dots. But then again, maybe we are all overthinking into this thing."

Tracy nodded that she understood and listened to Crooks's obnoxiously loud truck pull away from the front of the house.

After a little while, she said, "okay, honey, let me know what Josh has to say. I would like to have that information in my back pocket before I schedule a meeting to speak to Lucas and his father at the school."

Rhonda Otten pulled up next to Adam's yellow Toyota Celica parked next to the library entrance on the other side of town in the school parking lot. Adam said goodbye to Misty and gave her a quick squeeze on her hand instead of a different physical expression. Then, he reached into the back seat and retrieved his tuxedo while also hiding Misty's corsage. But, before Misty closed the door, Adam thanked Rhonda for everything, who, in turn, said, "no problem."

Adam turned and opened the driver's side door to his car and pushed forward the seat. He carefully hung up his tuxedo on the hangar latch located above the backseat window. Then he stood up and waved goodbye as the pickup drove by him.

Adam turned once more and sat down behind the wheel. Then he inserted his key into the ignition and started his car on the starter's first crank. It was after he turned on his headlights and the beams reflected off of the building's exterior that he saw it. Either someone or some people had written in soap on his windshield "*5-19*" and below it, the word, "*LOSER.*"

* * *

January 31, 2013
10:25 a.m.

By that point in our drive north from Casper, Hope Granderson and I had already exited I-25 and were heading northbound on Highway 259. We soon rounded a large, sweeping bend in the road that revealed the spot where East Teapot Creek merged with the main body of Teapot Creek.

While I paused in retelling the story, Hope turned off her recorder.

"It seems to me that so far, you aren't a central figure in this case, am I correct?" she asked

I nodded my head. "Yes, at this point at least, but I don't want to spoil the story yet."

Just then, I let off of the accelerator, and the Department Blazer immediately began to slow down. Then I turned on my turn signal and slowly exited the road.

"Is there something wrong with your vehicle, Sheriff? Why did you pull off of the road?

I shrugged. "I just wanted to show you the most famous landmark in the entire area, that is all."

Hope looked out of her side window. She noted the prairie grass; the sagebrush choked draws and the rock-topped hill surrounded by stout-looking Ponderosa Pine trees. Then she looked left through my window and saw yet another rock-topped mesa with even more pine trees.

She finally shrugged. "I guess I don't see what you want me to see. Can you give me a hint?"

I smiled and pointed my index finger straight ahead. Hope followed my suggestion and immediately spied a strange-looking rock formation. To her, it looked as if it were a child's magnificent sandcastle only ruined by a kid brother pouring a bucketful of water all over it. It seemed, at least to her, that the monument had seen its better days.

"You mean that eroded rock over there?"

I smiled at her again. "Yes, it is the exact item I wanted to show you. That is none other than Teapot Rock or the *Rock of Twenty Nine's Bane* as I come to know it."

Unfortunately, I confused her. "The rock of what?" she asked.

"Never mind, that is another story or another time. Anyway, the spout of Teapot Rock has severely eroded, though, at one time, it did look like a teapot.

Then I witnessed Hope recall something from memory. "Is that from the Teapot Dome Scandal?"

"It is."

Hope pressed the window button and lowered it. Then she took out a digital camera and took a nice photo of Teapot Rock for her file.

Then she asked, "is Teapot Rock a part of the story you were telling me?"

I shook my head, and then I saw a slight disappointment in Hope's eyes.

"So, where were we in the story?" I asked rhetorically. Then I said, "So, we are up to two days before the Prom."

* * *

12

THURSDAY, APRIL 19, 2002

OTTEN HOME, SEVEN MILES WEST OF MIDWEST, WYOMING

Misty anxiously stared out of the kitchen window while she waited for the bus to arrive. She looked at the wall clock again, and she shook her head. It was unbelievable that Naomi Wright was late, considering it never happened before. Misty looked at the clock once more and decided to walk out to the corral to talk to her mom.

Rhonda had just finished giving each of her two horses a part of a hay bale and was filling up the water trough when she spotted her daughter approach. She lifted her left wrist and pulled the flannel jacket's sleeve to expose her watch with her right hand. It read *08:05*.

"Mom, the bus driver hasn't come yet, which means I will be late unless you take me to school," Misty explained.

The mother nodded at her daughter that she understood, and then took a deep breath. She thought about everything she needed to do that morning and driving her daughter into town was not on her list.

Rhonda had secretly planned to leave the house at 8:15 that morning for a doctor's appointment in Buffalo. A month ago, she noted a mole on her thigh had changed color and had grown to the size of a dime almost overnight. Because she didn't want to alarm anyone, the appointment was a secret. But then an idea came to her mind.

She stood up and wiped the sweat off her brow with her jacket sleeve. Then she chinned over toward their Ford flatbed ranch truck. "You could take the ranch truck today because I have too much on my plate already."

In her excitement of being trusted to drive herself to school, her mother's remarks about being too busy went right over Misty's head.

Instead, Misty asked, "you mean I can drive today?"

"Yes, the keys are in it, but make sure you don't drive it too hard. It is old and worn out."

The girl could hardly believe her fortune. Like most teenagers, she'd wished and prayed for the day when she could start driving herself and not feeling like a placated kid all the time. But, instead, she withheld her excitement and quickly said, "thanks, Mom," and collected her things.

Ten minutes later, Misty travelled east on Highway 387. She was extra careful while exiting the yard around her house and up the long driveway to Smokey Gap Road. But as she passed under Interstate 25, she had thought about opening up the throttle on the old pickup truck but decided against it. Instead, her dad's voice entered her head, telling her that *"a part of one's character is doing what is right, even when nobody else was looking."*

She looked at herself in the rear-view mirror and shook her head from side to side. Then, finally, Misty diverted her eyes back onto the road in front of her. She soon approached the intersection of Fitzhugh with the highway on the north side of Midwest.

When Misty came within 50 yards of the turnoff, an ultrafamiliar work truck with an *OTTEN SERVICES* logo affixed to the door sat idle at the intersection. Then she spotted her father sitting behind the steering wheel. so she waved and then saw her father's mouth gape open.

Afterward, she repeatedly looked behind her through the rear-view mirror to see what her father would do. To her surprise and relief, he simply drove over the highway and onto Light Plant Road toward another job location, perhaps.

But her greatest surprise came as Misty parked next to Adam in the school parking lot. After she bounded out of the truck, Misty caught Adam's expression on his face that bore a mixture of confusion and delight.

Still dumbfounded, the only thing that Adam could say was, "hey."

Shaking her head, "Don't make anything out of this. The bus driver was a no-show, so my mom told me to drive myself."

Adam shrugged, which in his mind communicated that he was "okay" with it. But that was not how the girl took his nonchalant gesture. Instead, his lack of enthusiasm spoke volumes to Misty that the boy never intended or even thought.

"What's wrong? Can't a girl drive herself to school? Is this how it is going to be in the future, Adam? Are you going to put me in my place? Huh? Say something!" she demanded.

Her tirade drove him further into an emotional shell. It bewildered him how everything went off the rails with her so quickly. But instead of saying something to explain how Misty misunderstood his intention, he stood there in silence.

"Say something?"

The boy had no idea what to say, so he just said, "hi."

Misty spun on her heel and walked away, obviously upset. When she entered the school through the doors next to the library, she turned left and went down the high school wing. Then at the end of the hallway, she stepped into the school office on the right.

"Hi, Ms. Burrows," Misty said.

Edna Burrows lifted her eyes off the paperwork she was reading and looked over the top of her reading glasses at Misty. Then she smiled.

"Good morning, Misty! What can I help you with this morning?"

"I don't know; I just want to report that my bus driver didn't show up."

Edna removed her glasses and set them down on her desktop. Then, she said, "well, that is a little weird. Naomi would have called if she couldn't make her route this morning or if she weren't feeling well."

Misty nodded in reply.

Edna took out a scrap piece of paper and asked Misty, "so, what students are on your bus so I can smooth things out with their parents?"

"Well, there is Lucas Gagnon, the O'Hara twins, Stephanie Merrick, and Brandon and Benton Boyer."

Edna jotted down the names but then asked Misty an odd question.

"Did you see Stephanie Merrick on the bus Tuesday or yesterday? Unfortunately, she was absent both days, and I presume she will be absent today as well."

Misty thought back, but she hadn't noticed Stephanie's absence on the bus, in all honesty.

"No, ma'am, I didn't. I am sorry."

"No problem, Misty, now you had better get going to class, or you will be late."

Over at the Midwest Police Station, Chief Tracy Crandall entered her office door and immediately spotted Deputy Jackson at the impish desk.

"You are in early. I saw you pull up an hour ago when I was making breakfast," Tracy quipped.

"Yep, I have a few things on my plate," CJ replied.

"Oh, okay. So, how did your meeting go yesterday?"

CJ smiled. "It went well. That is one reason I am so busy."

Tracy nodded. "Okay, I understand. I will leave you alone then."

CJ shook his head. "No. That is not what I am trying to say. I also have to serve a couple of court summons first thing this morning, and I was hoping you could give me directions of where to go?"

Tracy replied, "sure," and set her bag down on her desk in the adjoining room. When she re-entered CJ's office, she asked, "what is the name on the first one?"

"Teapot Oilfield Services, LLC."

"Oh, that is Pete Searcy's old company before he merged with an outfit out of Casper. His place is easy to find in Edgerton. What is the other name?" Tracy inquired.

"Umm, let's see. Where can I find Roger Sands?" CJ asked.

"Roger Sands? Give me that envelope," Tracy said and quickly snatched the parcel away from CJ.

Tracy looked at the address, and sure enough, it was labeled correctly to *Roger Sands.* Moreover, it included his longtime Edgerton address on Center Street.

CJ was confused, so he asked, "who is Roger Sands?"

Tracy grimaced. "Oh, Roger is a decent, hard-working guy that has lived in the area for a long time. Unfortunately, his ex-wife has made it a habit to sue Roger for more and more support over the years."

Tracy paused to think and then continued, "but his daughters are adults now. So, I am curious to know what this is all about?"

"Well, why don't you come with me and help me serve these. In the meantime, I can bring you up to speed on the special project that I am working on."

"Okay, let me grab my jacket."

They had found Pete Searcy inside his massive workshop off of Lewis Avenue in Edgerton. It seemed to CJ that every male over the age of 50 in that part of Wyoming owned a detached garage that was larger than the house. The structure housed a brand-new fifth-wheel camper trailer, a pair of snowmobiles on a trailer, a new Honda Fourtrax ATV, and a boat. Collectively the worth of the recreational toys was more than the entire property of Searcy's.

CJ handed Pete the folder, which he acted like he was expecting being process served.

After getting back into CJ's vehicle, Tracy directed him to drive east on Center Street, which they followed to the end of town. Then they parked outside Roger Sands' trailer.

Tracy noticed that Roger had recently installed a sidewalk and a concrete driveway. Years before, when Tracy had served Roger a court summons, she noted that Roger used lengths of 2X6 boards to suffice as a walkway over of the mud. Seconds later, CJ and Tracy knocked on the door of the trailer home. Roger opened the door, but when he saw us standing on his doorstep with a manila envelope in CJ's hands, his face lost all expression.

CJ spoke first. "Roger? Roger Sands?"

"Yes, that is me."

"I am Deputy CJ Jackson, and I have to serve you this," CJ said and handed him the packet.

Roger stepped down the steps and grabbed the envelope. He then looked over and said, "Hey, Tracy. How are you doing? The baby is due soon, I see."

"I am doing well, Roger; thank you for asking."

Roger turned the package over and started to tear it open. Then he said aloud, "well, let's see if this is from you know who?"

The man pulled out the court summons and gave it a quick scan. Then he looked over to Tracy with a defeated expression on his face.

"Is it from your ex-wife again, Roger?" she asked.

"I'm afraid so. The ex wants part of my retirement now."

Tracy shook her head from side to side in disbelief. Then she protested, "but Roger, the two of you split up nearly twenty years ago. So how can she take you to court for your retirement benefits now?"

Roger shrugged and suggested, "I dunno. Maybe it is because after MERP sold out, the new company offered us a 401K plan. As a part of the merger, my retirement funds transferred over as well. So maybe the ex thinks she is entitled to my money?"

CJ was baffled, too, and let out his exasperation about the situation with a long-expelled breath. "Roger, how many times has your ex run you into court?"

Sands looked down at his stocking feet and thought. Then he raised his head and replied, "counting this one, it will make eight."

"Eight times! You are kidding."

"I wish I were, Deputy, but that is what I get for marrying the wrong woman. I see here in the paperwork that she has changed her last name again. She is on to husband number four now."

CJ shook his head again. "I am sorry, man. If there is anything I can do, I will."

Roger looked down the driveway, over Center Street, and fixated his eyes on the large sagebrush choked draw to the south. Then he focused back on the deputy. "Well, if you know of a good lawyer that won't run-up charges just to make a buck, then I would appreciate it."

"If I hear of anyone, I will refer him to you. But, again, I am sorry."

As they drove back to Midwest, CJ filled Tracy in about his meeting on the joint task force. After each case briefing, the task force members separated the obvious runaway cases from those that hinted at an obduction.

Tracy interjected that kidnapping cases were an anomaly in Wyoming. Maybe it is due to Wyoming's low crime rate, but then again, each household owned at least one gun. Perhaps that last fact was deterrent enough for would-be criminals.

"The big thing that I put together was that all of the girls were athletes."

"Really? What sport?" Tracy asked.

"Well, most of the girls were in multiple sports, but all of the ones on this list went missing during volleyball season."

"Where were the girls from again?"

"Umm, I know that one was from Upton and another from Hullit. But there are other small towns, but I forget. I would have to look at my notes."

"Hullit? Oh, I know what you mean. You pronounce the town as *HUE-LET*."

"What did I say then?"

"Hullit."

"Okay, thanks for the correction. I don't want to sound like an idiot around the other deputies."

Then after a few seconds, Tracy asked, "was there a missing girl from Big Horn? Or Arvada? Or Moorcroft? Or Sundance?"

He looked at his notes and affirmed, "yes, to Big Horn and Arvada, but I also remember another one from Dayton and a girl from Kaycee, too."

"CJ, you just stumbled onto something that I don't think anyone of your Deputies could connect."

He listened while turning off of Lewis Street and onto Shannon Ave. Then he asked, "what do you mean?"

"Oh, I would bet that all those Deputies you met with were from Buffalo, Sheridan, and Gillette, correct?"

"That's right, but I still don't get what you are saying, Tracy?"

She smiled. "Those six girls went missing from towns that used to comprise the Powder River Conference. Of course, you would have to be from a small town in northeastern Wyoming to know it."

When it was apparent that he didn't seem to connect what Tracy implied, she continued. "You see, Tongue River-in Dayton, Big Horn, Arvada-Clearmont, Hulett, Sundance, Moorcroft, Upton, Kaycee, and Midwest all made up that conference."

"I am sorry, Tracy, I still can't follow your reasoning?"

Tracy laughed. "Come on, CJ. Think! You said the missing girls played volleyball, so I would bet that the perp or perps selected them out by watching them play at a tournament."

Pulling the Silverado into the parking lot, he stopped outside their shared office. Then he shut the engine off and turned in his seat toward her.

"That is a little bit of a leap suggesting that the perp was at a tournament, isn't it?"

Smiling again, she replied, "no, it is not a leap at all. Every year in late August or early September, the Powder River Classic volleyball tournament takes place. You see, all of the schools that used to comprise the former conference still come together annually to play even though they are from different classifications now."

Tracy reached out with her right hand and opened the door and swung her legs outside. Then she stood up and made her way into the office. Meanwhile, CJ followed behind her. But, before sitting down behind the desk, he stood in front of the map on the wall. Then while looking at the push pins correlating with each missing girl's hometown, a thought hit him.

"Tracy? Can we get a copy of the volleyball schedule from the school, so I can verify the date of the tournament you spoke about?"

"Sure, I will just email the school office."

A few minutes later, Tracy called out, "Hey, CJ? I just received an email from the lab with the results of the testing on the party poppers in Adam's locker."

He walked into her office, and she waved him to walk around the desk. She then pointed to the text displayed on her computer monitor. It read:

Tracy,

The sample provided contained traces of potassium chlorate and red phosphorus. Under examination, the cardboard cylinders show modifications to accept more explosive materials. The standard amount of these chemicals in this particular party poppers' brand is 1 gram for each device. The samples you provided would have spent at least 10 grams each.

I hope this helps,

Carrie Ortiz

Tracy looked up at CJ and asked, "what do you think?"

CJ walked around to the front of Tracy's desk while he thought. Then he looked at her and shrugged his shoulders. "Those chemicals are key. But I would hedge that we could find all the materials in the chemistry lab at the high school."

She narrowed her eyes and asked, "really?"

He nodded and said, "yep. I had experience with explosives while I was in the army. The chemicals listed in that email are common in explosives and fireworks."

Then he rubbed his chin and thought about what they should do next. "How about we head over to the school to fill in Dr. Isom on the case's status, and you can schedule some interviews with both of those boys and their parents. Plus, I can also get a copy of the volleyball schedule to help me with my case."

Tracy smiled and said, "cool, let's go!"

* * *

13

The sulking mood that started in the morning continued for Misty the rest of the day. During lunchtime, instead of meeting Adam like usual, she walked over to the cafeteria. Not only was she still angry at Adam, but she also felt dismissed by him. It wasn't the first time that she'd felt that way.

After setting her tray down at a table in the rear of the room, she thought back to the first occurrence of Adam being dismissive. In the week before the infamous attacks on 9/11, his girlfriend had not only planned but pulled off a special picnic lunch for them. The logistical hurdles she cleared were incredible since she had to sneak everything out of the house over three consecutive mornings before school. The first thing that Misty stored in her locker was a tablecloth and two sets of silverware. Then on the next day, she carried plates. Finally, on the day of the picnic, she brought the food.

When the lunch bell rang that day, they hurried to get everything into Adam's car, and they drove down the football field parking lot. There they ate under the Cottonwood trees, and for 20 minutes, everything seemed perfect in the world. But, on their way back to school, Adam hadn't reciprocated the level of appreciation that Misty expected. Instead, he drove the car in silence as their lunch digested. When he pulled into the parking lot, all the boy said was, "thanks for lunch. It was delicious." Once again, she felt underappreciated.

Later that day, at track practice, Misty continued to distance herself from Adam. Instead of running hurdles like her usual routine, she ran for a solid hour. Afterward, she told her coach, "I'm heading home," and walked off without receiving permission to do so.

Adam tried to talk to her once again but was ignored. Instead, Misty walked determinedly up the hill to the school. She briefly stopped long enough to pick up her things in the locker room, and without changing clothes, she left the school parking lot in the ranch pickup truck.

Misty held onto her dour mood long into dinnertime as she sat across from her parents. Oddly, her mother didn't have a plate in front of her-just a glass of water. Then, suddenly, Rhonda cleared her throat and looked around as if she had an announcement.

"I went to the doctor today."

"For what, Mom?"

Steve set his fork down and gave his wife his full attention.

Rhonda continued, "well, I wanted to get this funny-looking mole on my thigh, checked."

"Where? Show me," Steve inquired.

"Not right now, honey. I don't want to undress at the dinner table."

"Mom, what did the doctor say?"

After taking a sip of water, she revealed, "the doctor didn't like the look of it, so she took a biopsy of it. Then she checked the rest of my body."

"Did she find anything else, honey?" Steve asked.

Tears welled up in Rhonda's eyes, and her lower lip quivered. She knew she had to say it to face it. "The doctor found a large patch on my back between my shoulder blades that is Melanoma, but she thinks it is malignant too. So, she wants to remove it all tomorrow."

Steve stood up, walked behind his wife, and said, "let me see."

Rhonda carefully pulled her shirt up to her shoulders to reveal her back. It wasn't hard for either Steve or Misty to find, which caused the girl to gasp when she saw it. The area in question was similar in size to that of a large egg yolk. It also had an odd dark color that was far different from the freckles next to it. The tumor appeared in a place that wasn't easily seen unless she used multiple mirrors. Furthermore, she had even quit changing her clothes around her husband years ago. He wouldn't have seen it either.

Steve knelt beside his wife and hugged her, which Rhonda hugged him back. Meanwhile, Misty stood by in stoic shock. Rhonda noticed her daughter's expression and assured her that she would be alright and that she had faith that the doctor could remove it all.

A little while later, Misty cleared the dishes from the table and began cleaning up the kitchen. Her parents remained seated at the dining room table and made plans for the surgery the next day. Misty had already unsuccessfully lobbied to go with them to Buffalo in the morning. Instead, her parents insisted she go to school and track practice and then come home afterward.

Steve had already cleared his calendar and gave foreman instructions on what to do with their work out by Bothwell Draw the next day. Likewise, Rhonda used the phone next to call her best friend, Cassi Mondragon, to come by to care for the horses. Misty overheard the exchange and openly challenged her mother by insisting that she tend to the horses before school. Rhonda waved Misty off and gave her a quick "shhh."

The girl quietly returned to the kitchen sink. After placing a clean plate in the dish strainer, she looked out the window and caught the last glimpse of sunlight. What captivated her attention most was the lone Sage Grouse in the middle of the driveway. The male grouse danced in a tight circle with upward tail feathers and cupped wings. Then two female grouse emerged, and then three more. The hens all focused their attention on the male who rhythmically pounded his feet soliciting for a mate. As suddenly as the lek of grouse appeared, they disappeared into the sagebrush.

It finally dawned on Misty that she had behaved terribly that day toward Adam. She knew that her behavior was a little like the male grouse demanding attention. *I owe him an apology,* she said to herself and planned to call her boyfriend after finishing her chore.

The sun had finally set when she looked out the window again. In that part of Wyoming, after every sunset came incredible dark. Even the yard light behind the house had a hard time penetrating the curtain of darkness.

But when she looked out the window once more, the lights inside the house reflected against the glass like a mirror. She could see her mother and father still talking at the dinner table in the reflection behind her. It gave her pause to appreciate the seriousness of her mother's condition. But, more importantly, the image of her parents inspired Misty to pray for her mother.

An hour later, Misty had assumed her usual position atop the step in the garage. In her right hand was the telephone receiver with its ridiculously long cord stretched through the crack of the partially closed door.

"I am sorry to hear that about your mom," Adam said. He was then surprised and relieved that Misty broke her silence and explained her feelings to him.

"Thanks, I just don't know what to think about it."

"You said that she is having surgery tomorrow, right?"

"Yes. Mom will have that thing taken out of her back and will be home tomorrow night."

"Do you want to cancel Prom on Saturday and stay at home with your mom?"

"I already suggested that to my parents, but they told me in no uncertain terms was I to miss either the track meet in Douglas or the Prom Saturday night."

Adam smiled. "Good. I am looking forward to our date."

"Me too. Forgive me if my mind is elsewhere. I hope you understand?"

"I can empathize. It seems you catch me in moments where something else is dominating my mind, and I miss telling you how much I appreciate you."

"Stop, Adam. It feels like you are making fun of me."

Adam shook his head even though Misty couldn't see him. "No, I mean it. Sometimes I catch myself comparing the two of us with how my parents used to interact. It is just sad that my dad is never around anymore."

"I know, and I am sorry for you too, Adam. But please use words to express what you are thinking. Agreed?"

"I agree that I will do a better job with that."

Silence fell onto the conversation, and it sounded like to Adam that Misty had just covered up the phone with her hand. But, in reality, she had done just that.

"Adam?" Misty asked.

"Yes, I am here."

"Hey, I have to go. My mom needs the phone to make a few calls. I will see you tomorrow, okay?"

"Okay, good night," Adam said and hung up the phone.

* * *

14

C STREET AND NAVY ROW, MIDWEST, WYOMING

It was early morning when Chief Tracy Crandall walked from her home to her tiny two-room office located behind the town hall. Though it was less than 100 yards, the walk felt much longer, considering it was her 37th week of pregnancy.

For the last month, sleep became impossible. No matter what position Tracy tried, she could get comfortable. Then whenever she was up and moving around, it seemed like the baby was standing on her bladder.

As Tracy neared the office door, a sudden urge changed her course. Instead, Tracy veered over to the town hall's back door, where a restroom sat just inside. But within a few feet of reaching the handle to the door, CJ Jackson called out from the office entrance, "good morning, Chief."

She looked over at him and replied, "Hi, CJ. Give me a second, will you? I have to use the restroom."

"Okay, I will make some coffee then."

Stepping back inside the modest workspace, he then walked over to the Mr. Coffee pot that sat on a table and reached for a jug of water underneath it. Since the office lacked even a sink, the officemates had to fill empty milk jugs with water to make coffee. They also managed to bring in a small refrigerator and placed it next to the coffee pot.

As CJ filled the coffee filter with grounds, he considered himself fortunate to have such a place for his office. It was not that it was lavish or even possessed any aesthetics of being a quality office. On the contrary, it was a glorified closet. But it felt cozy, perhaps because CJ didn't have to share his time or space with more than one person, and Tracy was great company.

The deputy then thought about the Salt Creek community of Midwest and Edgerton, plus Linch, though he hadn't been out there yet. He discerned that for every nicely kept place was another house falling apart next to it. If one house had a nice yard, the next one would be overgrown with waist-high weeds.

He recognized the negatives about the place, like no grocery store, no retail shopping, and little to no entertainment except for the three bars, a bowling alley, and Jr/Sr High School sports. But he also struggled to understand why area residents lived in the area. An even bigger question was how the community endured each change from one oil company operating the Salt Creek Field to another or how residents withstood each economic boom and bust.

CJ shook his head and then said to himself, *"I have to admit it, but they are a resilient bunch out here."*

His musings were interrupted when Tracy stepped into the door. She looked up at him with an air of exasperation. "Hi again. Sometimes being pregnant is such a pain."

"Hey, I am glad you are here because I have a couple of things to share with you."

Tracy moved by CJ and into her office. Once there, she set down her jacket and her new backpack on her desk. Then she returned to the other room.

"Okay, so what is your news?" she asked.

"So, guess who is moving to the area?"

She smiled again. "I knew it, CJ. So, did you contact Liz over at the café?"

"I did. The house is on Stock Street here in Midwest." Then he quizzed, "but how did you know?

Tracy placed her right index finger on her chin and playfully said, "oh, I just had a feeling. You see, I was once in your position too. But then I kind of fell for the community because of the people."

CJ nodded. "So, what was it exactly that helped you like this place?"

"Mine? Umm, it was an evening spent in the gym during basketball season. It was like the whole town showed up, and I just felt so comfortable. What was it for you?"

The deputy shook his head. "No, for me, it was nothing magical like that. I just have a sense of this place as somewhere I can fit in to make a difference. You see, in Casper, I am just one of many other deputies. But here, I think I can be a useful asset to the people." CJ thought for a brief second that he had lost Tracy's attention, so he added, "I'm sorry, that is just how I feel."

"No, don't apologize. I like it that you have character. I was just wondering about my husband. There is certainly something about this area that has called him too since he is going on nearly 20 years of being a part of the community."

The coffee pot stopped gurgling, which told the law officers that it finished brewing. He quickly poured a cup for her and then one for himself.

After a quick sip from her cup, Tracy asked, "so, what is the other news?"

CJ walked over to the map on the wall that he had put up a few days before. He pointed to a pushpin centered on the Wyoming town of Upton and said, "last night, I came up with a theory."

She moved closer to the map. "Really? What do you think about the missing girls?"

CJ tapped his finger next to Upton on the map, "this girl is April Moreau, age 17. She's an honor roll student and was an all-state volleyball and basketball last year."

Then he moved his finger and tapped on the tack next to Sundance, "this girl is Heather Searcy, also 17 and has an interest from Black Hills State College to play volleyball." CJ then moved his hand toward the left and stopped at Big Horn. "This girl is Brittany Stover, age 18, and has a verbal commitment to play volleyball at Montana Tech." He moved his hand to other parts of the map, "there is a pattern here. All of the girls played volleyball. There was one girl reported missing from Chugwater down by Cheyenne, and she too played volleyball. What I am trying to say is that you suggested that volleyball was the connection."

Tracy furrowed her brow, trying to follow the insinuation. "I'm sorry, CJ, what are you getting to?"

CJ smiled. "Remember when we went to the school yesterday, and we got a copy of the Midwest Volleyball Schedule?"

"Of course, we did so to verify the date of the Powder River Classic tournament."

"Yes, but that is not all. You see, Big Horn and Kaycee went to the State Tournament in Casper in the class 1A bracket. Then Upton and Sundance made it in the class 2A bracket. I also verified that Chugwater had also made it to State last year."

Tracy looked over the map and stared at all the push pins. It pained her little because she was the assistant volleyball coach for the last two years, and her Oilers did not qualify for the State tournament. The problem wasn't turnout. In all, 23 girls tried out, but only two were either a senior or a junior. Instead, the most massive problem was talent. Aside from Jessica Norman, her best player, and Misty Otten, the rest were freshmen and first-year players. Then his intimation hit her.

"So, you think the perp was at the State Tournament in Casper? Is that what you are thinking?"

CJ smiled. "Precisely. But how do we narrow it down to a suspect? I mean, just knowing the suspect was at the State volleyball tournament still leaves us too many questions."

Tracy sipped her coffee. Then she asked, "were there any eyewitness reports of the girls' abduction?"

He shrugged. "Well, there was one. In Dayton, where Kelly Stevens disappeared, a neighbor reported seeing a white panel van leaving the girl's property. Other than that, there is no clue a vehicle description."

Tracy's head spun around. "Not so fast. The girl in Kaycee that went missing a few days ago, didn't a witness say they saw a dark late model Ford F150 pickup?"

"Yes, you are correct. Maybe we have something."

Then after a few moments of silence, CJ asked Tracy, "so what do you have going on today?"

She shrugged. "In a few minutes, I will meet with Robbie Lepsis and his parents, plus I am to meet with Lucas Gagnon and his father. Maybe we can get to the bottom of their harassment of Adam Riley."

He nodded. "Yes, that would be good. Did your husband get with your FBI contact?"

"You mean Josh Anderson?"

"Yes."

"Well, last night, Eddie did speak to Josh. Unfortunately, however, he was unable to give us any other information on the fingerprints that the Secretary of State's office masked."

"Well, that is a bummer. Did Josh offer anything else?"

Tracy shrugged her shoulders. "Well, yes, umm, kind of, Eddie asked Josh to look up the Gagnon family. So, Josh did, and it came back devoid of information."

"Devoid? As in nothing on the family? Isn't that a little weird? I mean, I am sure if the FBI ran my mother's name, they would come up with something?"

"Yep, that is what Eddie and I thought too, but Josh said that every system he had access to was blank." Tracy suddenly looked up at the clock on the wall and said, "O my gosh, I have to go, or I am going to be late."

Then she got up, grabbed her purse, and walked outside to her Department Explorer. When she set her bag on the passenger seat, she noticed that she'd left her cellphone behind. So, she retraced her steps into the office and found the device sitting atop her desk. Then Tracy picked it up and saw that she missed a call from me.

For the last couple of months, I had called my wife at various times throughout the day to ascertain that she was doing okay. The calls always amused her that perhaps I was more anxious about the pregnancy than she had been.

A few minutes later, Tracy found a parking space next to the swimming pool entrance in the front row. As she gathered her things, Tracy thought back to when she first moved to Midwest. Then, it seemed odd that the school possessed a competition-quality 25-meter, six-lane pool despite a lack of a swimming team.

Rumor had it around the Salt Creek community that the pool was built as reciprocity for Midwest joining the Natrona County School District. Before then, Midwest was a stand-alone district and was incredibly wealthy from the severance taxes on all the oil siphoned out of the nearby school sections.

However, since the merger, the Casper high schools received massive upgrades to include new football stadiums. Meanwhile, Midwest begged for table scraps at every annual budget planning meeting.

Tracy entered the school and turned toward the high school office. As she reached the junction with the hallway, she turned right and almost ran into two students, Lucas Gagnon and Robbie Lepsis. The boys darted out of the way, and then Robbie raised both arms over his head like he was surrendering. "Don't shoot. I am unarmed."

The boys turned toward each other and laughed while moving over to the gym entrance, where two adults stood. Tracy recognized the man's face from all his car dealership ads as Robbie Lepsis' father, but she did not know the woman. She was the same height as her son and just as thin. But what was striking was the woman's straight jet-black hair, dark chocolate-colored eyes, and olive complexion. She would have been quite beautiful if it weren't for her dark-colored clothing and the black scarf around her neck.

Tracy said "hello" to the parents, but only the elder Lepsis acknowledged her.

While entering the school office, she heard, "Hey, Chief. Why don't you come into my office?" said the small female voice of Dr. Isom.

Tracy walked around the attendance desk and proceeded down a short, recently refurbished hallway complete with the overwhelming scent of fresh paint. The office used to be a part of the teacher's lounge.

Still, most schools chose to eliminate the teacher sanctuaries under the current climate and used the space for other purposes.

Tracy turned toward Dr. Isom and inquired, "what is it those two?"

"You mean Lucas and Robbie?"

"Yes. Those boys just don't seem to fit with the rest of the kids around here."

Dr. Isom smiled and said unabashedly, "that is because those boys are not originally from the Salt Creek area. Plus, neither boy has any intention of fitting in with others. Robbie is here because, well, it is no secret that he has no other choice because of his suspensions from both NC and KW. And as for Lucas, well, he is from a lot of places-Asia mostly."

Tracy nodded her head. "I was thinking more along the lines of a character flaw."

Dr. Isom shrugged her shoulders. "Well, there is that then."

Once inside, Dr. Isom waved Tracy over to one side of the conference table and took a seat for herself.

"Before I get to the reason I called you, I want to let you know that I already met with Robbie and Lucas along with their parents without you," Dr. Isom explained.

Tracy asked, "Is this about Adam Weiss' locker?"

Dr. Isom shook her head. "No, not necessarily, though I believe with every fiber of my being that those boys were behind the locker explosion. But, no, this talk was to put to end all the daily verbal abuse that those boys dole out on Adam Weiss."

"I agree, he is a good kid, and I think we all know that he is exercising immense constraint around those agitators."

"Yes, which is why I called the meeting with the parents. That reminds me, have you met Lucas' Au Pair?"

The question left Tracy confused.

Dr. Isom smiled, "She is like a nanny, but the woman corrected me and called herself an *Au Pair*."

"Ah, I see. So, what is her story?"

Dr. Isom shrugged. "I don't know very much. Her name is Hira, and she speaks only in the faintest of whispers."

"Hira? Hmmm, that is an original name. I wonder if she has Middle Eastern heritage?"

"It is hard to say, though, with the way she spoke, I did not detect an accent. But considering I haven't been anywhere other than Wyoming, Colorado, or Utah in my whole life, I would be the last person you want to ask."

Dr. Isom lifted the large, red-colored Nalgene bottle off the desk, opened it, and took a sip of its contents. Then she set the container down once again. But, she continued, "all I know is that Hira dotes on that boy Lucas, which for him is a blessing."

Tracy nodded that she understood but then asked, "so, Doc, what is going on? Why did you call me?"

Dr. Isom pushed away from her desk and stood up. She briefly turned toward the window overlooking the large paved common area between the three wings of the school. Then she slowly turned back to Tracy.

"I will be blunt. One of our drivers, Naomi Wright, hasn't been seen for two days now. What is more, one of our four-wheel-drive Chevrolet Suburbans that we use as a school bus in the rural areas went missing with her."

"Why didn't her husband report it to me?"

"That is a good question."

Tracy tapped her pen against her lip. "Did the other two drivers see her?"

Dr. Isom responded by shaking her head.

Tracy nodded that she understood since it was common knowledge that bus drivers drove busses home. Instead, she asked, "so, how tall would you say Naomi is? I think five foot one?"

"Yes, that is accurate. I would also say Naomi is about 150 pounds too."

"Thanks, I have all the other particulars to put in the bulletin, like her hair color-brunette and eye color-brown. But, as to the Suburban, do you have a license plate number?"

Dr. Isom reached over to the bookcase to the right of her desk and removed a plain white three-ring binder off of a shelf. Then she placed it on her desk and opened it to a specific page.

"The plate is the standard yellow background with black colored letters that spell out *SCHOOL 3030*."

Tracy jotted down the information and then began to rise out of her seat when the phone rang. Dr. Isom motioned for Tracy to sit back down while she answered the call. Rather than listening in on the phone call, Tracy used the time to look over her notes. However, she did pick up on many utterances from Dr. Isom of "it will be okay" as she spoke to the person on the line. The phone call ended abruptly, and Dr. Isom set down the receiver.

"I'm sorry for that inconvenience, Tracy, but I now have something else for you."

"What is that Doc?"

"That was a very concerned grandmother from Gas Plant that has reported her granddaughter as missing."

"Oh my gosh, who could that be?"

"The girl is Jessica Norman."

* * *

15

Distracted by thoughts of her mom, Misty only half-listened and half-ignored Lucas Gagnon's diatribe in her Biology II class. It had begun from an innocent question from the teacher about genes. Lucas hijacked the conversation and discussed how polymorphic variants of a gene are responsible for becoming a disease. Then Lucas explained to the class that the term polymorphic used in this case meant an organism possessing more than one adult form. Hence, new strains formed literally out of nowhere.

Misty sighed and shook her head. She didn't understand why the science teacher let Lucas drone on. Luckily, the bell rang and saved her from losing other minutes that she would never get back.

She entered the hallway to walk to her next class. Then Misty overheard Jessica's name and the word *missing*. Up to that point, it hadn't registered that she hadn't seen her friend that day. But, after passing by Mr. Crooks's classroom, Tosha Holland approached Misty.

"Hey, did you hear that Jessica is missing?" the girl asked.

She shook her head. "No, I haven't."

"From what I heard, Jessica didn't come home last night. So, when was the last time you saw her?"

"Yesterday afternoon at track practice. Jess said she was going for a run north of town."

Tosha spun on her heels and walked away from Misty. The news of Jessica continued to spread like wildfire. In a small school like Midwest, secrets were nearly impossible to keep. That was a good thing in most cases, as teenager conflicts tended to abate themselves quickly once out in the open. By the time Misty entered the art room, she had overheard various suggestions as to why. One kid suggested that terrorists abducted Jessica. Then another theory centered around the mysterious dark green Ford F150 that spooked the community for decades now. Yet another notion held that Jessica ran away.

She didn't believe any of the hallway gossips because she knew her friend. First of all, she intuitively knew that Jessica would have told her of trouble at home. But Misty also knew that her friend was not above tasking risks since Jessica had a penchant for cross country running. The girl was often spotted running over open land throughout the area. If Misty had to guess, Jessica stepped in a hole and broke her leg or had tripped over some abandoned cable. Yet, she dismissed even her theory as nothing more than gossip.

Meanwhile, in Gas Plant, Tracy pulled into the driveway to the only yellow house on Ash Street. Gas Plant was an incorporated parcel of Midwest, located a half-mile south of town. The settlement's origins were the same as any other in the Salt Creek Oilfield-it began as a camp town to house workers and their families. The house in question belonged to Pearl Norman, though everyone referred to her as Mrs. Norman.

Tracy walked up to the front door and pressed the doorbell button. As she waited, she turned and looked two houses down to the Corbin place. She fondly remembered the first time she met Wesley Corbin as a boy when she first arrived in the area. Wesley was now playing basketball for Northwest College located in Powell, Wyoming.

The sound of a chain rattling on the door snapped Tracy out of her reminiscent trance. As the door opened, she saw Mrs. Norman, who looked confused.

"Can I help you?" Mrs. Norman asked.

"Hi, Mrs. Norman, it is me, Tracy Crandall. Can I come in for a minute or two?"

Mrs. Norman stepped back and opened the door fully to allow Tracy to enter the house without a word.

When Tracy's eyes adjusted, she found the front living room neat without a speck of dust on any furniture surfaces. She then thought about her own home and how it was a chore to dust, and it showed. But what also struck Tracy were all of the pictures of Jessica from various ages.

Mrs. Norman asked, "So, what can I help you with?"

The question surprised Tracy. "Mrs. Norman, didn't you report to the school that Jessica did not come home last night?"

Mrs. Norman's eyes widened and asked, "my Jessica didn't come home?"

"Yes, Mrs. Norman, that is what you reported to the school just a little while ago. Don't you remember?"

Mrs. Norman remained motionless, and suddenly it became clear that her memory had returned. "Why yes, dear, I did phone the school. But unfortunately, Jessica did not come home last night, I didn't see her this morning at breakfast time."

"Jessica has a car, correct? I mean, I've seen her driving around the area." When Tracy's question went unanswered, she took a closer look at Mrs. Norman. It appeared that Mrs. Norman didn't understand Tracy's inquiry, or it was that she couldn't hear or both.

Tracy inquired loudly, "Mrs. Norman, Jessica drives a Dodge Daytona, doesn't she?"

"You don't have to shout, dear; I can hear just fine." Then Tracy watched Mrs. Norman gained clarity. "Yes, it is silver, and the plate number is *1-813AB*. It was my husband Frank's license plate, and after he died last year, I transferred it to Jessica."

She had a hunch. "Mrs. Norman, did Jessica have a medical appointment today in Casper that you may have forgotten about?"

Mrs. Norman's face turned red with embarrassment. "No, I would have remembered that, plus I would have written it on my calendar."

"Can I see it?"

"Sure, let me get it from the kitchen. I keep it near the phone."

As Tracy followed Mrs. Norman into the kitchen, she momentarily became enamored by the sight of the late '60s pale yellow matching appliances. But then she watched Mrs. Norman remove the calendar from its hook on the wall and handed it over. Tracy immediately recognized the work of Charles Wysocki in the picture. The artist's Americana renderings always included a United States flag.

First, she looked at the blocks for that week and noticed *"Aunt Judy"* written across both blocks for Thursday and Friday, the 19th and 20th, respectively. Then she also saw an entry in pencil on the 19th with the letters *TAS* and *7:30.* She also noted that Jessica had a track meet in Douglas on the 21st.

"Mrs. Norman, what does *TAS* mean?"

"Oh, that is my bible study class at the church. TAS stands for Teaching and Sewing."

"Did you go this morning?"

"No. After I called the school, I also phoned the church to let them know that I wasn't coming."

Tracy took out her notebook from her left breast pocket and scribed some notes. In doing so, it enabled her to think of anything additional questions.

"Mrs. Norman, one last question: what was Jessica wearing the last time you saw her?"

The woman thought for a moment and then replied, "she had on blue jeans, running shoes, and a grey hooded sweatshirt with Midwest Athletics written across the front in maroon ink."

"Thank you, Mrs. Norman. One last thing, do you mind if I could have a recent photograph of Jessica so I can put out an alert?"

Silently, Mrs. Norman moved through the kitchen and out into the front living room once again. She stopped at an antique roll top desk and opened one of the drawers above the writing surface. Then she handed Tracy a wallet-sized photo school photo of Jessica, but it was one from elementary school.

Tracy smiled. "Thank you, Mrs. Norman. I was wondering if you had a photo that was a little more recent?"

Mrs. Norman appeared confused. "I gave you a recent picture, didn't I? Jessica is in the fifth grade."

Tracy hid her shock well and passed off Mrs. Norman's assertion as a minor mental lapse. "I'm sorry, I thought Jessica was in high school?"

Mrs. Norman's eyes slowly opened wide, and a blush rose from her neck to her cheeks. Then with charm and grace, she excused her lapse. "Oh, I thought you wanted my favorite photograph of Jessica."

Returning to the desk again, Mrs. Norman then produced the latest school photo, and handed it to Tracy.

Tracy smiled and said, "I will get back to you shortly as soon as I find out something. But I want you to call me if you find out anything as well."

"Okay, dear, thank you for stopping by to see me."

Tracy left the last remark without retort. Instead, it seemed an odd thing to say, considering that the woman's granddaughter was missing. She climbed into her department vehicle and managed to maneuver the seat belt around her pregnant belly. After starting her unit, she made her way back to Gas Plant Road.

At the stop sign, Tracy turned right towards the creek. Upon reaching the bridge, she had realized her error-Tracy had another interview for a separate missing person case.

Tracy spun her vehicle around and hurriedly drove back to Gas Plant. She turned onto Ash Street and whizzed by the Norman house and around the corner. Tracy then stopped outside the Wright place on Aspen Street.

Walking up to the front door presented Tracy with an unexpected challenge. The Wright's didn't have a sidewalk but a half dozen homemade cement pavers set upon a muddy yard from recent rains. While stepping over a rusted Tonka truck in her path, Tracy's foot slipped on cement. Her arms flailed like a windmill blade. At one second, she thought she was about to fall face-first into the muck, and the next second, she straightened her back like a gymnast on the balance beam about to fall off of it.

Just as Tracy walked up to the front step, she heard a young child's cry, and a father frantically tried to soothe her. She knocked on the storm door and waited. No answer. Instead of a knock, she balled up her hand into a fist and authoritatively pounded it against the storm door. Additionally, she yelled, "Police."

The curtains covering the living room window parted slightly, and within a few seconds, Kirk Wright's face appeared. Then, a few seconds later, Tracy heard Kirk struggle to unchain the door. When he did, she saw why. Kirk had one child riding his right hip and another, a much smaller one hugging one of his legs.

"Hey, Tracy. I assume you are here because of Naomi?"

Tracy nodded her head and waited quietly for an invitation inside. It became readily apparent that Kirk didn't get the hint, so Tracy rubbed her bulging belly and asked, "Kirk, do you mind going inside? I could use a seat."

He stepped aside. "Sure, come on inside. I think you can find room on the couch."

As Tracy stepped by Kirk, she noticed that he appeared mortified by the appearance of the place. After a quick look around, she validated his embarrassment since toys littered the living room. Plus, there was a heap of unfolded laundry on the couch.

Tracy took out her notebook from her breast pocket and opened it to a clean page.

"So, Kirk, you know why I am here, so why don't you start telling me what you know."

"What I know, huh?" he repeated. Then Kirk replied, "two days ago, Naomi left the house to drive her bus route. That afternoon, our babysitter called me on my cellphone while I was at work and wondered if I could come to pick up the kids."

"What did you do then?"

"I called my boss and took a few personal hours off, and then I picked up my kids as requested. But unfortunately, when I got here, Naomi was still not home."

"Then what happened?"

"I made supper for the kids and me, and afterward, I started calling Naomi's cellphone."

"Did you reach her?"

"No."

"She didn't answer it?"

Kirk took an exasperated breath. "Naomi left her phone on the dresser, so when I called, I heard it ring."

"Could I see it?"

Kirk got up and went into the bedroom and came back with the phone. "I don't know if it still has a charge or not, but here you go," he said.

Tracy looked at the phone's display and scrolled through the call directory. Then she asked, "why didn't you call me two nights ago to report her missing?" She looked over at Kirk to see his expression as he answered the question.

Without expression or any sign of uneasiness, Kirk said, "she has done this before."

"What is it that Naomi has done before, Kirk?"

"Before our youngest kid was born, she ran out on me. She and her boyfriend went to Sheridan for a couple of days. The fact is, I didn't know the baby was mine until I saw it."

Tracy nodded her head. "I agree. The resemblance of both of your children to you are uncanny." Then she shifted her weight on the soft couch. "So, you think she is running around again?"

This time, Kirk did look away and then stared at the ceiling as if searching for words. "Yes, I thought so, but I think something else happened. I mean, why would she take off in the school Suburban?"

Tracy's eyes opened wide, and she admitted, "good point. But have you tried contacting her family members, and have they heard from her?"

"Nope, nobody knows anything. I even called her old boyfriend, but he was at home with his new wife. He swore to me that he was through with Naomi and hadn't seen her in a couple of years."

She took some more notes and asked for the phone number of her ex-boyfriend. Kirk took out his cellphone and read the numbers aloud as Tracy wrote them down.

"One last question: do you know the route that Naomi drives?"

Kirk shrugged. "I don't know exactly, except that it is west of I-25 and as far out as the South Fork of the Powder River. If you want specifics, I think you will need to go to the school."

She stood up and rubbed her belly. Then she asked, "do you mind if I use your restroom?"

Kirk's first response was a bright red blush of embarrassment, but then he managed to say, "sure, it is in between the two bedrooms."

Tracy stepped around the virtual obstacle course of toys and stepped into the children's room. She found an unmade full-sized bed, more toys, and dirty clothes on the floor. However, the bathroom was not much better since it had a filthy sink, a floor littered with used towels, and a dry bathtub with even more toys. But Tracy wasn't looking for cleanliness; instead, she looked for apparent signs of a struggle. Unfortunately, as hard as she looked, there was nothing other than a messy house.

Before returning to the living room, she snuck into the master bedroom and found it much cleaner, albeit the unkept bed was the same. But again, there was no sign of blood or anything to indicate a physical altercation between Kirk and Naomi. When she entered back into the bathroom, Tracy flushed the toilet and then made her way back out to the living room.

"Well, Kirk, I think I have got everything I need except for what she was wearing. Could you give me a description?"

Kirk thought for a second, "Naomi had a pair of women's Wranglers, tan Laredo boots, and a white with maroon lettering Midwest Oilers hoodie. I don't know what t-shirt she had on underneath, though."

"That is okay, Kirk, but what size of boots does she wear?"

"Size 8, but she tells everybody that she is a 6."

Tracy smiled reflexively but then asked her final questions. "Just a few more questions, and then I am done. I know she is about five foot one inches tall, but how much would you say she weighs?"

"She is 165 pounds, but if you see her, promise me that you don't tell her that I told you her real weight."

Tracy nodded. "Deal. Now, I already know her eye and hair color, but does Naomi have any particular marking like a birthmark or a surgical scar?"

Kirk cut her off, "she has a *Little Mermaid* tattoo on her left shoulder blade. She put it there so nobody but me would see it."

"I understand. Thank you for your help. Now, if your wife does contact you or show up, please let me know immediately. Deal?"

Kirk nodded. "Deal."

Tracy turned and let herself out the door. Then she made her way across the muddy obstacle course. But this time, instead of stepping over the Tonka truck, she nudged it away with her foot.

* * *

16

As Tracy drove back to the office from the school where she obtained Naomi Wright's bus route; she looked at the clock on the Explorer's dashboard. It read *2:15*. "Good," she said aloud and began planning out her making a dessert and transporting it out to the Otten place since Rhonda had undergone surgery earlier that day. But first, she had to finish up at the office.

When Tracy approached the junction of Lewis and Ellison Streets, she turned left to go to the Post Office instead of going home. When she pulled into a parking spot off of Stock Street, Tracy thought back to Mrs. Norman. It seemed to her that Jessica's grandmother was a little absent-minded.

But what bugged her was the bible study Mrs. Norman mentioned. Though Tracy and I were members of the Community Church, it was typical for all churches in the area to share resources like bible studies. However, Teaching and Sewing was not one of the studies that she'd heard of, ever.

After retrieving our mail out of box 1125, Tracy turned to exit. In doing so, she almost ran over Connie Albright, an Elder at the Methodist Church.

"I am sorry, Connie! Either I didn't see you, or my baby is sticking out further than I thought."

Connie smiled. "That's okay, Tracy. How do you like your new job?"

"Oh, the job is fine. You would be surprised how busy a small-town cop can be, even while pregnant." Then a thought entered Tracy's mind. "Connie, can I ask you about one of your bible studies at the church?"

"Sure, Tracy. Are you thinking about joining us?"

"Maybe, but I am curious about one with the most peculiar name: Teaching and Sewing."

Connie guffawed. "Oh my, we haven't had that class for nearly 25 years. Reverend Nealy would preach while the ladies would stitch quilts that the church gave out to newlyweds in the area."

Tracy sighed.

"But we have a women's group that meets every Wednesday morning. Would you like to join us?"

"No. Thank you, Connie, not at this time, though, perhaps after things settle down after the baby comes?"

Connie smiled and nodded and then held the door open for Tracy to walk through.

After sliding in behind the steering wheel in the Explorer, she inserted the key and started the engine. Almost immediately, her radio came to life. Since she was a one-person department, the mobile radio received and transmitted on the County Sheriff's frequency.

"Midwest Chief, Sheriff 45."

"Hey, that is CJ," she said aloud to herself. Then Tracy replied, "this is Midwest Chief. Go ahead, Sheriff 45."

"Hey Tracy, could you meet me at our office? There is something you need to see."

"Okay, Sheriff 45, I am en route to your location."

A few minutes later, Tracy spotted Deputy Jackson and Christian Mercy leaning onto the front fender of the department pickup truck parked outside the office.

Tracy pulled into the gravel parking lot and came to a stop next to the Silverado. As she stepped out, she asked, "what is going on, fellas?"

CJ chinned upward as if waving hello with his face. "While you were away from the office, Christian stopped by to show me something."

Tracy turned her head from CJ to the other man. "What was that Christian?"

He nodded. "Well, I heard that Jessica is missing, and I remembered that on Wednesday during track practice that she went for a run instead of doing speed work with the others."

"So, where would Jessica have run normally?"

Christian turned his body and pointed due north. "She liked it out there on Light Plant Road where there isn't much traffic and where there is good dirt to run on."

CJ looked at Christian. "Do you know the area north of town very well?"

"I do up to Coal Draw, but not north of there."

Tracy dropped her arms down to her side. Then she asked, "why not? I mean, you could run from here to Kaycee along backroads that border Salt Creek as it flows north to the Powder River."

Christian nodded in agreement. "I tried doing a run like that once before, but when I got to the old Electric Plant, I had to turn around."

"Why?" Tracy asked.

The runner suddenly appeared uncomfortable and pushed himself away from the truck. "I just felt uneasy when I approached the old building. It was like it was hiding some evil secret."

Tracy looked over at CJ and shrugged her shoulders. Then she directed her attention back to Christian. "So, what did you guys want to show me?"

Christian reached into his backpack and produced a digital camera. It seemed odd that a man like Christian, who did not have a phone or a television, would own a digital camera. Nonetheless, he opened the file and showed Tracy and CJ the screen.

The photo displayed a single set of footprints in some soft dirt alongside a road.

CJ asked, "what are we looking at here, Christian?"

"That is a picture of Jessica's footprints."

"Where was this photo taken?"

"A mile north of Highway 387."

Then she asked Christian, "how do you know these tracks are from Jessica?"

"I see her print every day since we have a cinder track. Jess only wears the Asics Gel Kayano running shoe, which leaves this specific print. Now, scroll to the two next photos."

CJ slowly scrolled through the second and third pictures. Meanwhile, Tracy rubbed her belly while she thought.

"It looks to me like Jessica got into a vehicle. First, you can see her stride narrow from a running to a walk by the distance between each print. Then you can see her come to a stop and turn. But then it looks like she turned another 90 degrees, and her tracks disappear just like it would be if Jessica climbed into a vehicle."

CJ then scrolled back through the photos again. Then he asked Christian, "were there any tracks further north of these?"

"Sorry Ke-mo, I ran another half-mile further, and there is no indication she got that far. I think like both of you that she just left with someone off of this dirt road."

After a minute's pause, Tracy shook her head. "I am not buying it."

"What are you not buying?"

Tracy motioned her hand around and explained, "all of this. I mean, the tracks tell us that Jessica got into a vehicle. For all we know, she could have run off with a boyfriend."

CJ stood up straight from leaning on the pickup. "Well, maybe we need to interview the girl's parents then."

"You mean, grandparent. Jessica's folks died when she was very young and raised by her grandmother ever since. I just came from her house, and Mrs. Norman said Jessica did not come home last night."

Tracy shook her head once more. "Again, I don't buy it. A girl doesn't just walk away in the middle of track season in her junior year, especially when she is as good of a runner as Jessica. Plus, her Prom is tomorrow night. She wouldn't miss that now, would she?"

CJ had a thought hit him. "Do you have a photograph of her? I just realized that the missing girls I am tracking in the task force all have something in common."

Tracy nodded and walked back over to her vehicle and retrieved the wallet-sized photo. Then she handed it to CJ.

As soon as CJ looked at the photo, he shook his head. "No, she doesn't fit the profile. Jessica has more round-shaped eyes, while all of the abducted girls have almond-shaped eyes. Plus, Jessica has light sandy blond hair, and the others have brown." Again, CJ shook his head. "I just thought for a second there that Jessica might have some connection to that other case." Then CJ handed back the photograph.

Tracy further questioned aloud, "my gut tells me that Jessica is not missing. So, therefore, I am reticent of putting out an all-points bulletin for a girl that could be shopping in Casper for all we know?"

CJ shrugged his shoulders. "It is your call since it is your jurisdiction."

His remark sparked another thought in Tracy's mind.

"Speaking of jurisdiction, CJ, I have a job for you."

"What is that?"

"It seems that one of the bus drivers, Naomi Wright, had gone missing along with her school district-owned Chevy Suburban. I have already interviewed her husband, but what I need help with is driving her route."

CJ furrowed his brow and shook his head slightly that he wasn't following her intimation.

Tracy explained further, "CJ, the bus route is out west of I-25 and in your jurisdiction. I think we, I mean you, should drive the route to look for the Suburban off the road or something? Maybe even stop and talk to the parents at each of the houses?" Then she handed him the directions to each of the stops to pick up children.

Christian moved in closer to CJ and read each line silently. Then he said, "Don't worry, Ke-mo, I can guide you if you want. I don't have anything going on the rest of the afternoon."

CJ looked over at Tracy to explain Christian's nickname, but she cut him off. "That's okay, CJ. I heard through the Salt Creek Pipeline that Christian gave you that name after the real Lone Ranger."

"Oh, so you know the story of Bass Reeves too. What? Was he a local legend around here or something?"

Tracy smiled. "No. I saw the story on *The History Channel*. You should give it a try sometime. You would be amazed at what you will learn."

Before the men could retort, Tracy explained that she needed to go inside the office to put out all-points bulletins on Naomi Wright. But, just before entering the office, she spun around and suggested, "why don't you guys stop at the Otten place last. A bunch of us are going out there around supper time to deliver food and our support to Rhonda, you know, Misty Otten's mom?"

CJ nodded. "Okay, I haven't met her yet, but what is going on with her?"

"Cancer."

* * *

17

The C-word hung in the air as if suspended from a string. For Deputy "CJ" Jackson, cancer was very personal since his mother died recently from it. It started when Maria Jackson found a lump in her breast. Then, over the next 24 months, she went through a double mastectomy, radiation treatments, and multiple chemotherapy rounds. Regardless of treatment, cancer made its way into the lymphatic system. Soon, malignant cells popped up in her liver and lungs, and eventually, into his mother's brain. The sight of her severely dilapidated body still haunted him to that day.

"You okay, Ke-mo?"

CJ snapped out of his trance and observed that Tracy had already walked back into the office. Then he looked over at Christian Mercy.

"Did you say something, Christian?"

"I did. I asked you if you were okay because it looked like you had seen a ghost."

"It's nothing," then he asked Christian, "so where do we go from here?"

"Well, do you have a water jug in this rig?"

The deputy shook his head. "I don't see why we need to bring water with us. I mean, we aren't venturing across the Red Desert."

"No, not the Red Desert, Ke-mo, but you should get into the habit of carrying emergency supplies, like water, whenever you go venturing off of paved roads. So, how about we go to the junction and buy a couple of water bottles each."

Ten minutes later, they drove westbound on Highway 387 toward Interstate 25. The cab of the pickup filled with the smell of fresh-baked chocolate chip cookies. Christian spotted them at the junction store and couldn't resist buying some after CJ purchased a six-pack of bottled waters. As they crossed over the bridge that spanned the Salt Creek to the north and west of Midwest, Christian handed over one of the giant cookies. CJ noted that it felt warm in his hand.

"Thank you," and after a few seconds, CJ quipped, "Tonto."

Christian smiled wide enough that it looked like he was missing a few teeth since the melted chocolate chips covered his front teeth.

"Thanks, Ke-mo. I'm glad you are on board with calling me that."

It puzzled CJ, so he asked, "but don't you think that by my calling you Tonto is at least a little bit racist?"

"No, I don't see it that way."

"Why not?" CJ insisted.

"Well, the real Indian guide to Bass Reeves went by the name of Grant Johnson."

He couldn't follow the intimation, "Grant who?"

Christian smiled. "See, you made my point. Tonto is easier to say." He lifted a chunk of the cookie to his mouth and talked while he ate. "Don't get me wrong, how they portrayed Indians in television and movies in the 50s and 60s was terrible, but I do like the name Tonto."

CJ refused to argue the point further; instead, he let Christian win that debate round. They had already driven under the interstate over-pass, and CJ focused on the cattleguard across the road ahead.

He looked over to his companion, "so, where do we go first?"

Christian looked down at the bus route directions. They decided to stop at the Otten place last, but first, they would visit the Cottonwood Creek Ranch owned by the Boyer family. After that, they would head over to the O'Hara homestead near the South Fork of the Powder River. Next, they would go to the Scarlet Ranch, where Stephanie Merrick lived, and her father worked as a foreman. Then they would go by the Gagnon place.

"Stay on this road, then turn right onto Long Canyon Road."

"Are the roads marked out here?"

Christian shrugged. "The main ones like Long Canyon, 33-mile, and most of the BLM roads are marked. But I have also found that if you need to find help out here, all you have to do is follow the powerlines, and they will bring you to a ranch house."

As the Sheriff's Department pickup crested over the hill, both men became enamored by the view of unspoiled land for as far as their eyes could see. To the north, they could see the southern foothills of the Bighorn Mountains plus the snow caped behemoths beyond. There was also a faint indication of a crimson-colored rock formation to the west. To the south, three hulking hills miles apart from one another stood as silent sentinels of the land. In any other part of the country, those tors are called mountains. But in Wyoming, they were just another hill.

The smell of sage was almost overwhelming. The aromatic plants dotted across the sea of grass in front of them. Here and there, a few barren hilltops of bentonite or sandstone stood out against the prairie. Interestingly, the more prominent hills held Cottonwood tree-choked drainages and stands of pine trees as well.

"So, this is what all of Wyoming used to be?" CJ mused aloud.

"Yep, Kemo, that is why I love to run out here. In doing so, I feel a little more connected to my ancestors. Just to the north of here is the Hole-in-the-Wall where Butch Cassidy and the Sundance Kid hung out."

"I see. Who owns all this land in front of us?"

Christian shrugged. "I don't know for sure who owns what, but most of the land is federal BLM sections." The look on CJ's face intimated that he didn't follow, so Christian elaborated further. "You see, it is a known fact that a lot of ranchers in this area do not own a lot of acres but sustain their operations by leasing federal land for grazing. In some cases, these rights have gone back two or three generations. Look at it this way; if you own a section of land and then lease the sections to the north, south, east, and west, you will control almost 6000 acres."

CJ nodded that he understood, but the grand vista still lingered in his thoughts. It seemed surreal to him how the topography changed so drastically in Wyoming. In all of his travels, he had rarely seen anything like it.

An hour later, they turned down a gravel path that led to the Scarlet Ranch headquarters. The stone and mortar two-story house with a wraparound porch sat in the center of a cluster of corrals, outbuildings, and a large ancient barn.

Before they came to a stop, three Australian Cattle Dogs and two Blue Merle colored Shetland Sheepdogs bounded off the porch. The canines quickly encircled the Sheriff's Department pickup with a series of loud barks and yips. The cacophony of noise from the herding dogs even drowned out the truck's radio.

CJ didn't know what to do, so Christian instructed, "stay put. The general rule about driving up to a ranch or farmhouse is to wait for the owner to call off the dogs."

Seconds later, an old cowboy walked out of the house and stopped on the veranda. Then he shouted a single firm word: "OFF," and the dogs miraculously went silent and returned to their place on the porch. The Shelties, however, continued to yip incessantly.

Christian gave CJ a nod and said, "Okay, now we step out."

As CJ walked around the department Silverado, he watched the older man painfully sidestep down the stairs and onto the gravel. Though he didn't mean to stare, CJ winced because it was evident that the man had suffered a severe back injury sometime in the past. But, above all, the rancher was an anachronism to the modern cowboy.

Before CJ could offer a greeting, the old cowboy spoke. "You must be the new Deputy I heard about?"

"I am. My name is Cory Jackson. But I am curious, sir, where did you hear about me?"

The old cowboy laughed. "I heard about through the Salt Creek Pipeline. It seems everyone has taken a favorable opinion of you."

CJ tilted his head to hide his embarrassment. Then he asked, "what is your name, Sir?"

"I am Ben Combs, and I own this ranch." Then he looked over to Christian, "I know you too, Mr. Mercy. I admire your work and how you ran Badwater last year?"

Christian smiled wide enough to expose a couple of silver-filled molars in the corner of his mouth. CJ seemed confused, so he asked his friend, "what is Badwater?"

Christian explained that *Badwater* was the pinnacle ultra-marathon in the country. The thing that made the race so special was its difficulty. Not only was the course a brutal 135 miles across Death Valley, but it was also in the extreme heat of July. Just finishing a race like that was an accomplishment.

Christian then looked over to the rancher, "yes, sir, I was pleased with third place."

Ben reached up with his right hand and adjusted his sweat-stained cowboy hat. "So, what brings you out to my place, Deputy?

"Well, sir, I am looking into the disappearance of a bus driver, Naomi Wright. I know that her route stopped here to pick up Stephanie Merrick." Then, after a momentary pause, CJ asked, "when was the last time you saw her?"

Ben rubbed the two-day whisker growth on his chin. "I last saw her on Tuesday. But every day after that this week, I have driven Stephanie to school. Her dad, Chuck, is my foreman. Since he is busy running things around here, I step in and help them out when I can."

CJ tipped his hat. "Alright, sir, we appreciate your time. But please let me know if you see either Naomi or the school's Chevy Suburban."

Ben nodded that he understood but then asked a curious question: "So, where are you gents off to next."

"Umm, we are heading over to the Gagnon place to finish up retracing the route, but we have to double back to Mondale Road," Christian offered.

The older man smirked. "You don't need to do that. I mean, the front entrance is just over there about three miles away," Ben said while he pointed southeast.

"Where exactly?" Christian asked.

"Go down the main road and turn left onto BLM Road 6 and then a right onto BLM 37. It will take you up to the edge of the property." Ben looked down at his rugged boots. Then he looked at CJ sternly. "Be careful is all I can say."

"Why is that?"

"No reason other than the road to that place has many eyes."

"What do you mean about *eyes*?" CJ asked.

Again, Ben rubbed his chin. "Up until six months ago, I held the lease on the BLM section of land adjacent to the Gagnon place near Chalk Reservoir. It is aptly named because the shoreline has a layer of alkali, but the water is good enough for livestock."

CJ looked puzzled, and Ben caught the expression. "Anyway, about a year ago, one of my hired hands was checking for newly dropped calves from cows we were pasturing when three men from the Gagnon compound braced him. Each of the men, I might add, carried sidearms."

The eyebrow over CJ's left eye raised. "Well, that isn't too unusual. But, of course, we are still in Wyoming, aren't we?"

Ben snapped, "Of course, but we don't point guns at people unless we intend to shoot."

The older man briefly looked down at his scuffed boots, and then he lifted his head. "My hired hand called over the radio that he needed help, so my foreman and I went over there. That Gagnon clan has placed cameras all over the place. You can see them along the road, in the trees, and along the creek bottom. It seems like it is more of a compound than a ranch."

"How did you defuse the situation?" Christian asked.

Ben shifted his weight again and placed his left thumb into the front pocket of his jeans. "Well, I convinced the big guy, Burris is his name, that they were impeding my ability to manage my cattle operation. I also persuaded him that my cows were on land rightfully leased to me."

CJ asked, "that is it? They just left?"

A playful smile broke across the older man's mouth. "Well, yes, but I think Burris and the others were more impressed with my Ruger Mini-14 that I carried in front of me and ready to use."

Christian interjected, "you said you used to have the lease adjacent to the Gagnon place?"

Ben nodded, "yep, I did. But a funny thing happened. Last year, I got a letter from the Bureau of Land Management saying that I could not renew the lease. They gave me some lame reason that I overgrazed the place, which I didn't."

CJ nodded and started to turn away, but Ben offered another piece of information. "Wait until you see their welcome sign at the gate."

"I don't know what you mean?"

"Don't worry, you will. But can you do me a favor if you are heading over to the Gagnon compound?"

CJ shrugged. "Sure, what do you need?"

"Tell them to keep their boy, Lucas, from pestering Stephanie and sending her inappropriate notes."

Curiosity struck CJ. "What kind of notes? I mean, if it is a teenager lover quarrel, it is not my position to interfere."

Ben stepped forward one step toward CJ and looked hard toward him. "That boy is sexually harassing Stephanie, and it has to stop."

"Do you have one of the notes by chance?"

Ben turned suddenly and stepped up to the porch and quickly ducked inside his house. A moment later, Ben reemerged with a piece of paper in his hand, which he handed over to CJ. "I saw this fall out of her pocket one day as she climbed out of the school Suburban."

The Deputy opened the note while Christian moved in behind to see. The handwritten block-style print revealed a disgusting proposal so suggestive that it was unworthy of further comment. CJ took the note and carefully folded it.

"Ben, is it okay that I keep this?"

"Yes, please get it out of my house. I have adopted the girl and her father since her mother died four years ago. Frankly, it is nice to feel like I have family around this place again, but that is another story for another time."

"No problem, sir, I appreciate your time. If you happen to stumble across the missing school Suburban or Naomi Wright, please give me a call," CJ said and handed Ben his business card.

* * *

18

The Gagnon place remained hidden from view against one of two enormous sentinel hills. To get there involved a succession of turns from one BLM road to another. As CJ and Christian followed the road that took them to the edge of a grove of pine trees, they got a glimpse of a small pond or lake in the bottom of a massive draw.

CJ quipped, "this must be the section that Ben Combs used to lease?"

Christian nodded. "Yes, it is. I ran up here once looking for a place to traverse over that hill to the east and closer to Razorback Reservoir."

"What is the name of that hill?"

"Grummond Hill named for a Lieutenant who died in the Fort Kearney Massacre up by Buffalo. Do you know the story?"

"Umm, if memory serves me correctly, that battle is tied to the Wagon Box fight?"

"It is. Just think, Crazy Horse, along with ten other Sioux, Cheyenne, and Arapaho braves, destroyed 81 Union Soldiers." Christian squinted his eyes and looked up through the trees toward the top of the hill once more. "Yep, that hill should be called Hoka-he. That is a Sioux expression that means *it is a good day to die.*"

CJ nodded, then asked, "Forgive me, but I have been wondering something."

"Go ahead, Ke-mo."

"So is Christian your given name. I mean, do you have a native name?"

"My birth name was David "Moss-on-the-turtle," but I went by Dave Moss."

The deputy looked at the road in front of the pickup and then back at his companion. "Why did you change your name?"

"It is complicated, man. Let's just agree that it isn't easy growing up on the reservation. But I managed to go to college, and while I was there, I had a profound awakening."

"Ya, what was that?"

"I read two books. The first one was the Bible after accepting Jesus Christ as my Lord and Savior."

"What was the second?"

"I read the book Centennial by James Michener. Although it was fiction, the story resonated with me because it followed the exploits of my people along the North and South Platte Rivers. But more importantly, I learned to appreciate the efforts of the only decent white soldier in the whole story by the name of Maxwell Mercy."

CJ lifted his chin to insinuate that he understood. "I see, so you are 'Christian' because of faith and 'Mercy' because of the character.

The runner smiled. "Exactly, Kemo. But I also started applying Dr. Martin Luther King Jr's assertion to judge a person by their character and not the color of their skin. You see, for too long, I saw only skin color, and now, I see the hearts of people around me."

"Makes sense to me," quipped CJ as he negotiated the pickup around a mud bog in the middle of the dirt road.

As they rounded the next bend in the path, CJ spotted a closed-circuit-style camera strapped to a tree. He could see cords running down the tree and into a conduit near its base. Then, about 20 yards further, they spotted the sign that Ben Combs had forewarned.

CJ came to a stop before the closed barbwire gate strung across the cattleguard. Then he placed the pickup transmission into the *PARK* position. The sign read:

> *IF YOU CAN READ THIS*
> *THEN YOU ARE WITHIN RANGE*
> *TURN AROUND NOW*
> *THIS IS YOUR ONLY*
> *WARNING*

CJ chuckled. "Well, I think they are a little obvious with their intention. I mean, they aren't parsing words."

Christian stared at the sign. "What do you want to do now, Ke-mo? Shouldn't we turn around?"

The deputy's hand then bypassed the shifter to the radio microphone. He lifted it out of the cradle instead of placing the truck into reverse. He called out to the County dispatcher and listened through the heavy static for acknowledgment. Then CJ gave his position, but he wasn't sure it went through. Christian interpreted CJ's move as cautionary since he had yet to observe the Deputy call in his physical location before.

A few minutes later, the high-pitched whine of an off-road vehicle filled the cab of the Department pickup. When CJ and Christian looked up, they spotted a John Deere Gator ATV course down the road toward them from the other side of the cattle guard.

As the gator came closer, they saw the driver as the giant man Ben Combs previously described. Curiously, though, Lucas Gagnon sat in the passenger seat. When the ATV came to a stop, the big man stepped out, causing the machine to spring a few inches upward as if suddenly relieved of a burden on its axles.

CJ reached over and flipped the switch that turned on the wig-wag lights. Then he gave Christian these instructions: "I want you to stay put. But do roll down the window so you can hear everything. If this goes sideways, grab the microphone, say *Sheriff 45- shots fired, request backup*. Then I want you to get out of here pronto."

Christian nodded that he understood. "Don't worry, Ke-mo, I've got your back."

CJ stepped out of the pickup and walked toward the cattle guard. He was alert to both the big man and Lucas, who remained in the ATV.

"Obviously, they don't teach you Sheriff's Deputies to read. The sign says to turn around," the big man said.

He smiled as to diffuse the hostility, but it hadn't yet worked. "You must be Burris, correct?"

"I am, and you are trespassing."

CJ looked at his feet and then back up to the man. "I am sorry, but I'm on BLM property, which is public domain. Additionally, this road is a BLM-maintained thoroughfare, so I have a right to drive it if I wish. But that is not why I am here."

Lucas stepped out of the ATV and walked up alongside Burris, who dwarfed the boy.

The big man bristled, "so, what are you doing here?"

CJ hooked his thumbs into his weapon belt. "I am here to speak to Liam Gagnon."

"What about?" Lucas sneered. "My father is a very busy man."

The deputy repeated, "I am sorry to intrude, but I wish to speak to your father."

Lucas shook his head.

CJ tried another approach. "What is it that keeps your father so busy, ranching?"

The boy stammered, "no, my dad is an important scientist, and his work cannot be interrupted."

"What kind of scientist?"

Burris took a giant step forward. "You ask a lot of none of your business questions. Now, you heard the boy. His father is busy. Either state your business or scat. It is your choice."

"Okay then, Lucas, your bus driver, Naomi Wright, was reported as missing. Do you have any information about that?"

The question seemed to shock the boy, and he unwittingly took a step backward. Then Lucas looked up to Burris. It was a tell. Instead of asking another question, he stood silently by and waited for one of them to answer his question.

Finally, after thirty seconds of staring at one another, Lucas offered, "I haven't seen her for a few days, so Burris had to take me to school."

"Fine, so you will let me know if either Naomi or the school Suburban shows up?"

Burris nodded. "Yes, I think I can find you at the closest donut shop."

CJ liked the challenge. It reminded him of his days in the Army. Then he said, "Okay, fellas, I guess I will be going."

Burris smiled, "ya, go back to where you came from then."

CJ turned his attention back toward Lucas. "Nope. Since I am new around here and this area is part of my district, I intend to continue driving along this BLM road through your property and to the other side."

The atmosphere became a challenge of wills. In the moments that followed, Lucas looked to Burris and then back to the Deputy. Finally, the boy shook his head at Burris.

Then the big man said, "not a chance. It is calving season, and ranchers have the right to limit access during those times."

"Really? What kind of cattle are you running up here?" CJ asked incredulity.

Lucas swallowed hard. "We run a few head of short-horns, but that is none of your business."

CJ nodded to acknowledge. Then he asked, "Is there another way through your property so I can get over to Mondale Road?"

Burris grumbled, "you can follow around the fence line since BLM surrounds this place."

CJ nodded, but before he turned to leave, he looked at Lucas. "Before I forget, Lucas, leave Stephanie Merrick alone."

The Deputy then pulled the note out of his pocket and unfolded it so Lucas could see the sheet of notebook paper. It was intuitively obvious that the boy recognized the sheet as his blood drained from his face leaving it an ashen hue.

"If I hear about this kind of stuff again, I will be back out here to have another talk, but with your father. I won't take a no that time, Burris."

Lucas swallowed hard and nodded his head.

"Tell your dad I said hello," CJ said as he turned and walked toward the truck.

As CJ stepped back into his department pickup, he could see a heated exchange between Burris and Lucas. It was evident that the big man did not like how the boy handled the situation. He then turned off the wig-wag lights and turned the ignition key to start the pickup.

Christian hadn't yet said a word but looked contemplatively toward his friend. Spotting his companion's expression, he raised both of his hands that indicated "what?"

"So, what was all that about?" Christian asked. "Wasn't that a little risky to push so hard? I mean, we could easily turn around and head back the way we came instead of driving through their property."

The deputy shrugged. "I know it was the sensible thing to do. But I have a hunch that they know more than they are letting on."

"What told you that?"

"By the way that Lucas and the big guy stared at one another when I asked about Naomi."

"Okay, but that doesn't explain why you pressed them, Ke-mo?"

CJ shrugged. Then he asked, "have you ever gone around the property? I mean, is there even a trail?"

"Yes, there is a trail. Just follow the fence on the right, and we will go up that ridgeline to the south."

"Good. Once we get up above, we can stop and get a look at the entire compound. Then perhaps we might be able to tell what is going on?"

"Okay, Ke-mo."

Ten minutes later, the Sheriff's Department Silverado strained to crawl over the ruts and boulders, even in four-wheel drive, as it climbed to the top of the hill. CJ and Christian winced as they listened to rocks popping under one tire and then the next.

CJ did his best to navigate the trail, but he had difficulty seeing the ground in front of the pickup. Then the trail narrowed as it rounded a rock the size of a Volkswagen, only to funnel them into an even narrower thicket.

As the truck entered the narrows, both men cringed at the high-pitched sound of scrub brush scraping the paint. Then, without warning, the left front tire dipped into a hidden hole that shook the truck. After that, everything shifted inside the cab, including a spare water bottle that found its way under the accelerator pedal.

Thoroughly annoyed, CJ reached down and removed the container and placed it inside a cup holder. Then he looked over at companion.

"I thought you said you have driven on this goat path that you call a road?" CJ quipped.

Christian kept his focus ahead of them. "Keep to your left up here. And, by the way, I never said that I drove over this trail. I ran it."

The pickup continued to climb, and soon they had powered up to the top of the hill where the trail turned easterly on the other side. The fence surrounding the Gagnon place had stopped a half-mile before the summit along a ten-foot-tall sandstone wall.

A few minutes later, CJ stopped the truck.

"What's going on, Ke-mo?"

"I already told you, I want to take a look around. With any luck, we can see the compound. Now, grab those binoculars and follow me."

CJ got out of the truck and reached into the backseat. From within its nylon case, he retrieved a spotting scope that he used at the rifle range. Then the duo hiked toward the top of the hill, though the men flattened themselves out as they neared the top to become invisible from below.

CJ inched forward behind sagebrush and set down his spotting scope. Christian was next to him and found cover as well.

As they peered down into the valley, the outline of the ranch showed itself. CJ and Christian could see the gate where they met Lucas and Burris in the trees to the West from their perch. Then they traced the BLM road through the copse of Cottonwoods along the creek toward a ranch yard.

From above, they spotted the pond Ben described beyond the barn. The creek made a big horseshoe bend to the north and then to the south once again. In between the bow in the watercourse was a flat area approximately a half-mile across. Upon that tract of land sat the buildings that formulated the Gagnon place.

CJ then glassed to the east, where the stream originated. It seemed to divide the gigantic hill from the much smaller one that towered about the ridge where they remained hidden. He also identified another road that ribboned around the slope that Christian called "Hoka-he."

The deputy moved his optic back toward the yard. He thought the house itself was an ordinary rectangular home with an entrance in the middle facing the ranch yard. Behind the house sat a large greenhouse. Additionally, there was a large steel building and a barn aside from each other. The steel structure looked like a shop of sorts, and Burris stood in its doorway facing the house.

CJ nudged Christian and whispered, "take a look at the barn. Are those individual stalls outside?"

Christian took up his binoculars and looked where the deputy had instructed. While he did so, CJ quipped, "I don't know much about ranching other than working on a hay crew during high school, but those stalls don't look right."

His companion shrugged because he didn't know either. But then he saw something else. Next to the large vacant corral were two mushroom-looking objects, a thin radio antenna, and a large satellite dish that pointed west. But the sudden sight of Lucas Gagnon walking from the house and over to the greenhouse broke CJ's gaze at the mysterious object. Instead, he watched the boy open the greenhouse door and vanish inside. But the door remained open.

He aimed his spotting scope to the greenhouse and tried to see inside it. He quickly made out a planter full of tomato plants and another filled with lettuce. However, the view beyond the plants remained hidden by a large black object.

Christian pushed himself backward away from the hill's crest, then tapped CJ on the boot.

"Are you about done, Ke-mo? I don't know how long it will take to drive out of here, and I certainly don't want to do it in the dark."

He sighed. "Okay, maybe you are right."

As he pulled back the spotting scope, CJ caught a whiff of an odor that wafted in front of his face. For a second, he thought he smelled the ocean. But just as soon as the aroma found him, it departed.

Thankfully, the trail going east became an easier two-track pasture road to follow. Soon, the pickup rounded the ridge that separated themselves from the view of the Gagnon place and drove downhill toward a small creek. Unfortunately, the truck pitched again as it crossed over the stream bed, which dislodged the water bottle from the cup holder. CJ caught the container in mid-flight and set it between his legs for the remainder of the off-roading.

Minutes later, the two-lane track merged with an improved road that was presumed to be the extension of BLM Road 37. Before he turned east again, CJ rolled down his window and looked down onto the route. He immediately spotted tire tracks that would fit most all-terrain vehicles or certainly an ATV like the one they saw before.

CJ pointed out of his window, "I see tire tracks that I would bet belong to that John Deere Gator we saw before." Then a thought hit him. "Come to think of it, did you see any other vehicles in the ranch yard? How about people? Did you see anyone other than Burris or Lucas?"

"No, I can't say that I did, Ke-mo. But maybe they keep everything parked inside that big shop of theirs. And maybe, everyone else was inside the house?"

The deputy nodded and looked off in the direction of the Gagnon place. "I suppose you are right."

The new route improved as they pressed easterly; however, the rutted tire tracks in the dried gumbo mud reminded everyone what happened to the road during wet conditions.

They climbed slightly in elevation and skirted the southern side of the "Hoka-he." Above them, CJ and Christian could see a series of rocky ledges that stepped down to the road and toward the deep draw on the other side. On the opposite slope, they could see the full extent of the hill they once traveled over. Still, the unnamed sentinel lacked the height of its neighbor.

For CJ, who was on his first outing in this part of the state, the scenery was still overwhelming. The growing shadows trekking to the east from the setting sun behind them were particularly mesmerizing.

About 15 minutes later, they could see another stock pond alongside a straight line of vertical uplift of rocks.

Christian pointed forward and said, "that is Razorback Reservoir."

CJ nodded. "I see that." Then he had a thought. "Take a look at the bus route directions. I thought I read that Lucas gets picked up next to Razorback Reservoir on Mondale Road."

"It is, Kemo. Why don't you stop at the junction, and we will have a look around before we lose daylight?"

After Christian opened the barbed wire gate strung across the road, CJ steered the pickup through the opening and stopped on the other side. Christian quickly strung the gate closed again and climbed back into the truck.

As CJ drove forward, he asked Christian, "if three men are wearing Stetson hats and sitting abreast of one another in a pickup, which one is the real cowboy?"

Christian shrugged. Then CJ answered, "the one in the middle."

"How can you be so sure?" Christian asked.

"It is easy. For one thing, the guy in the middle doesn't have to drive anywhere, and, secondly, he doesn't have to get any gates."

The men simultaneously chuckled as CJ turned the Department pickup over a patch of grass and came to a stop just short of Mondale Road. After the men stepped out of the vehicle, they walked to the junction. There they spotted the distinct Gator tire imprints and another large vehicle like a pickup truck that used the intersection as a turn-around.

As CJ stood up, he spun around and looking toward the route they had just taken. The lack of an ominous billboard sign warning off visitors on this side of "Hoka-he" Hill was glaringly absent. Then a question filled his mind, *why does Lucas get picked up on this side?*

* * *

19

Thursday, January 31, 2013
10:40 a.m.

We were still driving north on Highway 259 when I took a break from retelling the story to sip from my travel mug briefly. I was appreciative that I had the time available in my schedule to devote to telling the story. Even more, I welcomed that Hope was a great listener. Throughout the tale, she kept eye contact with me and didn't interrupt. Instead, Hope took in every word. But then I detected that she wanted to ask a few questions, so I paused. Hope didn't disappoint.

"So, let me get this straight, this boy was Lucas Garcon."

"Gagnon," I corrected.

"Gagnon, thank you, and his father lived out away from town, and nobody knew where they lived? That is kind of hard to believe."

I nodded my head. "Yes, you are right, it does sound a little far-fetched, but I assure you that it is true."

Hope shook her head in disbelief. "I still don't understand. I mean, you said it yourself that all of the lands in that part of the County were under your watch. So, how is it that even law enforcement didn't know exactly where everyone lived?"

I let my foot off the accelerator and slowed down to pull over in a turnout on the east side of the highway. After coming to a complete stop, I turned and looked at Hope.

"Let me put it to you this way, Hope. Wyoming is pretty much a live and let live State. Meaning that your business is private and it is re-spected."

Hope still didn't seem to understand, so I asked her a question. "Has your neighbor suddenly popped over for no reason at all other than to say *hi*?"

Hope shook her head.

I explained further, "you see, when the Gagnon family arrived in the area, I never had reason to figure out where they lived exactly and show up unannounced. Only CJ dared to do so."

Hope nodded her understanding and then turned her head to look out the passenger side window. She was surprised to see a large mesa dominating her view to the east. Then, while shifting in her seat, she spotted a much smaller butte by itself. The sheer Shannon sandstone cliff jutted skyward 100 feet out of the grass and sagebrush steppe.

Without taking her eyes off of the formations, she said, "wow, what are those? I suppose that I was so involved with your story that I missed taking in the scenery."

I smiled. "The large mesa in front of you is called the Rimrocks, and the lone one is called Castle Rock."

"Have you ever been on top of those rocks?" she asked.

I nodded even though Hope couldn't see me. Then I heard my wife's voice in my head telling me to use words and not gestures. "Yes, I have been on top of the Rimrocks. Though it is not what you think, since the backside is a slope that you can drive up."

"Well, it is pretty striking. I mean, the rocks remind me a little of Monument Valley in Arizona and just as lonely."

I guffawed. "I'll say. When my wife, Tracy, and I just started working together, we got caught in a blizzard and spent the night in a small cave on the backside of the Rimrocks. But that wasn't the amazing part of the story. It is the fact that we were so relatively close to town, and we could have died." After a short pause, I added, "if you look out the windshield, you will see the town of Midwest about four miles ahead."

Hope turned her eyes toward the north and followed the highway. Fortunately, the water tower gave away the town's location, along with its abundance of trees juxtaposed to the treeless plain.

"That's it? That is the town?"

"It is. Were you hoping for something bigger?"

Hope shrugged her shoulders. "I guess I was," she said disappointedly.

"That's okay," I assured. "I had pretty much the same reaction the first time I came here myself. But, yes, this is my home."

Hope spanned the area from the north along the western horizon and back to the south. The scenery stood in stark contrast to her home within the urban sprawl's confines throughout the Colorado Front Range. To Hope, this part of Wyoming was altogether different. She felt awash in a plain of grass and sagebrush. Only the distant township or the distant hills displayed any kind of tree.

"Is that another town over there?" she asked.

"Well, that is Gas Plant, which I told you about in the story."

Hope nodded and then asked, "where is the other town you mentioned?"

"That would be Edgerton. You can't see it from here, but it is only a mile east of Midwest."

I placed the Blazer into *DRIVE,* and as I pulled out on Highway 259, I asked Hope, "It is still a little early yet for lunch, so how about I show you around?"

As we approached the junction of Highways 259 and 387, Hope beheld a large metal structure not unlike a radio tower, only not at tall but much more expansive.

"What is that?" Hope inquired.

"That is an old steel oil derrick. But, of course, nowadays, drilling rigs are mobile, and you don't have to erect a new tower with every well. But, if you want to see an old one, there is a wooden derrick on the corner of Poplar and Highway 26 in Casper."

As I turned the Blazer onto Lewis Street and crossed over the cattle guard demarking Midwest's city limit, I motioned toward the Junction store.

"Are you thirsty, or do you need a bathroom? I can stop?"

Hope shook her head. "Nope, I am good for now." Then after a beat, she observed the school marquee. "So, that is the school."

"It sure is. There aren't many schools left in the nation that have all students from Kindergarten to High School within the same building."

As we passed by the playground, a group of boys stopped their touch football game long enough to wave at us. Then we rode in silence as I turned up Ellison Street, and after a few blocks, turning again to the west.

"This street is aptly named Navy Row since the row of houses on your right used to house Naval Officers who oversaw Naval Petroleum Reserve #3. We passed by it south of town."

"I see. Does the Navy still have a presence here?"

"Nope, they left a long time ago. The school district owns these homes now and rents them out to teachers. Incidentally, that blue house is where the new football coach, Scott Merino, lives."

Hope smiled. "It seems quaint, especially with the park across the street."

"I agree, but when I moved here, that park was nothing more than a vacant lot. But now they host movies in the park during the summertime." I paused for a second while I made a slow turn onto C Street. "On your right is my home, and then on the left is the museum and further left is my wife, Tracy, walking out of her office from behind the Town Hall. She is still the Chief of Police in Midwest."

I pulled into the gravel parking lot outside of the puny Police Station and came to a stop. I waited for a second for the dust to settle outside the Blazer before rolling down the driver's side window. When I did, Tracy strode over to say hello.

"Hi, hon. Who is this with you?" Tracy asked.

I proudly introduced Hope to my wife. I explained to her that Ms. Granderson was the reporter from Denver I had been expecting. I also remarked that I intended to give Hope the whole tour as part of our interview.

Tracy looked beyond me toward Hope. Then she asked, "are you doing a story about the Salt Creek Community?"

Hope shrugged, "well, not exactly. I wanted to do a piece on the glass ceiling breaking decision of your husband's to hire a black Undersheriff."

Tracy shifted her eyes to me and said, "I see," she said. "Eddie couldn't just give you an office interview, could he? He had to bring you out here too." Then she looked back to Hope with an apologetic look. "I hope he isn't boring you, Miss. But, unfortunately, he cannot resist showing off our community."

Hope waved off Tracy's comment, "it is okay. I am intrigued about this place and of the case we were discussing on our way out here."

Tracy looked confused. "What case was that?"

"The Early Dawn case when the Undersheriff, CJ, first started his duties out here."

Tracy bowed her head, and when she lifted it back up again, her face bore out a fantastic smile. "Yes, that case happened when I was super pregnant." Then Tracy looked at me, "so, can I meet you over at the café for lunch in a few?"

I nodded, "sure, give us about 35 minutes, and we will meet you there."

Tracy waved goodbye to both of us, then spun on her heels, and I rolled up my window.

From the Police Station, I drove over to Fitzhugh. Then, as we traveled south, I called out each street by name. Then I turned left onto Ellison and parked the Department Blazer on the cliff overlooking the football field.

"So, this is where Midwest made history with the first football game in the nation to play under the lights."

I smiled but shook my head. "I am glad that you are such a good listener, but no, this is the second field. The first one, Moses Field, is where that historic event took place. It is now a softball field across the road from the steel oil derrick that you spotted." Before Hope could respond, I pointed back to the field, "this is quite the view from up here. I can remember football games where vehicles completely encircled the field.

But also up here on the cliff, where people stood shoulder to shoulder to watch."

Hope nodded that she understood. Then she asked a peculiar question. "Is that the creek the teacher was following when he went missing."

"Yes, that is the Salt Creek, and the teacher's name again is Tim Savolt. But, again, that is another story and another case for another time."

Hope shrugged, "maybe someday you can tell me about it."

"Maybe I will." I paused long enough to bring up another subject. "So, what do you think of our community so far?"

"Honestly?"

I shrugged. "Sure, give it to me honestly."

Hope looked out the passenger side window for a second or two and then turned to me. "I guess I was expecting a little more. I mean, from what you described in your office, I anticipated a Normal Rockwell portrait or another Mayberry or something like that. But, instead, what I see are many tired-looking houses, rusted out outbuildings, and even mini junkyards encroaching the alleys."

I shook my head. "No, you are not wrong about your observations, but the character of this place is as I described it. Though it may not look like much to you, to me, I see our own Mayberry, and I wouldn't change a thing."

I reached up and adjusted my hat, and then I looked over at Hope once more and asked, "so, where was I in the story?"

Hope looked down at her notes in her lap. "I believe CJ and Christian had just seen the Gagnon place for the first time."

"Okay, then go ahead and turn on your recorder, and I will tell you the next part," I instructed.

* * *

20

FRIDAY, APRIL 19, 2002

18 MILES WEST OF MIDWEST, WYOMING

As they made their way back to Smokey Gap Road, CJ noticed a slight vibration within the Silverado pickup. He looked over at Christian and observed that the shudder caught his attention too. The men looked at each other, and in silence, they understood what each other thought. The deputy scanned the road to see if it was a simple wash boarding of the road. But, it was not. Then he came to a stop and exited the pickup. Christian followed and joined his friend on the other side.

CJ pointed at the front tire. "Go around to your side and see if we got some mud in our rims. That will sometimes cause vibration like that."

Christian nodded his head and quickly disappeared to the other side of the truck. Meanwhile, he inspected both his front and back tire rims and found both surprisingly clean. When he stood up, his friend shook his head, which he took as zero mud.

"I dunno, Ke-mo, maybe we bent a rim or something up there on the trail?"

CJ nodded. "Okay, let me drive forward a few yards while you watch the wheels."

The Deputy scrambled into the pickup and placed the transmission into *DRIVE*. He then slowly let off of the brake and rolled forward. Even before Christian called out to him to stop, CJ heard a slight noise coming from the right front wheel.

Christian walked up to the open driver's side window. "Ke-mo, I think you got a bad bearing?"

"Yep, I heard it too." The confirmation of his suspicion was overwhelming, and he struck the steering wheel with his hand. "Now, what do we do? I mean, we are in the middle of nowhere, and it is not like someone will be along to give us a ride."

Christian shrugged. "How about we drive it to Steve Otten's place? That is where we were going anyway."

"How far away is that?"

"It is nine, maybe ten miles tops. It has been a while since I have run this way."

CJ knew their options were few, so he looked at Christian and said, "okay, get in."

Near dusk, the Sheriff's Department Silverado drove down the half-mile-long driveway to the Otten place. The small squeak out of the wheel bearing had turned into a teeth-gnashing squeal. If all the people gathered at the Otten place had not seen the pickup turn off the main road, the noise certainly alerted them. Before they parked the pickup along the corral fence, it seemed like half of the community exited out of the house to meet the men in the driveway.

I was amongst the onlookers, including my wife, Bill and Lois Crooks, retired Chief Traynor, Carlos and Cassi Mondragon, and Steve Otten.

While CJ exited the vehicle, Steve asked, "what happened to your truck?"

The Deputy looked up to him shook his head. "I don't know. I must have tweaked the wheel hub and messed up the bearing."

"Which one?" Steve asked.

CJ pointed. "That one."

Steve moved to the passenger side and the front wheel. He knelt and reached around the tire to feel the axle. It was hot, which confirmed his suspicion.

"I wouldn't drive that another inch, Deputy. I think you need to take it into Casper for your Department mechanic to look at it."

CJ shrugged. "Okay. I will call it in and have a tow truck come out."

Steve cut him off. "That's not necessary. I'll have one of my guys put it on a trailer and haul it to the County garage on Monday."

The Deputy seemed taken aback a little, which Steve sensed. "It's okay, CJ, you are one of us now, and we take care of one another out here. Besides, I already have a contract with the county."

To seal the deal, Steve extended his right hand to CJ, who took it. "Great, that settles it. Now, how about I introduce you to my wife and get you and Christian something to eat. You guys look like you could use it."

Thirty minutes later, CJ wandered out of the front door and walked off of the porch. He wasn't avoiding people as much as he felt uncomfortable at times in a crowd. A trait he long linked to his time in the military.

Christian had already left, choosing to run home rather than wait for a ride. Unfortunately, CJ wasn't so lucky. But he did get to meet some more residents in the area, and even Ben Combs, whom he'd met earlier in the day, managed to come by the house. Then he had a long talk with both Steve and Rhonda Otten. He was surprised to hear Rhonda's excellent prognosis. First, the doctor removed all traces of melanoma, and, secondly, Rhonda avoided chemotherapy or even radiation treatments.

As CJ leaned on the corral's top rail, he became captivated with the early springtime evening. The western horizon in front of him sported a thread of orange with the sun setting not long before. Now, some stars to include Venus shone brightly in the darker, eastern sky. As he inhaled, the air still carried a freshness to it from the new grass sprouting everywhere. But with the setting sun, the temperature dipped into the 40s. It was chilly but tolerable since everyone welcomed warmer weather following the cruelness of winter.

Then a deep voice beckoned behind him, "the heavens declare the glory of God. Don't you think?"

CJ was startled for a second and snapped his head around to look in the direction of the voice. From the aid of the yard light, he could see Bill Crooks approaching.

CJ asked, "what was that?"

Crooks moved in next to him, threw both arms over the top rail, and allowed his hands to hang free. He looked at CJ. "That was from Psalm 19. *The heavens declare the glory of God. The skies display His craftsmanship.*"

CJ tilted his head. "I didn't take you as being a religious type?"

Crooks let out one of the infamous hearty chuckles that only enticed those in the vicinity to join him. "No, CJ, I am not religious."

"But you quoted scripture," the deputy protested.

"There is a big difference between someone having religion and someone having a relationship. The first one is restrained to a mere worship ritual, while the second seeks a relationship with the Lord." Although, after a few seconds, Crooks continued, "anyway, that is not why I came out here."

"Okay, what did you need?"

"So, I heard from Christian that you guys went out to Gagnon's place."

Even in the darkness, Crook could see CJ nod his head. He continued, "I haven't been out there in a while. Did everything seem on the up and up?"

CJ pushed back from the corral fence and turned his body toward the hulk of Crooks. His dower demeanor seemed exacerbated by the prospect of having to tell his supervisor that he damaged his department pickup and wasn't in the mood for a protracted discussion."

"Isn't that your job? I mean, don't you patrol BLM sections around here? The sole reason I tore up a wheel bearing was that the Liam Gagnon closed off the BLM road going through his property," CJ snapped.

Crooks turned and raised his hands to palm out to suggest CJ calm down. "Take it easy, brother! First, it isn't unusual for a rancher to temporarily close a road for certain cattle operations like calving. Secondly,

I cannot patrol every BLM section in an area fifty miles long by 25 miles wide. The last time I visited out there, I rode my four-wheeler around their place from the east. Again, did you see anything unusual?"

"Why?"

"I have my suspicions."

CJ thought for a second or two. "Aside from them blocking off the road, the obnoxious sign, and the fact that the only cattle we saw were in small pens along one side of the barn."

"Anything else," Crooks grunted.

Then something sparked in his memory. "Yes, there was one more thing: both Christian and I thought we smelled the ocean from on top of the ridge."

"Hmmm," Crooks mused. "That makes a little sense."

"What does? I don't follow?"

Crooks waved his hand. "Oh, nothing. Just something I am crunching on. I will let you know if something comes out of it."

They stood in silence and listened to the wind whisper its mournful song through the fence rails. Then Crooks nudged CJ with his arm.

"You grew up in Green River, correct?"

CJ nodded. "Yep."

"Have you ever heard of Superior?"

CJ scanned the extent of the corral as if looking for an answer. Finally, after a brief silence, he answered, "I don't think so. Should I?"

"It is not far from Rock Springs and seeing how you were from the next town over, I thought you might know of it."

CJ tilted his head to one side. "Come to think of it; I do remember seeing the exit sign on I-80."

"That is correct. Superior has a lot of parallels to the Salt Creek community."

CJ squinted his eyes. "How is that?"

Crooks explained, "Superior was a huge coal-mining district that supplied the Union Pacific Railroad. As a result, the area boomed for over 50 years. It even had an opera house."

"What happened?" CJ asked.

Crooks shrugged. "I suppose it was nothing more than simple innovation. You see, once the Union Pacific began using diesel locomotives, the company closed the coal mines. Without work, the town bled down from a few thousand to a couple of hundred folks. Then the high school closed after my class graduated in 1962."

"Why are you telling me this?"

Crooks stood up straight and tucked his massive paw of a right hand into his Wrangler jeans' front pocket. "Well, I guess I am trying to establish some common ground between the two of us, which we have when you consider that we grew up in southwestern Wyoming."

CJ nodded while he maintained his stoic silence.

Then after a long pause, Crooks spoke up. "You and I served in the same unit; you know? Though we served decades apart."

CJ spun his head around. "You are kidding? Which one?"

Crooks smiled, and even in the faint light, CJ could see his teeth. "Let me put it this way: what unit were you assigned to in Mogadishu, Somalia? You know that little firefight where you worked alongside Rangers to nab that monster, Aidid?"

CJ protested. "Just a second, a lot of men died in that *little firefight* including two men I idolized as a young officer."

Crooks reached over and patted CJ on the shoulder. "I know. I met both Shugart and Gordon early on in their careers during a reunion." Crooks drew his arm away from CJ and folded it across his chest with the other. Then he continued, "I also know that you volunteered to join your fellow snipers on the ground to protect the downed Blackhawk pilot, but the General refused."

"Seems you know a lot about me, but you don't."

Crooks inhaled deeply and expressed it out. "Listen, I know that you still hurt over that deal, and I am willing to talk to you about it. I saw way too many of our brethren die, too, except when I served, people still called us 'baby killers' of all things. But, again, I am a brother to you."

CJ nodded. But before Crooks could leave, CJ reached out and grabbed his sleeve.

"I have to ask you something?"

"Sure," Crooks replied.

"I know I am new here, but isn't it a little weird that everyone is out here at the Otten's house considering that Rhonda was just diagnosed with melanoma? I understood what Steve said about the surgeon believes she got everything, which is good news, but it feels out of place to share in someone else's agony."

Crooks smiled again. "Ya, I could see your point of view. But this is what we do. We take care of one another even if our support is just showing up with a covered dish or offering to mow a lawn or just spend time together."

He stopped and stroked his beard and tried to read CJ's face in the dim light. Then Crooks added, "it is about character. You see, the character of a community is best observed by its resilience and by the way citizens care for one another."

While CJ and Bill Crooks reminisced about their military service, the men suddenly ceased their conversation when the eyes of the buckskin horse inside the corral lit up from a reflection of light. The horse's ears also alerted to the south, which was the direction of the light source. As the men turned toward the beam, they could also hear the distinctive sound of gravel popping under a rubber tire.

In most cases, those who lived outside of town enjoyed having the ability to spot visitors long before they parked outside the house. It was no different that night. Misty and Adam, who settled their differences, also saw the twin beams. Misty abruptly stopped the porch swing with foot and stood up.

From inside the house, Steve saw a reflection of light streak across the living room wall. He stood up and walked over to the picture window to look toward the driveway to see who had just arrived.

From behind Steve, his wife asked, "who is here?"

Steve placed both hands on his hips. "It looks like Jessica Norman's car."

His announcement met with a few gasps that included Tracy, who followed with, "you have got to be kidding?"

Steve turned and looked at Tracy. "I wish I were."

Tracy wiggled her pregnant body forward to get up off of the couch. Before she could stand up, Steve asked, "where are you going?"

"I have to do my job, Steve. You know that I will need to interview her."

Steve nodded his head and then waved Tracy over to the window. Next, Steve pointed to Misty on the porch, who was already moving off in the direction of the car.

"Why don't we see how this plays out," Steve urged.

Misty left Adam behind on the porch swing and stepped quickly and purposefully down the steps. She made a beeline across the front lawn toward the vehicle that stopped behind Crooks's ancient Willy's pickup.

From inside the car, Jessica Norman turned off the ignition and removed her key. As she grasped to door handle with her left hand, Misty came into view. Then, Jessica got out of the car and shut the door.

"You had better have a good reason for not being dead!" Misty bluntly exclaimed.

Jessica spread her arms out at waist length with her hands tilted palm up. "What are you talking about?"

Misty shook her head. "Don't play games with me. You had everyone scared to death that something bad happened to you."

"I still don't know what you are talking about?" Jessica pleaded.

Misty folded her arms across the top of her belly. "You know what I am talking about; how about you explain where you have been the last two days."

"I was in Denver." After a few seconds, she saw that Misty didn't understand. So, Jessica explained further, "I was in Denver. I told you about that!"

Misty nodded her head. "You did, but I didn't know when you were going."

Jessica dropped both of her hands simultaneously and allowed them to strike against both hips. "I don't know why you are so mad at me. I thought I told you?"

"Well, you didn't, and your grandmother reported you missing."

"What? Why would she do that? I mean, Granny knew where I was going. She even picked me up on Light Plant Road as I told her to so I could get ready to leave for Denver in the morning."

Misty relaxed her posture and stepped closer and hugged her friend. As they held one other, Tracy approached from behind.

"Jessica?" Tracy asked.

"Yes, ma'am."

"First of all, like Misty, I am happy you are okay. But I need to ask you a few questions."

"Umm, am I in trouble, Chief?"

Tracy shook her head and calmly motioned for Jessica to follow her to the porch. Then, while clutching her underbelly, Tracy explained that she needed to sit down. When they reached the steps up to the porch, Tracy sat down on the second step.

"Okay, that is better, now. Why don't you sit down next to me?"

Jessica did as instructed and sat down next to her.

Tracy explained, "just like Misty said, the reason everyone is so shocked to see you is that your grandmother reported you missing."

The girl shook her head in disbelief and looked toward her friend and then back at Tracy.

Tracy further explained, "I even went to your house in Gas Plant, and your grandmother honestly did not know where you were. Can you explain that?"

Jessica shrugged. "I don't know. She forgets things sometimes."

Tracy nodded. "How long has that been going on?"

"I don't know, a while, I guess. I leave Granny notes to remind her of things just in case her memory isn't working."

"Did you leave her a note about your trip?"

Tears welled up in Jessica's eyes, and she raised both hands to cover her face. Within that instant, Misty moved in closer and threw her right arm around her friend in support. Jessica lifted her head and turned back toward Tracy.

"I did, Ma'am. I left Granny a note to call the school to excuse my absence for Thursday and today."

"I see," Tracy replied. Then she turned her head and looked out into the darkness to think of what to ask next. What distracted her was that the night seemed to grow colder by the instant. Then, she involuntarily shivered.

"Alright, Jessica, so tell me for the record where you were exactly."

"Well, like I told Misty, I went to Denver to see my mom's best friend."

"What is her name?"

"Well, I call her aunt Judy, but her full name is Judy Parker."

"Why did you go see, umm, Aunt Judy?"

"I stayed with her while I visited the campus of Regis University and meeting with one of the assistant track coaches."

"I see, so are they recruiting you for a scholarship?"

Jessica nodded.

Tracy struggled to get up, and Jessica stood up quickly and helped her get to her feet.

"Thank you, sweetie! This child inside of me has got to be as big as a bowling ball." Tracy once again cupped her belly and then wiped her forehead with the other hand. But before turning away, she looked at Jessica and said, "I suppose I can close out this investigation. But what concerns me is your grandmother and her forgetfulness. I mean, what if she forgets to shut off the stove and burns down the house?"

Even with the dim light of the porch, Tracy could see Jessica's cheeks blush with embarrassment.

"No, we'll be alright," protested Jessica.

Tracy pleaded, "I am not trying to take you away from your grandmother. Instead, I want to figure out how to help both her and you."

Jessica nodded that she understood. "Granny is all the family I have left in this world. I mean, I have to be the only person in the world that has no real aunts or uncles or even cousins. So, it is just Granny and me."

"I understand, sweetie. I do. Now, let's go inside and figure out a way to help both you and your grandmother. Okay?"

Jessica nodded and followed as they crossed over the lawn toward the house.

As Misty turned and started to step off, Adam reached out and took her hand, which stopped her. She slowly turned to him and saw a half of his face illuminated by the porch light.

"Misty, I think I will be heading home now," Adam declared.

"Why not stay a little longer? I don't understand?"

Adam shook his head. "I do want to spend time with you, but we both have a track meet tomorrow, and then we have prom right after we get back in town."

"I see. Well, I will see you tomorrow morning then."

As Adam turned to walk over to his car, Misty grabbed him and whispered into his ear, "I can't wait for tomorrow night."

* * *

21

SATURDAY, APRIL 20, 2002

COMMUNITY CHURCH, MIDWEST, WYOMING

11:45 P.M.

Slowly over the past ten minutes, cars started arriving at the church. As part of a long-standing tradition borne out of necessity, most prom attendees accepted the invitation to eat a late-night meal following the dance. Since driving to Casper was not a consideration because it was 45 minutes each way, it was the only place for the kids to eat, aside from the café in Edgerton. Hence, it became a tradition for community members to gather together each spring to host the event. As usual, one of the volunteers was Steve Otten.

Since Rhonda was still recovering from surgery, Steve went solo that year and worked in the kitchen. Alongside his lifelong friends Pete LaRouche and Carlos Mondragon, Steve and his buddies put together a fine meal for the couples. The dinner course included a restaurant-quality sirloin roast from Steve's cattle, rosemary potatoes, green beans, dinner salad, and white cake with buttercream frosting for dessert. While the three men took care of the kitchen, other parents were on hand to wait on and bus the tables.

Teenaged couples continued to trickle into the fellowship hall and quickly found their seats. Every time Steve heard the door open, he bent over and peered through the serving counter window to try to catch a glimpse of his daughter and Adam. But soon, the entrance stopped opening. Then he became worried.

Steve peered over the batwing doors that separated the kitchen from the dining area and searched carefully around the room. He soon spotted the boy he wanted. His name was Jack Sonnenberg, who was also

Adam's best friend. Steve untied his apron and set it aside before pushing through the swing doors and into the main fellowship hall.

Jack must have heard him walking up behind because the boy turned his head and smiled respectfully at Steve. "Can I help you, Mr. Otten?" Jack asked.

Steve nodded and then pulled an empty folding chair from the table adjacent to Jack and his company. He then straddled the seat backward with his forearms resting on the metal backrest.

"Yes, you can help me, Jack." Then Steve motioned with his fingers that instructed the boy to lean forward. At a whisper, Steve asked, "Where are Misty and Adam?"

Jack nodded and leaned close to Steve's ear. "I don't know, Sir. I didn't see them at the dance."

Steve's voice boomed, "what do you mean they never showed up at the dance?"

The question was so loud that everyone in attendance heard Steve, which he now realized that fact as he looked around the room at the stunned faces. Instead of embarrassment, he refocused on Adam's friend.

"When did you see your friend and my daughter last?"

Jack again leaned forward near Steve's right ear, "I saw Misty get into your ranch pickup at the school after we all got back from the track meet."

"And, what about Adam?"

The boy shook his head, "same thing, sir, Adam got into his car after getting off of the bus."

Steve stood up and placed both hands on his hips. Then he bowed toward Jack. "Did Adam or even my daughter say anything to you about not going to the dance?"

The boy laughed aloud, which annoyed Steve. "What is so funny?"

Jack immediately pleaded, "no, sir, it is not funny."

"Well, what is it then?"

"Your daughter talked all day today about that dance. I honestly think that she wouldn't miss it for the world. Besides, Adam is afraid of you."

"I see. Thank you, son," Steve said and then patted Jack on the shoulder before turning around and walking back to the kitchen.

After arriving at the kitchen door, he called out, "hey, guys, my daughter didn't show up, so I am going to try to find her. So, can you cover for me?"

"Sure, buddy, we can do that. But where do you intend to look?" asked Carlos

Steve shrugged. "I dunno. Maybe I'll drive around here in Midwest and then maybe over to Adam's house in Edgerton. Why?"

Pete's lips formed into a small smile, not that the situation was funny to him. But, instead, he could readily empathize. He looked back at Carlos first and then at Steve. Then he suggested, "if you don't find them in either town, try looking where they might be parked."

"Parked?"

Pete nodded. "I know what you are thinking but trust me on this one. Remember, I have two grown daughters in addition to the one still in school. So, this situation isn't my first rodeo."

"So, where did you look?"

Pete grinned. "The first time this sort of thing happened to me, I drove out to all of the places I used in high school. You remember, don't you? Coal Draw in the trees. Lewis Camp. Even baby graves."

Steve shook his head in disbelief. "Unfortunately, I do, and thanks for putting that image into my head of you on a date in high school. So, where did you find your daughter?"

Pete chuckled to bring a dose of levity to the discussion. "Well, Coal Draw lost all its trees when some yahoo cut them all down. But kids these days are different in that things have to be easy for them, or they won't do it. Most of them drive these Japanese cars with coffee can exhausts, so I doubt they would ever venture far off of paved roads. I would try places close to town."

Steve furrowed his brow. "Really?"

"Yes, places like the dump or even behind the buildings on the golf course. Any place that is close by and easily accessible."

Steve lifted up the previously discarded apron and carefully folded it, then left it on a side table. He then lifted his jacket off of the peg and threw it on. As he turned to head out of the door, he stopped and said, "thanks again, guys."

Pete smiled. "Don't mention it."

In the parking lot, Steve started up his pickup and allowed it to warm up. The outside temperature hovered the freezing mark, which was not unusual for a Wyoming springtime night. He then reached into his pocket and drew out his phone.

Steve pressed the #1 button on the keypad to speed dial the home phone. After two rings, his wife, Rhonda, said, "hello."

"It's me, hon. Adam and Misty never made it to the church, and from what I can tell, they never made it to the school for the dance either."

"What do you mean they never showed up?" Rhonda fumed.

Steve sensed her anger, and he took a deep breath. "Trust me; I am mad too. But, yes, they never made it."

"Did you ask around? Did any of the other kids see them?"

"Yes, of course, hon. I did ask around. That is how I come to know the kids didn't show up at the dance."

"What are you going to do?"

"I don't know. I think I am going to drive around Midwest and Edgerton to see if I spot Adam's car." Then after a brief silence, he asked, "what time did the kids leave?"

Rhonda huffed. "That was an experience. Adam showed up here a half-hour after Misty. So, I had to sit around and entertain him for the next thirty minutes while she finished getting ready. Then I took some pictures, and I think it was 8:30 by the time they left for the school."

His phone abruptly went silent. Steve thought that perhaps he'd lost his cellphone signal, which happened to him all the time around the Salt

Creek area. But he continued to listen in silence, and he finally heard the sound of tiny and shallows breaths of air move across the receiver.

"Hon, are you still there?" Steve asked.

"Yes, I was thinking to myself for a second." Then following another brief stillness, Rhonda said, "okay, why don't you go look for the kids while I phone Adam's mom. Call me back when you find them."

The muscles in Steve's neck tightened like a thick braid of rope. "If and when I find them, there won't be much left of the boy."

"Steve, please control yourself," Rhonda warned. "I know you want to wring Adam's neck for this, but I want to know Misty is okay. Promise me you will bring our daughter home before we discuss anything with her."

Steve sighed heavily. "I promise, and I will call you as soon as I know something."

Then he closed his phone and placed it back inside his pocket.

Steve's truck had warmed up by the time he backed away from the church building. The clouds above opened up, and snow fell relentlessly around him in large cornflake-sized snowflakes that only come in Wyoming's springtime. The moisture had already turned the gravel parking lot surrounding the church into a sloppy soup of gumbo mud that stuck to everything it contacted-especially tires.

Mud flung from the treads in all directions as Steve drove onto Ellison Avenue. He then turned east onto Burke Street, and once he reached Shannon Avenue, he intended to crisscross the East-West streets of Midwest in a grid-like pattern starting with Peake Street. Yet, when he drove up the southern leg of what comprised Ellison Avenue, he hadn't spotted Adam's bright yellow Toyota Celica.

Steve suddenly remembered what his friend Pete suggested about where kids park their cars. He then yanked the steering wheel of his pickup and came to a stop on the parking pad that provided the grand overlook of the football field. Instead of getting out of his truck, Steve unbuckled his seat belt and slid across the bench seat to look out the window. But he couldn't see anything due to the half-inch of slush that had gathered on the glass. So Steve quickly toggled the switch and lowered the glass.

In the black void in the bowl below the cliff, he only made out the white outline of the football field since the snow had stuck to the blades of grass. Everything else was dark and without shape, including the equipment building at the east end of the track. But as Steve started to roll up the window, something else caught his attention. He looked more closely and noted the light color of a small car parked amongst the stand of Cottonwood trees in the field's parking lot.

In his immediate haste, Steve forwent securing his seat belt around him, and, instead, he placed his truck in gear. A new adrenaline rush caused his heart to beat faster, and a slow rage engulfed him. It had been a long time since Steve had felt this way-the last time was when a man shot him through the shoulder. That was long ago, but the surge of alertness he felt was ultrafamiliar. His vision focused, and every muscle fiber in his body coiled like a spring waiting to explode.

It took him less than a minute to navigate down to the entrance to the football field lot. The headlights of Steve's pickup illuminated a teenage boy and girl embracing one another in the front seat of the car. It was also evident that the girl wore a dress.

"I knew it!" Steve growled to himself as he threw open the door of his pickup and quickly exited as rage consumed him.

He promptly walked around the car and stopped adjacent to the driver's side window. With a clenched fist, he rapped on the cold glass with force. As the startled boy turned around, his heart sank.

It was not Adam. Nor was it Adam's car; instead, it was a mid-90s white-colored Toyota Corolla.

"Mr. Otten?" the boy asked.

Steve looked down once again and recognized the boy as the son of his longest employee, Will. The anger that he felt just a moment ago fled within a flash.

Steve bent forward toward the rolled-down window. "Billy, you haven't seen Adam or my daughter, Misty, have you?"

The boy shook his head.

"Okay, thank you. Now, Billy, don't you think you should take your date home before her parents get worried and come searching for her?"

"Yes, Sir. Right away, Sir!"

As soon as Steve stood up, the boy started his car and left without another spoken word. But that didn't solve anything for the concerned father. Instead, he reached into his coat pocket and retrieved his cellphone and flipped it open. Then he pressed "1" again to call home.

It rang once on his end before he heard his wife, Rhonda, say, "Hello?"

"It's me again, hon. I haven't found the kids yet. At least they aren't in Midwest."

"Have you looked around Edgerton yet?"

Steve shook his head as if his wife could see him. "No, hon, I haven't. But that is where I am going next."

He heard Rhonda breathe heavily into her phone's receiver. Then after the brief pause, she asked, "you don't think they went parking somewhere in the oilfield, do you?"

Reflexively, Adam nodded. "I was thinking that too, but I doubt it now."

"Why?"

Steve reached out his arm and swept it horizontally across the landscape before him. As he did so, he replied, "because this wet snow will have turned everything into a slick gumbo mess."

"It snowed? When did that start?"

Steve shook his head again. "I don't know. It started falling after I got to the church. Was it snowing when the kids left the house?"

"I'm not sure. I didn't look outside."

Steve shook his head, "no, I doubt those kids went to park somewhere. So, what do we do next?"

"I don't know yet. So, why don't you go through Edgerton and then come home? If the kids haven't shown up by then, we will have to make another plan."

Steve signed off of the phone call and closed up his phone. The wind picked up and blew an icy reminder of winter against his neck that caused him to shiver. As he climbed back into his pickup, Steve realized he was no longer mad; instead, he felt something that rarely gripped him in the past. He felt scared.

* * *

22

After coming to a stop outside the café in Edgerton and shutting off the engine to the Sheriff's Department Blazer, I cautioned Hope to bundle up since the wind would chill a person in an instant. She nodded that she knew the drill and stepped out of the unit. Once inside the café, the longtime owner, Liz Martin, greeted us with her trademark smile and genuine pleasantness.

"Hey, Sheriff, your wife is sitting at a table in the back," then Liz gestured to the woman accompanying him, "who is your pretty guest with you?"

My cheeks blushed. "I'm sorry, this is Hope Granderson, who is a reporter from Denver."

Liz beamed a huge smile again. "Well, welcome honey, I am Liz. Is this your first time in the Salt Creek area?

Hope returned a warm smile herself. "Yes, it is. The Sheriff has been giving me a great tour of the area and giving me a taste of the history here."

Liz nodded. "Well, if it is history that you want, you will get it by the truckload here." She held up her hand and began counting off facts. "We have the first nighttime football game in the nation, first paved road in Wyoming, first steel pipeline in Wyoming, first arc weld, and first heated public swimming pool."

I cut her off. "Well, the last fact is not fully verified, Liz, but I think Hope got your point."

Liz nodded. "Be sure you take her over to the museum before she leaves town." Then she spun around, grabbed two menus from behind the cash register desk, and handed one to Hope and me.

Tracy saw us walk around the corner and waived to us. When we reached the table, I offered to take Hope's coat, which she obliged. I then walked to the back of the room, hung it up on the coat rack. I, too, took my jacket off and placed it on an empty peg. By the time I made it back to the table, Hope and Tracy were already in the middle of a conversation.

Tracy looked up at me as I pulled a chair back from the table on her immediate left, then she looked back to Hope. "As I was saying, it took me a little while to adjust to living out here."

I looked over to my wife and teasingly chided, "ya, that was all of about two weeks if I remember correctly."

She smiled and admitted, "yes, that is true, but I have to say I felt displaced."

The three of us looked over our menus, though it was unnecessary for Tracy and me since we knew it by heart. Hope gave us both a quick, brief look and saw that we had refolded each menu. Then she returned her gaze to the menu.

Looking up again, Hope asked, "so, what do you recommend?"

Tracy offered, "if you want something lite, then go for the avocado chicken salad, but if you want something a little bit heartier, then go for the Reuben."

As if on cue, Liz arrived at the table and took our orders. Then after we received our drink order and Liz left the table, Hope once again took out her digital recorder. She looked over to me and asked, "so, we were telling me about the kids not showing up at the after-Prom dinner."

I nodded. "Yes."

"So, did Steve find his daughter and her boyfriend?" I shook my head. Then Hope asked, "okay, what happened?"

Tracy interjected. "We woke up at 2 a.m. to someone pounding on our door. When Eddie opened it, he found Steve and Rhonda Otten standing on our porch."

Liz appeared once more with three lunch plates and quickly passed them around. While we ate, I resumed the story. I recalled that not only were the Ottens in our living room demanding action from the Midwest Police and the Sheriff's Office. But with them were also the Mondragons, LaRouches, and Adam's mother.

"What did you do?" Hope asked.

"There wasn't much I or we could do back in 2002 since it was before we could issue an AMBER Alert." I then picked up a fry and bit off a piece of it, and then I added, "no, eleven years ago, we still needed 24 hours to elapse, even with children. But I did go out and patrolled around the area. Plus, Deputy Jackson drove out from Casper to join me right after sunrise."

Hope smiled. "I was wondering when he was rejoining the story."

I nodded. "Yep. CJ and I retraced the only possible route that Adam could have taken from the Otten place to go to the dance at the school."

"Did you find anything?"

I shook my head. "No, not really. I mean, by that Sunday morning, the wet snow overnight had wiped out any possible tracks on the dirt road that ended at the pavement. But CJ found something."

Hope leaned forward to the table and eagerly waited for me to reveal that small clue.

"As I said, we were en route back to Midwest where County Road 115 ends and Highway 387 began at the interstate when CJ caught the glint of glass in the gravel next to the road. So, we stopped and looked around and found a handful of spare glass fuses, you know, the kind that goes into older cars?"

She nodded.

"Well, Adam's car was notorious for blowing fuses and other electrical problems. I mean, I had helped the boy a few months before this episode when I found him stranded alongside the road between here and Midwest. I ended up giving him a small tin of glass fuses from the glove compartment of my old pickup."

Hope's eyebrows raised, indicating she understood. "Did you think Adam broke down? On that night, I mean?"

I nodded. "Well, there is where things were unclear early on in the investigation. You see, neither CJ nor I had any evidence that Adam had pulled over. Remember, the wet snow had obliterated any tire tracks in the dirt shoulder if there were any."

I paused long enough to take another bite of my cheeseburger. Meanwhile, Hope eased away from the table and sat back in her chair. She looked reflectively out the window toward the long before shuttered bank across the street from the café.

When she returned her gaze to me, she asked, "I know you will eventually tell me, but at this point, I wonder what was going through those kids' heads?"

I nodded as I reached for my glass of iced tea to wash down the bite of the burger. Then I said, "let's just say that things start to come together rather quickly from this point on."

Without warning, I reached over and grabbed the digital recorder that sat in front of Hope. Then I pressed the stop button. Meanwhile, she seemed shocked about my sudden movement. So much so that Hope missed my reaching into my left shirt pocket as well.

"Hey, what are you doing? That is mine." Hope protested.

I looked at her with determined fixed eyes. "Can I trust you?"

Hope's eyes widened, and she looked physically taken aback by my question. Then, finally, she answered, "I am a reporter, and I always write the truth. If that is what you are asking me?"

I nodded. "That is what I thought." I picked up my iced tea and took another long drink and set it down on the table. "Here is the problem; the rest of the story is off the record. I mean, it must never show up in print. Can you agree to that?"

I could see the wheels turning inside Hope's head. I knew she wanted to hear the rest of the story, but I also knew she would like to write about it too.

"If I cannot guarantee, then what?"

Up to that point, Tracy was stoic, then added, "or, you will have a fluff piece that you can write. But the question my husband is trying to ask is whether or not you want to know why CJ is a rare man amongst others?"

Again, Hope demonstrated a great conflict inside her mind. Then, finally, she agreed. "Yes, I want to hear the rest of the story, and yes, whatever you say is confidential, and it will remain so. I promise."

"Good." Then I reached into my pocket, retrieved the micro tape recorder I had used for years, and pressed the stop button. "I have you on tape agreeing to our deal."

Hope rolled her eyes, unamused. "Okay, you got me. Now, let me hear the rest of it."

* * *

23

She felt disoriented, like she had napped too long into the afternoon and woke up unsure of her surroundings. But underneath her body wasn't a bed. Instead, it felt like concrete. As the fog started to clear her mind, she took inventory. She wondered if she was hurt, so she tried moving her arms but couldn't with her wrists tied behind her back. Then she tried moving her legs, but they too were bound.

It was too dark to see, but then she realized a cloth blindfold of some kind covered her eyes. Despite the bindings, she was unhurt except for a sore jaw and her aching back teeth, where she had fillings.

She felt like crying, but for some reason, she couldn't. Instead, there was a foreboding sense that she needed to keep calm and think her way out of the position.

She asked herself, *"What day is it?"* which naturally went unanswered along with *"where am I?"*

Then she heard something, so she held her breath and listened intently. Then she heard it again, and her head instinctively moved toward the tiny noise. It sounded like a single drop of water that fell into a small pool. She listened once more and caught the sound of the drip. This time she vividly pictured a drop of water forming and growing bigger. Then she fancied it was swelling up into a fat orb and suddenly falling into a pool. Then she imagined the drop becoming nothing more than a ripple on the surface of the puddle. Simultaneously, an actual water droplet struck an unknown collection of water, making a distinctive *kerplunk* sound.

Now she smelled something. It was as if someone flipped a switch and all her senses were once again at her disposal. What she smelled, though, wasn't pleasant. It was the overwhelming and undeniable scent of urine, which caused embarrassment to overcome her. But it occurred to her that her underwear felt dry. So, she asked herself, *"who peed their pants?*

She moved against her restraints, which only resulted in further frustration. Anger started to burn in her belly, and she desperately wished to scream out. However, as soon as that raw emotion began, it subsided because she knew that keeping calm would keep her alive. Yes, she admitted that she was in extreme danger, and then a stray thought wiggled loose from her memory. She remembered one of Pastor Robert's sermons. The Pastor reflected on Apostle Paul's various setbacks. Specifically, the man spoke about how Paul didn't let the stoning, the shipwrecks, or even imprisonments steal his joy.

Then another sound alerted her senses. This time it sounded like a doll that she once had as a young girl. It was her favorite, and it rarely left her side. What she liked about it most was that it would cry if left unattended.

But now, the sound she heard somewhere in her darkness was like the sob of a woman.

She wasn't alone! Someone was here with her!

Just as she was about to call out, another sound alarmed her. It sounded like a metal door unlocked and the sound of footfalls on the floor.

"I see you are awake. Don't worry. I will untie you in a little bit. I promise," said a strange, synthesized, sounding voice.

She remained speechless and motionless. She also squinted her eyes as if hiding herself from the man.

Again, the strange voice sounded, "you will be okay."

Then she felt a slight prick of pain in her arm. As fast as the pain came, it left just the same. Afterward, the strange man moved away, and she heard the door open and closed again with an eerie squeak.

She tried to think again about what had happened to her. Then she remembered seeing bright lights before everything went black. As soon as she recalled it, her memory went blank. She told herself, *"come on, back up to before the lights. Where were you?"*

Again, a memory started, and this time she saw herself sitting in a car and then the bright lights once again.

Then it hit her: she was with someone she loved the most! Before she screamed out the name on her tongue, her memory rebooted like a computer. Now she knew her name.

Her attention focused on the sobs in the dark, which began after the man with the strange voice left. Whoever wept in the darkness surrounding her must need help or an ally or both. She wrestled up the courage and finally said something.

"Hello?"

Unbeknownst to her, he, too, awoke from a terror that raced through his aching head.

"Oh my head," he said aloud. At least, that is what he thought he said, but it came out as one long muffled noise. Next, he felt a slight pinprick in his left arm. It was then he realized that a cloth of some kind gagged his mouth. His eyes were blinded too. Perhaps even more unsettling to him was the feeling like he was floating above the floor.

He drew a long breath through his nose, and the smell of saltwater overwhelmed his senses. He wasn't sure where he was or even alive since he felt unnatural. But then, his body began to come alive as if his nervous system were a machine starting up in stages. His neck ached for some reason, as did his lower back as well.

In an instant, he knew he wasn't alone. At first, he sensed contact against his left thigh like a feather brushing across it. Then, something rubbery bumped against the other leg, but this time with a little more force.

He was fully awake and aware now. He wasn't floating. Instead, he was sitting on the bottom of a tank of some kind. The water surrounding him was comfortably warm but not hot. However, his arms were outstretched and bound just like his legs. The invisible restraints prevented him from moving around.

Suddenly, a voice spoke behind him, though metallic and mechanical like a throat cancer survivor.

"Don't struggle too much, or you will entice them," the voice warned.

"Entice what?" He said, but it came out as another muffle.

"Silly boy, you are in a tank with 32 blackfin sharks, but don't worry, they already ate and won't be hungry again for hours."

His mind screamed, *"SHARKS!"* Then he asked himself, "sharks here, but where is here? Think, you fool, think," he said to himself.

"Wyoming," he tried to say aloud. He knew he was from Wyoming, a small town, yes, in Edgerton. He went to school in Midwest. Now things were coming online mentally.

But sharks? It didn't make sense.

The voice interrupted his thoughts, "oh, but you are a strong one. It took three blasts from the taser to subdue you. Then we had to drug you too, which is why your head hurts now. Don't worry though, all of that will fully wear off shortly, and then, perhaps, we can move you out of that tank.

He tried to speak again but could only make incoherent sounds.

"Shh," the voice said. "I hope you understand. I only did this to get your attention. If you don't do what I ask, then you will become dinner."

Then he heard the sounds of tiny footsteps departing away from him to the unknown area behind him.

He remained inordinately still and acted as a log in the water. But then, he thought hard once again, and he came up with his name. "I'm Adam," he said in his mind. Yet, the side effect of his revelation sent pulses of adrenaline throughout his veins. Now his thoughts became focused on one person: Misty. *"Where is she?"*

* * *

24

SUNDAY, APRIL 21, 2002

CORNER OF C STREET AND NAVY ROW, MIDWEST, WYOMING

8:30 A.M.

CJ and I had finished our sweep of the area where we failed to find the highly conspicuous yellow Toyota Celica or its occupants, Adam and Misty. Finally, the cold weather seemed to lift, and the morning sun felt warm on our faces as we made our way back to my place. What I didn't expect or prepare for all of the people waiting in my driveway.

In the few hours that elapsed since being awoken by desperate parents and their supportive friends, the mob had grown to 20 people, including my good friend, Walter Merino. It was a vigil of sorts, complete with a folding table set up on my sidewalk that held a thermos or two of coffee and boxes of donuts presumably from the café. All of them were anxiously awaiting news from CJ and me. But unfortunately, I didn't have much to tell them.

We pushed past the crowd and entered my home to talk to Tracy, only to find her not there. So, instead, we went back outside and, spotting my friend, Walter, I shouted out, "Walt, have you seen my wife?"

Walt pointed in the direction of the Midwest Police office across the street and said, "she is in her office, Eddie."

"Thanks, buddy," I called out and led the way over the short distance to that portion of the Midwest Town Hall.

When we reached the office door, I opened it and allowed CJ to enter inside first. Then I followed. Even before clearing the entrance, I could hear Tracy speaking to Steve Otten. Until that point, I hadn't remembered placing him inside the large crowd.

"Steve," I said and nodded my head.

"Eddie," he replied curtly.

"Oh, hey, Eddie. I am glad you are back. As you can imagine, Steve is still very concerned about the welfare of his daughter," Tracy explained.

"It is true." Steve nodded. "But what I want to know is this: why can't you call in the entire Sheriff's Department on this?"

I cleared my throat, then I replied, "it is not that simple, Steve. First, we don't have a legal reason to assume she is missing. Secondly, it is against the policy in this county or any other in Wyoming to do a proper search within 24 hours of the person being unaccounted for or noted missing. I hope you understand?"

Steve gritted his teeth. "No, I don't understand."

My heart went out to him, though. Following a moment of silence, I dared to ask the question no protective father would ever appreciate hearing. "Do you think Misty and Adam simply skipped the Prom and drove to Casper or Buffalo to spend the night alone?"

As soon as I said it, I involuntarily took a step backward and bumped into CJ. It was as if I dropped a live grenade in the room. As fate would have it, Steve responded unexpectedly.

Steve shook his head. "No, I don't think they would do that. I mean, Adam is a good boy and was raised well. I also know that Misty would not pull a stunt like this no matter how in love she thinks that she is in."

CJ moved around from behind me. Then, he offered, "how about I make some phone calls to hotels in Buffalo and Casper to find out if anyone has seen them."

Steve shrugged. "I guess that wouldn't hurt, but why only Casper and Buffalo? If these kids ran off, then they could be anywhere like Rapid City or even Denver?"

I smiled in an attempt to bring the tone and tenor down in the room. Then I said, "you know that car of Adam's, don't you? Do you honestly think it could make it beyond Casper or Buffalo?"

Steve didn't think I was funny. Instead, he shook his head. "No, I had my doubts that boy's car could make it to my place and back to the dance, let alone drive to Casper."

Tracy tried to diffuse the tense situation further and expressed that she would do everything within her power to help. Then she asked Steve if they had a copy of Misty's most recent school photo that she asked for earlier? She further explained that her picture and the one of Adam supplied by his mother would become part of the all-points bulletin once the first 24 hours elapsed. Steve indicated that he did and reached into his Carhart jacket, retrieved the picture from his wallet, and handed it to Tracy.

"Thank you, Steve. I will personally keep you and Rhonda abreast of anything we find."

Steve mustered enough gratitude to tip his hat and then silently stepped past CJ and me and headed out of the door.

As soon as the trio heard the latch click back into place, CJ said, "well, I guess we have our work to do. I will start calling Casper hotels, so why don't you take the Buffalo area, Lieutenant?"

I nodded, "it sounds like a plan." Then I turned around to look at my wife, Tracy.

She must have read my mind because she offered, without prompt, "I will start contacting some of Misty's friends to see if I cannot locate the girl."

I nodded and placed my cowboy hat on my head. "That would be of great help, thank you."

An hour or so later, I sat alone in my office. I had already exhausted my telephone search of all the hotels in Buffalo. Quite frankly, I felt embarrassed by the whole exercise since nearly every conversation began with, *"we don't rent rooms to minors."* However, my temporary brooding evaporated when the phone on my desk rang unexpectedly. I reached out and pressed the speaker button to answer the call.

"Sheriff's Department, Lieutenant Crandall, how may I help you?"

"Hey, honey. It is me. I just got a tip that you will probably want to follow up on."

I reached for a pen and a scrap of paper and then replied, "okay, what do you have for me?"

Tracy continued, "well, I called Jessica Norman over in Gas Plant to find out if she knew Misty's whereabouts." Then she paused.

"So, does she or not?" I asked somewhat impatiently.

"No, she doesn't. But that is when the call got a little weird."

"Okay."

"Mrs. Norman got on the line after Jessica and asked me if I was calling regarding the strange pickup that is driving in circles around her block."

I sighed aloud and vented some frustration. "Darling, I hate to pull this on you but isn't Gas Plant your jurisdiction? I mean, I don't want to get dragged down by something Mrs. Norman thought she saw in her delicate state of mind."

Defensively, Tracy retorted, "yes, it is my jurisdiction, but I don't think this is something she made up. Now, according to her, the pickup was last seen headed toward Salt Creek on Gas Plant Road."

I started to say something, but she cut me off. "Eddie, Mrs. Norman described a late dark-colored model Ford F150. I think it is your phantom truck."

I dropped the pen from my hand, and it landed with an audible thud on my desk. I then reached down into the bottom drawer of the oak desk and pulled out the two files containing the facts of the Savolt case from 1984. I opened the manila folder and looked at the vehicle description contained inside it.

"Eddie, are you still there?" Tracy asked.

"Yes, I'm sorry. I was thinking."

"Well, stop doing that. I mean, I cannot see you think while we are on the phone," my wife scolded.

"Again, I am sorry. So, how long ago was this report?"

"Umm, about four minutes ago."

"Okay, I am leaving now. Is CJ still there?"

"No, he left about 15 minutes ago."

"Darn, I will have to take my dad's old pickup since I gave the department Blazer to CJ to use while his Silverado is in the shop."

"No problem, just keep your cellphone handy in case you need backup."

I ended the call with an abrupt "thanks" and pressed the speaker button again to hang up the call.

After I backed my pickup onto C Street, I turned west onto Peake Street, and then at the corner, I continued south along Fitzhugh. Having the full anticipation of meeting a 1978 dark green Ford, I was shocked to find the street empty.

I sped up, though I was careful to look down the alleys and streets until reaching Ellison Avenue, which I turned onto, and headed east. While above the football field, I pulled over momentarily and scanned the area south of Midwest. Just as I was about to pull away, I spotted the pickup as it emerged from the bank of the creek and re-entered the perimeter road in the direction of the school.

My heart began to race in anticipation of a day I had prayed would never come. Marvin Stiles's photo from the Savolt file burned into my psyche since I connected the man with the demise and disappearance of the teacher and my friend.

After jamming the accelerator pedal to the floor and spraying the metal railing with rocks and dirt, I made my way around the next corner by the post office. My intent was clear. I would intercept the pickup behind Teachers Row as it drove up the hill on the east end of town.

I sped down Lewis Street while my mind conjured up what Stiles looked like nearly twenty years later. When I drove by the school, I slowed down and turned behind Teachers Row and parked my truck across the road. Then I got out and removed my service .40 caliber S&W from its holster and used the hood as a sort of barricade.

Though it seemed like minutes, the target vehicle approached within a few seconds. When the driver saw me, he came to a stop.

I called out, "Turn off your engine and drop your keys out of your window."

The driver remained motionless behind the steering wheel. So, I repeated my demand. Again, no compliance. I raised my gun at that point and demanded one more time.

The driver rolled down his window and asked, "Is there something I can do for you, sir?"

As I looked closer, the man did not remotely resemble an older version of Marvin Stiles. Making matters worse, the woman in the passenger seat was in a full-blown panic as she screamed at the driver to turn off the vehicle. Finally, he abided.

Though still drawn, I kept my weapon pointed down at the ground in front of me while walking around my makeshift barricade. Finally, but ever so cautiously, I walked up to the driver's side window. Within minutes, the entire situation de-escalated, and, as it turned out, the driver was a Midwest High School graduate from 1962.

His name was Gary Anstey, a widower who was on vacation with his fiancée, Cheryl. He had left the Salt Creek Community after returning home from service in Vietnam. He had spent the rest of his life in a suburb of Dallas. He offered to me that they had already driven around the area earlier in the week. But, as they were heading for home in Texas after a few days in Yellowstone National Park, Gary wanted to show Cheryl his childhood home in Gas Plant.

I felt embarrassed and utterly demoralized. I did my best to apologize for the inconvenience and briefly described the reason for my roadblock. However, I assured Gary and his fiancée that they would have a great story to tell everyone when they returned home. Lastly, I offered, and they accepted, that I buy some refreshments over at the Junction store.

Only after Gary and Cheryl had departed the parking lot did I think to call my wife. It was then that I reached for my belt and pulled out my cellphone from its holster. As I flipped open the device, I paused and said to myself, *"what am I going to tell her?"*

* * *

25

My hopes that the crowd of concerned citizens had given up their vigil on my sidewalk dashed as soon as I turned onto Navy Row. If anything, the group doubled during my absence. Now, people grouped on both my sidewalk and over C Street and into the town park. Some of the crowd I attributed to people being ready to help. While others were out because it was the first nice day all spring to do so, while others, like one of my friends I spotted in the crowd, were there out of a higher purpose.

Naturally, the first person to greet me with a wave was my longtime friend, Walter Merino.

Over the years, I had come to know and respect Walter, and he was my Christian mentor for a long time. Once, he helped me work through the traumatic nightmares I had following one particular gruesome vehicle accident. To sum it up, Walt was my rock.

As I got climbed out of my pickup, Walt immediately asked, "so, do you have any leads on the kids?"

I shrugged and replied a curt, "no."

Walt nodded that he understood and then hooked both of his thumbs into the front pockets of his jeans. "I expected that, but, hey, we convinced Steve and Rhonda to go back home in case Misty suddenly appeared."

"That is good thinking, Walt, but is there anyone else out there with them?"

Walt removed his left hand from his pocket and pointed it in the general direction of the Otten place, west of Midwest. "Well, I know the Mondragons are over there." Then he shrugged, "maybe a few others that I don't know about."

I agreed that the Ottens waiting at home was a good thing. Still, I could not convince my friend that the vigil outside my house and now into the park was unnecessary. He reminded me once again that this sort of thing is what a true community does- it takes care of its own. Walt further explained that he was there to counsel those that needed it and pray for those that wanted it.

While I walked across the street to the police office, I felt like a failure for not doing more myself. However, it didn't take long for me to feel even worse when I retold the story involving the capture of the mysterious Ford pickup. My wife, Tracy, guffawed a laugh. However, CJ, who had returned to the office in my absence, seemed disapproving to me. It wasn't what the Deputy said. It was, somewhat, his silence that disturbed me most.

The only thing that CJ said was, "by the way, Sheriff Paulson wants you to call him."

I gave him a skeptical look and asked, "why does the Sheriff want to talk to me."

CJ shrugged. "I don't know. But I mistakenly let out that we were searching for the missing teenagers."

My eyes narrowed. "Really? How did that come about?"

It was now apparent why CJ seemed so outwardly aloof. It was because of his perceived failure. Then he explained further, "well, I inadvertently called dispatch to report my location when I ran over to Edgerton. Almost immediately, I got a call on my cellphone from the Sheriff."

"And?" I said as if waiting for the punchline of a joke.

"And I told him about Adam and Misty's disappearance and how we were helping area residents to find them."

I relaxed a little and felt a little empathy toward the Deputy. "It's okay, CJ. You were honest, and that is way more important to me than being deceptive."

"Thanks for understanding."

I nodded at CJ and then turned to Tracy and said, "I am going to go home and call Sheriff Paulson." I started to walk away, but I stopped and looked back at Tracy, who unceasingly rubbed her belly. Then I asked her, "shouldn't you go home and put your feet up?"

"Oh, I am fine. The baby is pretty active today, that is all. Besides, I feel useless in this situation if I am not doing anything to help out our friends. Besides, Naomi Wright is still missing, too, along with the school suburban that she drove. I have too many questions and not enough answers."

"I know what you mean. Anyway, I think you need to take a break, and soon."

Tracy feinted a salute to me with her right hand. "Yes, Sir! I'll get right on it." She then looked at each one of us and stated, "need I remind everyone that the odds of finding a missing person decrease as each day passes."

My wife's comment hung in the air like a cloud. Yet, each of us knew the implications of the statement.

Before I left, though, CJ told me he was heading home. Then he reminded me about his mandatory training for the next two days in Douglas and wouldn't be around the Salt Creek area until Wednesday.

I nodded and gave him a short wave.

A few minutes later, following my phone call with my boss, Sheriff Paulson, I felt even more useless. He told me my actions that day was, as he put it, "noble, but against all protocol." The Sheriff further reminded me that I couldn't go all "cowboy" on my own and run an independent investigation as a representative of the Sheriff's Department.

I acknowledged the criticism and admitted that from his point of view, it made sense. I mean, he was a solid administrator, and I respected the man.

I did, however, ask my boss to see things from my perspective within my home community. Unlike Casper, I asserted that anything out of the ordinary was a big deal to folks in this area.

But the Sheriff's response was an all too familiar myopic view of things. Although, I had observed that same attitude from anyone that lived in a city throughout the state. Then again, a city in Wyoming is any place large enough to have either a McDonald's or a Burger King and a stoplight.

Considering the Sheriff grew up and still lived in Casper, he had no way of empathizing with me or the residents of the Salt Creek community. I am sure it was unfathomable for him to conceive the idea of concerned parents at his doorstep when their teenagers failed to show up after the Prom in the middle of the night. Plus, I seriously doubt a vigil would form on his sidewalk either.

In the end, my plea fell on deaf ears. The Sheriff again reminded me that I couldn't investigate anything further until the teenagers became missing status described by the law. Lastly, Sheriff Paulson reminded me that my duties were to train new deputies, which by and large were in Casper.

Defeated, I hung up the phone and briefly stared out my office window while I tried to figure a way to help the situation.

Later that afternoon, Bill Crooks was locking the school's east entrance after stopping by his classroom to retrieve some homework assignments that he left behind on the previous Friday. As he turned to walk to his Willys Jeep pickup, Reed, the head custodian at the school, stepped out of his small apartment on the far end of the maintenance building.

Reed waved his hand. "Hold on, Bill," he called out.

Crooks stopped in his tracks and waited for Reed to come closer. "Hey, Reed. What's up?"

Reed extended out his other hand, which held a small journal of some type and motioned for Crooks to take it from him. Naturally, Crooks grabbed the notebook and began to open it.

"What is this?" Crooks inquired.

Reed shrugged his shoulders. "I don't know, really, but it has a bunch of mumbo jumbo that I cannot decipher. But it is alarming enough that I wanted your take on it."

Crooks nodded and scanned a few pages. Then he spotted something that indeed alarmed him because his demeanor changed entirely.

"Where did you get this, Reed?"

Reed looked down toward his feet and thought about how to respond. "Well, I found it."

"Where? And more importantly, how did you find it?"

Again, Reed wouldn't make eye contact with the giant of a man standing before him. Finally, after a moment, he pleaded, "as you know, Bill, I am the eyes and ears of this school. You know how it is, everybody pretty much ignores me, but like I already said, I see everything."

Crooks nodded. "Okay, but what about this journal?"

Reed hemmed and hawed. Finally, he said, "I found that journal on the floor last Friday. But it is not what you think. The student also left the locker door open."

"I see," Crook said. "So, why are you giving it to me instead of the Principal?"

This time, Reed stated directly into Crooks' eyes. "Considering what is on the pages, I think this needs the attention above the capabilities of a school administrator."

Crooks nodded again and conceded, "good point." Then he thumbed through a few more pages and again found something that alerted him. Crooks looked up at Reed again and implored, "I would keep this between us. I suggest for the time being that you forget seeing me today and even knowing about this journal. Got it?"

"I understand," and Reed abruptly turned and headed back toward the door of his apartment.

Meanwhile, Crooks turned around and unlocked the door, and then locked it behind him. Within seconds, he was in the school library and proceeded to turn on the computer paired with the scanner.

Thirty minutes later, Crooks exited the school parking lot and headed toward the football field along the perimeter road that would eventually take him to Gas Plant Road. Crooks glanced over to the journal and picked it up off of the passenger seat as he drove. He placed the book on the steering wheel and opened it up. Once again, the words, *Early Dawn*, jumped off the page.

Crooks looked over at the football field and track as he thought about the implications of his suppositions. He knew he needed help and started to compile a list in his head as to who to solicit.

He then turned left onto Gas Plant Road and went over the bridge spanning Salt Creek. When he reached the other side, Crooks placed the notebook back on top of the passenger seat for the remainder of the short ride home.

Lois Crooks heard her husband coming long before he pulled up in front of their home. The old Willys pickup truck her husband drove was infamously loud. Perhaps it was due to a new hole sprouting every week through the rusted original exhaust system. Then as each hole opened, her husband fixed it with a patch instead of spending money on a complete system replacement. She often thought it funny when Bill came home late from hunting, and he tried his best to keep quiet. It never occurred to Bill that she heard him coming from a half-mile away.

Bill Crooks parked his pickup and gathered the paperwork and the newly formatted compact disk containing a scanned copy of the journal Reed provided. He made his way into the front living room, where Lois greeted him.

"Well, hi. I thought you were just going to pick up your homework folder? So what is all of that other stuff you are carrying?"

Crooks looked down to the things he clutched against his chest and then turned back toward Lois. "I hate to say this, but it is time to make sausage."

Lois understood what her husband meant and stepped back and watched him trek through the house and out the back door, across the back yard, and into the garage.

The term *Sausage* was a code word they used when Crooks was working on something he could not disclose to her. The habit started early on in their marriage while Bill was a special operator in the military. She suddenly remembered hearing him say, "sausage" once, and Bill disappeared for four months without any contact.

Crooks managed to open the garage door and quickly stepped inside. He reached out with his right hand and turned on the light switch that instantly illuminated the space. On one side was a typical workbench and toolbox. In contrast, the other side sported twin stainless steel tables that Crooks used for butchering game animals every fall. So, naturally, a large chest freezer half full of game meat hummed in the back corner. Lastly, Crooks had also equipped the space with a TV to watch the Denver Broncos games while working on projects every Sunday afternoon during football season.

He set down the journal, the disk, and the paper copy on the other workbench that filled the short wall. Next, Crooks lifted a canvass cover to expose his state-of-the-art computer and digital modem, giving him incredible online processing speed. Then following a few button presses, the computer came to life. Lastly, he walked over to the old Hamm's Beer clock sign that hung on the wall to the left of the workstation. Behind the bear was a cutout in the sheetrock where a satellite phone sat inside its charger.

Now he sat down on a swivel top chair and stared down at the keys on the phone. Crooks selected the second phone number in the storage file and waited patiently for the connection to go through. Then, after two rings, a voice answered, "hello?"

"Brit, it is Browning; I need a recipe," Crooks said.

"Oh, you do? Okay, I will call you back in a minute."

Crooks ended the call and set the phone down on the desktop until his friend had the time and opportunity to respond. In the meantime, he inserted the compact disk into the slot. He then moved his mouse over the icon for his disk drive, opened it, and selected the pdf document within the folder he created just an hour before while still at the school. Then, impatiently, Crooks looked at the clock in the beer sign again and began to wonder whether or not his buddy Brit would get back to him.

Only Bill Crooks knew the real identity of the man he called Brit. However, his buddy was a long-time confidant whom Crooks served within a special operations unit. Now, his friend served as a civilian advisor for at least two clandestine federal organizations.

Brit's nickname for Crooks, Browning, stemmed from Bill's affinity for Browning rifles, especially his lever-action 1970 BLR chambered in .308.

Finally, the satellite phone vibrated on the desk, which caught Crooks' attention. He snatched it up and pressed the talk button with his hefty sausage-like index finger.

"Browning," Crooks dryly answered.

"Hey, brother, are you good are your end? Brit asked.

Crooks pulled the phone away from his ear and looked at the display. "Ya, I am encrypted."

"Good. So what can I do for up there in God's country?"

Crooks took a deep breath, and when he exhaled, he said, "I would like you to look into something further."

Brit grunted something unintelligible, then asked, "what exactly?"

"Early Dawn."

The phone suddenly went silent on the other end.

"Brit? Are you still with me?"

Finally, Brit answered, "yep, I am still here. But I am wondering why you are asking me about that group? Are you implying you've detected something in Wyoming of all places?"

Crooks nodded his head even though his friend had no way of seeing him do so. "Yes, that is exactly what I am saying. I found something I want to share with you over the secure network."

"What are you sending me?"

"It is a scanned copy of a journal plus a few loose pieces of paper I found as well. When you receive it, I want you to look over it and decide what to do with it."

Brit again grunted something and then asked, "if you suspect something, why not go to the local authorities? Or you could run it yourself being the BLM law enforcement in that area?"

Crooks paused for a second and replied, "I thought of that, and though I trust a few members of the Sheriff's department, I doubt the higher-ups will take this as seriously as you and me?"

"Good point." Then Brit paused for a few seconds. "You have my secure email address still, correct?"

"I do."

"Fine, then send it over soon so I can start working things tonight." But before Crooks could reply, Brit asked, "so, what kind of population surrounds the target?"

"Practically zero since it is in one of the least populated parts of the entire state. I will also include the coordinates as well."

"Great. But I can't promise you anything, and you will not receive word back from me unless it becomes necessary. Do you copy?"

"Copy. I will standby and watch from the cheap seats."

"Good. Whatever you do, don't engage by yourself."

The phone call dropped precipitously with Brit's last words, and Crooks powered down and stored his phone again. Then he uploaded the files and sent them to Brit.

* * *

26

Adam awoke to unfamiliar sounds echoing along the concrete walls surrounding him. He did not know when he fell asleep. His last memory was leaving the water tank and walking blindfolded across an open expanse and inside another building. Adam knew he was briefly outside because the wind blew across his wet clothing, which caused him to chill.

Then, inside the other building, he heard an audible *click,* and the door opened. But he also listened to the hum of an electric motor that accompanied the sense of slowly moving downward simultaneously. Next, Adam's escort led him to the right and placed him into the small room where he currently sat.

Then he sat up. Astonishingly, both the blindfold was gone, and his hands were free. So, he slowly stood up and felt his way around the bunker since it was too dark to see. He still wore the tuxedo shirt, trousers, and shoes, all of which had dried. But he did not know what happened to the jacket and bowtie.

Using his hand as a guide, Adam stepped forward and found the door. He quickly identified it as metal, then traced the walls to the left, and soon found where he began.

Suddenly, Adam heard what he thought was a key inserting into the lock, and then the door creaked open. Before he could make out who stood in the frame, his eyes burned from an intensely bright light shown on his face.

The familiar mechanized voice cut the silence in the cell. "How are you doing, Adam? Is your headache gone?"

Adam raised both of his hands in front of his face to shield his eyes from the light beam. Then, he replied, "yes, it is gone, but how do you know my name?"

"That is not your concern," the voice said.

"Who are you?" the boy asked.

"You can call me Khala."

"Why am I here?" Adam asked calmly.

"That is a good question, but I am not ready to tell you the answer."

Adam looked down, which he now felt something around his neck for the first time. He asked, "what is this thing?"

"Oh, that. It is your collar."

"Why am I wearing it?"

"I guess you could call it a control device since it can emit an electric shock into your neck and completely immobilize you. Do you want to get a feel of what it is like?"

"No, no, thank you."

"That's a good boy. Now, let me explain some rules. First, if you get caught messing with the collar, you go back into the tank at feeding time. Second, if you feel like you want to run away, I'll shock you and throw you into the tank as well. Do you understand?"

"Yes."

"Good. One of my associates will come to get you in just a little bit, and I ask you to follow him and do whatever he asks. Do you think you can do that?"

Again, Adam replied calmly, "yes."

He waited patiently for a reply but received none. Instead, the light beam turned off, and the door closed forcibly. Adam found the wall again with his right hand and braced himself as he sat down. Oddly, though, instead of feeling immense remorse for his situation, he found himself collected.

The boy carefully examined the collar and ran his fingers over the hardware securing it around his neck. He could tell it couldn't come off quickly, nor could he undo the clasp without a unique tool. The thick leather strap, he found, could not be stretched or torn either.

In the quiet, Adam thought of his favorite book, *The Worst-Case Scenario Survival Handbook.* Though once a curiosity, the guide provided him some practical things to keep in mind regardless of the situation. He also made a mental note of what his captor said, like the name Khala, which he couldn't determine whether it referred to a male or a female due to the altered voice. But Khala did say *he*, which told him that he faced at least two people, one of which was male. Perhaps he could gain some foresight into how many others made up the group of captors shortly.

Above all, Adam inherently knew that he had to persist long enough to find an opportunity to escape in his current predicament.

Concurrently, Misty found herself in a similar situation. Unlike Adam, she was unrestrained by a collar but was now all alone. However, moments before, the other person sharing her cell was forcibly removed. Although Misty said her name aloud, the door swung open before the stranger could reply. But from the wails emitted, the other person was a female.

Only then were her restraints taken away from her arms. Then, while still blindfolded, the person with the strange voice asked her to remove her prom dress and don another, much simpler loose-fitting smock. Lastly, the blindfold lifted off her eyes, though Misty struggled to see anything due to an intense beam of light flooding her face.

The concrete room still smelled afoul of urine, which kept Misty from moving around too much for fear of stepping into an unsuspected puddle. Instead, she slowly and carefully sat down on the floor.

Though Misty's memory returned in pieces, the reason for her detainment continued to escape her. She remembered leaving the house with Adam, and then it was a blinding light. Even that didn't make sense because she could not recall anything else for proper context.

Now, the silence, the waiting, and the unknown seemed daunting to her.

* * *

27

MONDAY, APRIL 22, 2002

SHERIFF'S DEPARTMENT HEADQUARTERS

CASPER, WYOMING

8:00 A.M.

I had returned to my desk after refilling my coffee. I set the mug on my desk and began sifting through a stack of training documents for all the newly hired deputies. Among the files was Cory Jackson's. I sorted him out first, considering CJ only needed my endorsement on a few items to complete his training log. Cory possessed a lot of experience and only needed departmental procedures and policies training, unlike the other new hires.

After moving CJ's folder to the file cabinet next to my desk, I heard a voice shout out behind me. "Lieutenant Crandall! Come to my office now!"

I immediately identified the voice belonging to Sheriff Paulson, and I stopped what I was doing and walked toward his office.

"You wanted to see me, Sheriff?" I asked.

"Yes. Close the door and sit down," Paulson commanded.

It is hard to describe the feeling one gets when abruptly summoned to visit the boss' office. Rarely was such a summons a good thing in my experience. So, I immediately made a quick mental inventory about what I possibly did wrong. *Did I fail to sign off a training record? No. Did I not train something incorrectly? Possibly.* I said silently in my mind.

The Sheriff sat directly across his desk from me with his arms folded. He was a physical specimen who worked out in the gym daily. By his bulging biceps that strained his uniform shirt, I could tell that this discussion would become a serious one. I anxiously awaited for the Sheriff to reveal the importance of this impromptu meeting.

Sheriff Paulson looked sternly at me and then stated, "a few minutes ago, I got off the phone with the Justice Department."

I interrupted, "what does the Wyoming Department of Criminal Investigation want with me?"

Paulson shook his head, "no, not the DCI, the Justice Department in Washington D.C."

I started to proclaim that I had no idea what that involved when the Sheriff lifted his hand, which intuitively meant I needed to hush.

"Someone has contacted the feds about a few of the county's residents in connection with those missing teenagers in Midwest." The Sheriff looked down at his notes, "what were their names? Oh, here they are, Misty Otten and Adam Weiss."

I waited for my boss to inquire further.

"Specifically, the inquiry involves Liam Gagnon and his son Lucas. Additionally, the agent I spoke to mentioned Robbie Lepsis' name as well. What do you know about that?"

My cheeks suddenly felt warm, which I knew also indicated that my face blushed red as well. "I don't know anything, Sir."

The Sheriff looked toward something to his immediate right and then turned his eyes back to meet mine. "Are you are telling me that you didn't inquire with the feds whether formally or informally?"

I shrugged and raised both hands. "Honestly, Sir, I haven't done anything of the kind."

"But you suspect Lucas Gagnon and Robbie Lepsis are somehow involved, don't you?"

I couldn't lie. "Yes, I have my suspicions ever since Adam Weiss's locker exploded, but I don't have hard evidence to tie both of the boys to the incident. But, considering the extreme badgering the boys have inflicted upon Adam over the last few months, I deduce they are somehow involved."

Sheriff Paulson pushed back from his desk and stood up. Next, he walked over to the large window and peered through it. Then he turned around.

"Here is the deal. Neither you nor any other law enforcement officer under my charge will investigate anything further concerning the Gagnon boy or his buddy, Robbie."

Again, I started to say something when my boss abruptly cut me off. "I mean it. I don't want to hear about even a parking ticket with these two. Got it?"

"I understand," I replied and allowed a few seconds of silence to envelop us. Then I asked, "what is going on here, Sir?"

The Sheriff shrugged. "I don't understand."

"Let me rephrase my question. Why would Washington call you to warn the department off investigating or even interviewing a county resident in Wyoming of all places? Doesn't that sound a little weird to you?"

The Sheriff nodded. "Yes, it is, as you say, 'weird,' but the feds have their reasons. Again, leave your suspicions alone, and that goes for Deputy Jackson as well."

I nodded, and the Sheriff ended the discussion by waving his hand toward the door to indicate the conversation was over. I stood up from the chair and quietly exited the office.

When I sat down again at my desk, I did my best to distract myself by completing the busy work of reviewing and signing off training records. Yet, try as I might, I could not keep my thoughts from wondering what was going on. Yet for every question I thought of was met with an equal amount of uncertainty.

My cellphone vibrated on my desk, which snapped me out of my musing. I lifted the device and flipped it open.

"Hello, Lieutenant Crandall."

"Hi, honey, it's me," Tracy replied.

"Hi," I curtly replied.

"What's wrong?"

I signed audibly. "Why do you think something is wrong?"

Tracy guffawed on the other end of the call. "Eddie, I know you. I am your wife, remember? So I always know when something is amiss with you."

"Okay, so you know me."

"Do you want to talk about it?"

I paused and stood up and looked over my cubical around the rest of the room. There were other deputies, as I could hear them talking in the background. Then I sat down again.

"I can't talk right now," I replied, hoping that Tracy understood my unspoken meaning.

She did, though. "Well, why don't you go someplace where you can talk about it and call me back?" She suggested.

I sighed again and then acquiesced, "Fine. I will call you back soon."

Five minutes later, I called Tracy from inside of my pickup. As I listened to the first ring, I made a mental list of what I wanted to say.

"That didn't take you long," Tracy blurted out without the formality of saying *hello*. "So, husband, what is bothering you?"

I quickly informed her of my meeting with the Sheriff and his impetuous warning of staying away from Lucas Gagnon and Robbie Lepsis. Tracy offered the same misgivings and doubts that I did, which didn't help. Then she asked a peculiar question.

"Who do we know would potentially have some pull inside the confines of the federal government?"

I paused to think for a few seconds, but Tracy interrupted my thoughts.

"Come on, Eddie, think. It was Bill Crooks. He is the only one I know that has any connections in Washington."

I shook my head. "Why would he do that?"

"I don't know, honey. I have long ago stopped worrying about why Bill does the things he does, but I do know his heart is always in the right place and is always on the right side of justice."

We both sat silently for a moment to allow our thoughts to continue. Then, finally, Tracy broke the pause by asking me, "so, what are you going to do?"

I shrugged as if she could see me. "I don't know if there is anything I can do?"

"I know," Tracy said empathetically. Then she offered, "oh, before I forget, I emailed you photos of Misty and Adam. Maybe you could persuade the Sheriff to distribute the pictures to the other deputies?"

"I dunno, maybe. It is worth a try, I guess."

I then heard Tracy moan through the speaker. "Are you alright?" I asked.

Again, I heard a slight grunt. Then my wife answered, "I'm fine. It is hard to stand up with a baby pushing on my insides."

Then I heard her gasp. Panicked, I inquired, "are you sure that you are alright?"

The phone went strangely silent as if the call had dropped. Again, I implored, "darling, are you okay?"

Finally, Tracy answered, "yes, I am fine."

"I heard you gasp," I started to say when she interrupted me.

"I was looking at the photos of the other missing girls, you know, the case that CJ is involved in?"

"Yes, the ones thumbtacked on the map next to his desk?"

"Yes. But here is my thought: all of those girls have a similar build plus athletic and good students. What just hit me is something that CJ pointed out right away."

"What is that?"

"All the girls have the same almond-shaped brown eyes. Doesn't that sound eerily like someone we know?"

"Misty!" I blurted out. Then I asked, "but how would that involve Adam?"

"I'm not sure. Maybe Adam was in the wrong place at the wrong time," Tracy suggested. Then after a few seconds, "perhaps Misty was targeted along with the other girls?"

I grunted. Then I added, "maybe, but again, I am not supposed to work on that case, remember?"

"I know, honey, I am thinking out loud." Then she changed the subject, "so, when should I expect you home today?"

"Supper time, same as usual."

"Okay, see you then."

* * *

28

I ran out of things to work on by late afternoon since all of the trainees went out on assignment alongside fully trained deputies. However, the rare lull provided me the excuse to follow up on an intimation I had earlier in the day. I logged out of my department page on the computer and opened my private email account. There I found the message from Tracy. With a few clicks of my computer mouse, I opened the first of two pictures attached to her note. It was the current school photo of Misty Otten.

Then I brought up the second picture of Misty, though it depicted her in a volleyball game. Again, I recognized the setting as the Casper Events Center, which hosted the East Regional Volleyball Tournament the previous fall. Yet, before I closed out the second photo, something else caught my eye. Lucas Gagnon sat in the background sitting alongside substitute volleyball players. Additionally, just a row behind Lucas sat Robbie Lepsis. It piqued my interest, and I even said aloud, "what are those clowns doing there?"

I closed my email account, and another idea came to mind that stemmed from an earlier training session that day. I had discussed how the department used closed-circuit camera capabilities within Casper. I emphasized to the trainees to always look around any crime scene for a camera. Be it a private security camera or even a live feed from a host of Wyoming Department of Transportation assets distributed across the state highways and the two interstates.

While ordinary civilians had access to the live feeds of the roadways, law enforcement also had access to the file storage of up to 72 hours of video. Thus, I pulled up the two Smokey Gap cameras at the north exit off I-25 to Midwest that day for my training session.

In the quiet of my cubical, I began scrolling through the video files of the Smokey Gap intersection. I singled out three in particular that covered 7:00 through 9:00 p.m. the Saturday before. Luckily, each video stream came with both fast forward and rewound abilities that made my search easier. Otherwise, watching a real-time video stream of an interstate exit in that part of Wyoming would equate to watching paint dry.

My supposition was simple: I should see Adam drive under the interstate overpass toward Misty's home to the west and out of view of the camera. As the tape neared the timestamp of when Adam picked up Misty that night, my heart began to race. Then, from the north-facing camera of the exit, I saw Adam's conspicuous yellow Toyota pass under the streetlight where the exit ramp met Highway 387. I then switched to the south-facing camera view and sped up the file to the same time mark, and I saw Adam pass by the exit ramp and proceed out of sight on Smokey Gap Road.

I carefully fast-forwarded the south camera file. Finally, at 36 minutes and 32 seconds later, I spotted Adam's car heading west through the intersection. Then the picture went blank. My heart sank, and at first, I thought I had done something wrong. But, instead, I fast-forwarded another 30 minutes' worth of video, and it was still blank.

I quickly brought up the view to the north and scrolled to when Adam should have passed by toward town. I watched. Then I watched longer for a total of 10 minutes of camera time. I began to think the video file had frozen. Still, I saw a semi-tractor trailer head northbound across the overpass. So I forwarded another 10 minutes.

I sat back and considered what I had witnessed. Adam had crossed over the cattleguard and onto the pavement but did not come out on the other side heading toward town. I then reversed the tape and watched again. I saw the headlights of Adam's car before coming into view, and then the screen went blank. I switched to the other camera. I could make out the pavement beginning to glow from a car's headlights, but then the area darkened in a flicker. As I scrutinized the tape further, a sudden intense beam of light radiated from under the bypass. Then it panned around to the other direction as if the source of the light spun a full 180 degrees.

I sat at my desk while briefly dumbfounded by the video files. It didn't make sense. But then I wondered if there were any other vehicles on either of the exit ramps before Adam headed to the Otten house and, in turn, returning with Misty to town. I carefully rewound the north-facing camera for another 40 minutes. I counted three vehicles exiting I-25, one sedan, and two pickup trucks. However, they all turned to the east toward Midwest. I also spotted a flatbed pickup drive from Midwest and under the interstate and onto Smokey Gap Road. But, later then, there was a non-descript white-panel van that appeared from under the overpass on the west and turned onto the northbound entrance ramp. I rewound the tape and watched a second time but could not identify who drove the van.

On a hunch, I switched once again to the north-facing view. This time, I spotted the white van approaching the overpass and disappearing underneath it.

It was early evening as I approached my usual exit onto Highway 259 that took me home to Midwest. I was already late for supper. Tracy called my desk phone and reminded me that it was time to go home thirty-five minutes before. Naturally, I apologized for letting time get away from me, and I briefly told her about my findings. She knew that I couldn't let Adam and Misty's disappearance alone and told me as much.

At the last second, I turned off my turn signal. I gently veered my pickup back into the northbound lane. I pulled out my cellphone and called home to inform Tracy of my sudden change of plan.

"Where are you?" Tracy asked.

I stammered a reply and caught myself and answered again. "I'm heading north on I-25, and I am going to check something out at Smokey Gap intersection."

Tracy sighed. "Do you have to do it now? I mean, can't it wait for to-morrow?"

She had a good point that I couldn't argue. "Yes, it can wait, but I think I have a lead on Adam and Misty's disappearance."

Tracy's silence on the other end of the call intimated to me that she was interested. So, I informed her about my observations on the two WYODOT cameras. Then I remembered to ask Tracy a question that bugged me.

"By the way, I saw the picture of Misty taken at the Regional Tour-nament. But, why was Lucas Gagnon sitting on the bench with the rest of the players."

I heard Tracy take a deep breath, then she replied, "he was the team manager last year." But as soon as she said those words, her mind must have synched with mine. "Are you thinking that Lucas has something to do with the other missing girls?"

"Yep. That is what I am thinking."

She paused for a second, then said, "okay, check out what you have to, but don't be too much longer. It will get dark within the hour."

"I won't be very long. I promise."

Then as I started to close up my phone, I heard something come out of the speaker. So I lifted the phone back to my ear and asked, "did you say something, darling?"

"I did. I tried to tell you that you need to call Bill Crooks tonight and find out if he pushed some buttons in Washington. I would also remind our dear friend to give you a heads up before he does something like that again."

"Noted. Is there anything else that you wanted to say?"

Tracy laughed. "Other than I am pregnant, uncomfortable, and can't wait for you to come home? No, only that I love you."

"Love you too. I will see you soon."

I hung up the phone and looked to the north and could see the exit a little over a mile ahead of me. After I passed over the overpass, I hit my left turn signal, slowed down, and crossed over the median toward the exit ramp on the other side.

It didn't take me long to discern what was wrong with the camera upon parking my pickup. I stepped out of my truck and zipped up my uniform jacket. Even though it was springtime, the late afternoon wind chilled me to the bone. I stuffed my hands inside my pockets and then looked above my head. I spied the device smashed and dislodged from its mounting bracket. The camera case hung listlessly by a stretched electrical cord. Next, I scrambled up into the pickup bed for a closer look. It was destroyed by a bird perhaps, but more likely an intentional act by a man.

Then another idea came to mind. Looking back on it, it was a foolish idea, but it marked one of those incidents where law enforcement intuition makes it hard to ignore.

At the end of the exit ramp, I turned west, crossed over the cattle guard, and passed by the buckshot blasted road sign for County Road 115. Over the crest of the hill, I spotted the turn-off for the Otten place. From the looks of things, it seemed they had company visiting based on the different vehicles parked in the yard.

Ahead of me, the road opened up into a wide-open range of pasture land absent without another home in sight for miles to come. I had traveled this route many times over my years in the Salt Creek community, and every time, including this one, the vast expanse left me in awe. Somewhere, miles ahead sat the Scarlet Ranch, which was my destination. The way I figured it, perhaps Ben Combs, the ranch owner, or his foreman, Chuck, saw something last Saturday night. It wasn't a whim necessarily since Chuck's daughter was in all probability at the Prom that night so that someone might have driven her.

About fifteen minutes later, my eye caught something that didn't appear natural. I realize that human sight is by a large proportion comprised of detecting patterns versus specific identification. I slowed down to a stop and stepped out of my pickup. On the southeast side of the road sat a brilliant white-colored flower in a clump of sagebrush about 10 yards on the other side of the ditch. I followed a muddy two-track pasture road that seemed to follow a powerline to the south. The trail was also complete with recent tire impressions from two distinctly different sets of tires.

I bent over, lifted the wilted flower off the sagebrush, and raised it closer to my face. On further examination, it was more. It was a wrist corsage.

Flummoxed as to where the adornment came from, I looked around. I briefly considered that it belonged to Stephanie Merrick. Though, as soon as the thought appeared, I deemed it not likely. I looked around again, and my eyes settled on the pasture road. Then I traced it as it meandered toward the direction of two prominent hills in the near distance. My heart sank with the realization that the tire tracks pointed toward the Gagnon compound and the power line must go there as well.

After retracing my steps back to my pickup, I made up my mind to see where the trail led me. But before I climbed inside, I went to each front tire and manually locked each hub into the 4X4 position. Lastly, I picked up my cellphone and checked to see if I had any signal. Just as I thought, there wasn't one, but I pushed onward anyway.

Fifteen minutes later, the two-track led me across the open grassland and into the once hidden creek drainage lined by stalwart Cottonwood trees. Luckily, the creek crossing was easy since whoever created the trail had also gone the lengths of dumping river rock across the void so a pickup truck like mine could ford. On the other side, the track joined another but improved and maintained road, which I assumed belonged to the BLM.

The setting sun cast long shadows on the road and the sagebrush around me. I then negotiated around a large puddle in the middle of the road and followed the path easterly as it weaved through a small clutch of trees.

A fence line appeared out of nowhere, along with a huge sign made out of a sheet of plywood. I slowed to a stop and read the sign carefully. The words were explicit that trespassers were not welcome. However, instead of turning around as the sign warned, I saw an open gate. I reasoned that my going onto the property was lawful because 1) I was law enforcement, 2) I wanted to collect information, and 3) an open gate is an invitation.

The ranch yard opened up at the edge of the Cottonwood grove, and I saw four buildings in all. One structure was the house, then a barn, another was a sizeable metal-sided shop, and the last one looked like a greenhouse. I also spotted a small reservoir in the creek basin behind the complex. But, by then, the sun faded fast to the west, and the area darkened by the second.

I saw that light illuminated from the open side door to the shop, so I decided to park adjacent to a white panel van with oversized tires. As I stepped out of my pickup, I noted the vehicle possessed a unique 4X4 front axle.

I closed my truck door and pushed gently to latch it as I didn't want to attract too much attention. Then I turned and looked around. A lone overhead yard light turned on and cast pale blue light to the gravel area below. The absence of dogs was most surprising since Wyoming had an unwritten code for any respectable rancher was to own four canines.

I stepped through the open door and took inventory of my surroundings. The floor was concrete which held two Dodge pickups, a Ford Explorer, a small Kubota yard tractor, and a more significant capacity Case 930 tractor. But there, in the back of the shop, existed a small two-sided metal stall. My nostrils suddenly filled with the smell of fresh paint, and my ears heard the hiss of a gun operating in long steady bursts.

I walked over to the stall and rounded the corner. As my senses told me, two men were painting a large passenger vehicle that I assumed was a Ford Excursion. But I couldn't be sure since paper and tape covered anything to help me identify the make and model.

"Hello!" I shouted over the sound of the spray gun and the hidden air compressor thumping away out of view.

The man closest to me snapped his head around and looked at me. Then, he took his finger off of the spray gun trigger and slowly stood up. When fully upright, the man's head was above the roof of the vehicle in the stall.

The man turned and called out, "Cal! Shut that thing down." Then, the compressor shut off a moment later, and the big man stepped toward me while slowly lifting his respirator mask.

"What do you want?" demanded the man.

Undeterred, I stated, "I am sorry to bother you guys and take you away from important work, but I would like to ask some questions."

The big man stopped within an arm's length from me and pierced my skull with a set of deep-seated eyes. Reflexively I stepped backward to create more space.

"Can't you read? You must have seen our sign that says stay out?"

The man named Cal laughed as he approached me from my left side. "Either he can't read, or he is too stupid to understand. So, which is it, Deputy."

I cast my eyes at Cal and then back to the big man. "I am Lieutenant Eddie Crandall. I am here to ask if either of you observed anything unusual last Saturday night at the interstate overpass just east of here?"

The big man's right eye twitched, not much, but enough that told me in my experience that I hit directly on target. Meanwhile, Cal gave the big man a quick yet nervous look.

The big man took a giant step toward me. Again, I stepped back.

"I take that as a no, then?" I said.

"No, that is not it at all. You are trespassing, and now you must leave. Maybe next time, you had better come here with a warrant if you want us to answer any of your questions."

Cal snickered through his smile of crooked teeth, "ya, get a warrant."

Knowing full well my predicament, leaving was a good decision. If I pushed these men any further, it could become volatile. I stepped to my right, and my foot struck against a pile of metal. My clumsiness sent a license plate skidding across the floor in front of me. When I picked it up, I flipped it over to the painted side. Instead of the familiar blue and white Wyoming plate of the time, it was yellow with the word *SCHOOL* and the number *3030* stamped into it.

My mind immediately recalled the plate belonging to the school Suburban that Naomi Wright reportedly drove., which also intimated the men busied themselves to alter the vehicle. I half-turned and tossed the plate onto the scrap pile as if nothing happened. Then I took a few steps toward the open door.

I could hear the sounds of rushing feet behind me when I exited the shop, so I lunged for my pickup and swung open the door. I unbuckled my weapon to raise it from behind my makeshift barricade. I then heard the pop of gravel behind me, forcing me to turn my head slightly. The big man reached around the door in that split second and grabbed the trapezius muscle above my left collar bone. The man's grip was immense, and pain shot through my torso. I felt so much pain that I forgot all about lifting my gun in defense. But as suddenly the man's grasp let go.

I felt another jolt, and my body went stiff. The fillings in my teeth arched from top to bottom in my mouth, and then I blacked out.

* * *

29

My mind couldn't recall everything that transpired after feeling the sensation of my body going stiff until the rush of tingles as my body reset itself. My head felt heavy, as did my arms and legs. Finally, I opened my eyes and found myself sitting inside the familiar surroundings of my pickup truck.

Oddly, it felt as though I sat on a decline with the front axle dipped lower than the rear one. I dropped my hands to my waist and found both my weapon and belt were missing. However, I still wore my uniform that included my jacket.

Then I sat up and looked all around. In front of me and out each of the side windows was blackness. It took some effort, but I managed to crane my neck around to locate the source of faint light behind me.

The back window looked odd to me since the bottom half of the window was so dark that I couldn't see anything beyond the plate of glass. However, I could see through the top half, and I could tell it was nighttime, although it seemed someone shined a flashlight onto the truck.

I started to shiver for whatever reason, and then I realized that my feet and legs up to my knees were underwater. Whether it was the epinephrine flowing through my body or some innate kind of self-preservation that set in, but I suddenly felt energized.

From the hidden storage files of my brain, I recalled lessons I taught to my deputies. Step 1- Assess the situation. Step 2- Formulate a plan. Step 3- Execute it with full anticipation of adjusting to ever-changing dynamics. "Okay," I said aloud and determined that I was in an unfamiliar place with an unknown number of aggressors, and I was about to drown. So my course was simple: get out of the truck, swim to shore undetected, find a directional bearing and head for help.

I grasped the door handle with my left hand and gently pushed my shoulder against it. Surprisingly, the door moved. I then had the awareness to reach through the water and under my seat with my right hand. I found and retrieved my Kel-Tec P-11 9 mm pistol that I kept hidden away for self-protection. While doing so, I must have dislodged my blaze orange-colored hunting fanny pack as it somehow bobbed to the surface of the water. Knowing I had some emergency supplies inside the bag, I snatched it up and buckled it around my waist.

The water level rose in a whoosh as my shoulder pushed the door open and filled the interior. Stabs of pain pierced every part of my body from the ice-cold water. Ignoring the tremendous shock of cold, I swam beneath the surface and around the front of my truck. After a dozen or so of hard strokes, I let my feet down and was relieved that they hit the soft, muddy bottom of the pond. I set my feet and slowly raised my head, and took in huge gulps of air. It also gave me a chance to look around. I saw the big man in the headlights of one of the ranch trucks I spotted earlier in the shop. The weasel-looking man named Cal was there as well.

I started to ease out of the water and did my level best not to make any noise. Then I looked beyond the alkali-crusted shoreline in front of me and saw the yard light glowing softly. Not only did the lamp inform that I hadn't left the Gagnon property. But, more importantly, it gave me a sense of where I needed to go, which was east to my left-hand side. About fifty yards away, I heard the big man shout angrily at Cal.

"You idiot! You must have rolled that pickup into the back of that boy's car. The truck isn't sinking anymore."

Cal pleaded, "it's not my fault, Burris. Dodd and I put it where you told me.

I made a quick mental note of the new name. Then I watched Burris sweep his flashlight onto the back window of my truck, still barely visible above the waterline. So, I decided I needed to get out of the water that instant.

With both feet on dry land, I started to climb over the small four-foot cliff next to the shore. Once again, Burris barked out behind me, but I did not turn around this time.

"The driver's side door is open, which means the deputy ain't in there."

"How do you know he is not?" Cal questioned.

"How about you swim out there and check then?" Burris strongly suggested.

"No way, not in that cold water."

Burris heard Cal's retort but refrained from replying. Instead, he panned his flashlight to shore and illuminated the ground all around me.

"There his is!" exclaimed Cal. "Get him!"

I didn't hear the shot's report for a split second after seeing the mist of my blood form a small cloud in front of me. I had no idea of my injury, nor did I want to stop to check things out. So instead, I heaved my soaked body over the rim and low crawled for a few yards on the other side. Then I rose to my feet and ran easterly.

Unbeknownst to me at the same time, another man was leading Adam back to his cell. However, his captors called it his "room" to soften the realization of his internment. Over the last day or so, the boy had kept his mouth shut and did everything his handlers told him. Even more helpful to him was keeping his eyes open since they no longer blindfolded him.

Slowly over the last few days, Adam pieced together what happened to Misty and him. Though parts of his memory were still blank, he distinctly remembered leaving the Otten house with Misty. It snowed that night, a hard fact, Adam quickly recalled. But when he drove over the cattle guard near the interstate bypass, his windshield wipers quit working. Thinking that the car blew another fuse, Adam pulled over under the protection of the southbound overpass bridge. After he stepped out of his car and knelt to inspect the fuse box, another vehicle pulled up behind and blinded him with an intense spotlight. The details went sketchy at that point, and his next recollection was waking up in the shark tank.

During his captivity, Adam encountered only adults. He counted three men, and he memorized their names as Burris, Cal, and Dodd. There was the other man, the smallish one who spoke with a disguised voice. But, earlier that morning, when Cal brought him a bowl of oatmeal, the man slipped and said, "you will like what Brenda does to the oats." He deduced that Brenda worked as the cook for the outfit.

Through bits and pieces of conversations around him, Adam also gathered that the ranch-raised blacktip sharks to harvest their fins and shipped them to Japan for consumption. The ranch also raised Kobe beef, which was a term he hadn't heard before. Whatever it meant, the cows he fed were isolated in a small pen and were enormously fat. The cattle, too, were butchered by a large man named Burris, then frozen and shipped. He also overheard that the delicacies brought in a sizable sum of money.

Aside from the agricultural oddities in the barnyard, below ground sat a peculiar subterranean structure that housed his "room." From all appearances, there was only one way in and one way out of the underground complex via a large freight-style elevator. The access of which ended up on one side of the house. The rest of the home, however, remained foreign to him.

When he stepped off the lift, it opened up into a large room equipped with three school cafeteria tables and a kitchen in the back. A metal vault door was on the right side of the room that accessed something he didn't know either. Then on the left side were two corridors, which the right side led him to his cell. Adam had the sense that other people were present around him, but just out of sight. For one thing, he ate only in his room, but there were moments he thought he heard the murmurs of faint female voices. He prayed that Misty's voice was amongst the others, which also meant she was safe for the moment.

Thirty minutes prior, while Adam he fed the cattle, Dodd suddenly ran up and forcibly turned him around. Then the man forced both of his wrists together and snapped a large zip tie around them. Then Dodd spun Adam around once more and placed a piece of duct tape over his mouth. But before the man left, he instructed the boy to sit on a bale of hay.

Not long afterward, Dodd returned, took the tape off Adam's face, and cut the restraint on his hands with a pair of pliers. Then, the man forcibly grabbed the boy by the arm and led him to the elevator access door on the side of the house.

A few minutes later, Dodd led Adam to his room. As the man reached to open up the door, an alarm beaconed loudly in the concrete surroundings. Dodd hastily shoved Adam into the room and raced down the hallway without fully closing the cell door behind him.

Adam now saw perhaps his only chance to escape, but he wouldn't do so without Misty. He must find her.

The boy eased the door open ever so quietly. The darkened hallway in front of him appeared empty, and he slowly eased through the opening and quietly closed the door behind him. After a few steps, Adam realized his dress shoes sounded heavily on the concrete floor. So, he stopped and quietly slipped both of them off and carried them with his hand.

When Adam emerged into the large, fully lit room, he glanced around and found it empty. He stepped past one of the tables and into the elevator shaft recess. The lift itself rested above him when Dodd exited the structure. Adam briefly thought about pressing the button to call the elevator but then stopped. Behind the safety cage, he spied a metal ladder mounted to the wall that rose the length of the shaft. Then an idea formed inside Adam's head.

The boy turned around and walked through the large room and into the other passageway. However, Adam didn't know if any of the captors were still present in one of the six rooms in the corridor. So, unhesitantly, he approached the first door on the right side and knocked.

"Misty," Adam said but with a deep guttural voice to disguise himself. He listened carefully and again knocked and called. This time Adam heard a slight whimper of a cry, but not from Misty. He repeated his actions on the second and third door, again to no avail. Next, Adam turned around and knocked on the last door on the left.

"Misty," he said once again.

"What do you want?"

"Misty?"

"Adam? Is that you?"

"It is," Adam replied. He grabbed the doorknob. It was locked. "Listen to me. I think something is going on because all the adults are gone."

"Then let me out of here!"

"I can't. The door is locked. I can go to the kitchen area to find a key, though."

"No, Adam, don't do it. There isn't any time. You have to get out if you can and get some help."

He sighed. "I can't leave you here alone."

"Adam, you have to try, but hurry." When he didn't immediately respond, Misty begged him to leave again.

He stepped back from the door and said softly, "I will come back," to which Misty replied, "you better."

* * *

30

Back in Midwest, Tracy opened her eyes and looked around the dimly lit living room. When she became fully awake, Tracy realized that she had fallen asleep in the recliner. I had bought her the chair as a pregnancy gift, and through each trimester, it became her only comfortable place to rest. Tracy looked at the clock mounted high on the wall behind the television. It read *9:03*.

"Eddie," she called out. But I didn't answer.

Awkwardly, Tracy partially rolled to her right side and reached for the lever to lease the chair's footrest. Then, she balanced herself, stood up, and walked to the master bedroom in the rear of the house.

Tracy parted the curtains and peered into the carport, but my truck wasn't there. As she walked back toward the living room, a foreboding sense consumed her. Admittingly, my coming home late from work wasn't that unusual though lately, she'd grown accustomed to me arriving no later than 6 p.m. nightly.

What was different from my routine was that I called earlier that night and informed her I wanted to check something out near Smokey Gap Road. Tracy checked her cellphone and did not see a missed call, so she dialed mine. After four rings, the call forwarded to my message box.

"This is Eddie. I'm away from my phone, so please leave your name and number, and I will get back to you."

After the tone, Tracy said, "Eddie, it's me. Call me back, please." She set the device on the end table, moved over to the front window, and looked outside. Then, while rubbing her belly, she tried to figure out why I wasn't home yet.

Tracy turned and picked up her phone again, and dialed my number. But, once more, I didn't answer. She inherently knew that my being three hours late wasn't that unusual, but still, that weird feeling continued to grip her.

Suddenly, a painful spasm quivered across her lower belly. But it subsided within a minute. In the meantime, Tracy sat down in her chair again and turned on the television. She scrolled through the cable menu for something to watch yet found nothing interesting. So instead, Tracy settled for a cable news show. She did so even while expecting that the anchors would drone on endlessly about conditions in Afghanistan mixed with shots at ground zero in New York City.

Then, out of the blue, another spasm hit, but this one hurt more than the first. Again, after 40-50 seconds, it too subsided. As Tracy's body relaxed, she looked up at the clock and noted the time. She tried my phone again, but I still didn't answer. Once more, the painful muscle spasm hit. While waiting for it to decrease, Tracy observed that only six minutes elapsed from the last bout.

At first, Tracy was in denial, but she knew the baby was coming after the next contraction. Then she picked up her phone and called Bill Crooks.

After the third ring, Bill answered gruffly, "Crooks."

"Bill, it is Tracy. I need your help."

Crooks instantly stepped out of the rough exterior he always projected and asked, "what's wrong."

"Two things, Bill. For one, Eddie hasn't come home yet, and I am worried. And, secondly, I think I am in labor."

Bill replied stoically, "hang on, I am on my way."

When Bill and Lois approached the door, he rapped on the exterior and opened the door. Then the couple let themselves inside our home. They found Tracy sitting in her chair, and both circled in front of her.

"How far apart are the contractions?" Lois asked.

"Umm, about five minutes now. I keep feeling like I have to pee, though."

Lois nodded and put her hand on Tracy's shoulder. "Do you think your water has broken? Maybe that is why you have that feeling."

Tracy shook her head. "No, no flood yet. But maybe I should go to the hospital."

"Okay, how about we do that?" Lois calmly suggested.

Tracy nodded and then looked over to Crooks. "Bill, I have a hospital bag ready to go in my bedroom. Could you grab that for me and my purse off the counter?"

Crooks nodded and disappeared. Meanwhile, Tracy started to stand, though Lois stepped closer and helped her up. At the same time, Crooks re-entered the room with Tracy's belongings.

Tracy looked at Crooks again. "Bill, don't argue with me, but I think something bad has happened to Eddie."

"Why do you say that?"

Tracy then briefly explained the hunch I came up with earlier that afternoon. She spoke of the photo with Lucas Gagnon sitting in the background and how I wondered if there was a connection to the other missing girls. Crooks was most attentive when Tracy described the camera files at the I-25 exit. She also retold my meeting with the Sheriff, who explicitly told me to stay away from the Gagnons and the Lepsis families. But generally, he nodded while she spoke, which indicated that he understood.

Then Crooks asked a peculiar question. "Where would you start looking for him aside from Smokey Gap junction?"

Tracy looked sternly into the man's eyes. "As I said already, Eddie has a notion that the Gagnon family is somehow connected. So, I'd start with them." But as she maintained her stare, she detected just a slight movement in the corner of Crooks' mouth.

"God, I hope not," he quipped.

"Why is that Bill?"

While Tracy waited for Crooks to reply, which he didn't, another contraction enveloped. Then, as she fought through the pain, she reached up and grabbed Crooks by his shirt.

Through gritted teeth, she demanded, "What are you not telling me?"

Crooks broke off eye contact and then looked back at Tracy. "There are some things I suspect too, but with God as my witness, I cannot divulge anything."

The contraction started to subside, and Tracy whispered to him, "tell me the truth, is he in trouble?"

Crooks shrugged. "Well, I don't know for sure, but your husband has found himself some sticky situations, hasn't he?"

"I'm not joking. I need my husband, and I need him now."

Crooks started to protest, but Tracy cut him off. "Bill, I need you to find my husband. Can you do that for me?"

Finally, Crooks nodded. He then looked over at his wife, but she interrupted, "time to make the sausage?"

He nodded. "Yep, I'm afraid so. But I'm going to need some help."

"Give Chief Traynor a call," Tracy suggested.

"I will, but not for what I have in mind." Then, after a pause, he continued, "look, we are wasting time. We need to get you to the hospital, and Lois, I need you to drop me off at home on the way." He smiled at her and gave her a small peck on her cheek. Then he said, "I will check in with you later when I can." Then to Tracy, "with any luck, I will find Eddie walking toward town because he broke down or something."

Tracy smirked, 'ya, it is always the *something* that I worry most about."

Within five minutes after his wife dropped him off at home, Crooks had already contacted his buddy Brit via the satellite phone. He forewent getting bogged down in a discussion of how the Justice Department got involved, but, instead, they discussed a plan. Crooks told Brit that he would call him back when the second phase of the operation was ready to execute at the end of the call.

Crooks powered down his phone and set it on the desktop. The problem with the plan was he needed a partner. Brit couldn't do it because he wasn't even in Wyoming. However, Wyatt Traynor was a capable and dependable man in difficult situations. Still, his limited ability to walk presented yet another problem. Then Crooks came up with another idea, and he grabbed his cellphone and made a call.

"Hello."

"CJ?"

"Yes, who is this?"

"It is Bill Crooks. Did I catch you at a good time?"

"You did. I just got home from Douglas, where I took a class."

Crooks harrumphed. "How did that go?"

CJ laughed. "Oh, you know how it is, they give you these pre-written slide show packets full of garbage. But, the good thing, I finished the material in one day, so I don't have to go back.

"Good." Then Crooks paused. "I need your help, but I have to warn you that it is the kind of help outside normal channels and without any backup."

"What's going on, Bill?"

"Eddie is missing, and I think he is off cowboying an investigation."

"Well, that's easy. I can call it in and let the department handle it."

"We can't do that because there isn't the time to go through the bureaucratic crap with the Sheriff, plus I doubt he would do anything. Additionally, we can't risk losing track of the targets."

"You aren't telling me anything, Bill. Why not?"

"I have reason to believe something is happening right under our noses. Something that I cannot speak to you about over an open line. Are you tracking me?"

"Well, if Eddie is missing, then I am on my way, whether above the table or not. What gear do you want me to grab?"

"Great, write this down."

Crooks agreed to meet up with CJ at the Smokey Gap junction off I-25 at 11:15 p.m. I had yet to contact Tracy or anyone else. A few minutes ago, she was still in labor and could begin delivering the baby at any time, according to Lois. Crooks rechecked his wristwatch. It read *11:12*.

After his phone call with CJ, he called Steve Otten to see if he'd seen me. Steve said he thought he saw my bright red late-model Ford pickup drive west by his place just before sunset. When Steve asked why Crooks wanted to know about me, Bill had a hard time explaining. Then their conversation took another turn when Steve made the leap that I was investigating his daughter's disappearance. When Steve volunteered to help, Crooks did his level best to explain that the authorities would handle it.

Next, Crooks called Wyatt Traynor and asked him to stay up that night if he needed some assistance. Traynor aptly accepted his part and would wait for Crooks to call. Then, while he drove up Highway 387 toward I-25, his cellphone rang again. It was Steve Otten. It was apparent that Steve took it upon himself to go down Smokey Gap Road and used his spotlight to see if he could see my pickup. Steve reported that a couple of miles short of the Scarlet Ranch, he came across a fresh set of tire tracks that matched my truck headed toward Grummond Hill. Crooks thanked him for the update and promised he would contact Steve later.

* * *

31

While catching my breath behind the cover of rock, I found myself with great respect for wild game animals because, like them, I'd run on nothing but fear since the first shot rang out. Once I maneuvered over the flat ground on the fringe of the ranch yard, I quickly ducked into the sagebrush and greasewood that lined the creek. For the first 400 yards or so, I never glanced back.

Instead, I clumsily pushed on into the darkness. I fell twice, and that second time, my right elbow landed squarely onto a patch of cactus. Yet, there was no time to pluck the painful needles from my arm or proverbially lick my wounds. Instead, I heard the snap of bullets hitting the ground all around me. I determined that my survival depended upon one thing: putting as much distance between me and my pursuers as possible.

Eventually, I no longer heard the report of shots behind me, but I pressed on, nonetheless. I then discovered a large Cottonwood tree and used the enormous truck to hide my body. At the same time, I tried to ascertain where I was exactly. As I peered around the ancient bark, I made out four men standing under the yard light of the ranch, with one of them sitting behind the wheel of what looked like a John Deere Gator ATV. Though I could hear the men talking, I couldn't make out specific words due to the distance. But it didn't matter because I knew they were coming up with a plan to search for me. I looked skyward, and I fixed upon the Big Dipper, which pointed to the North Star. From there, I knew that I needed to keep that constellation to my left while I made my way east toward the interstate highway.

I decided to cross the creek at that location. Instead of following the drainage to the point between the two giant hills, I began to climb. I presumed that my pursuers would look for me along the drainage first because that was the most accessible path I could take. When I reached the creek bottom, I knelt and scooped up a handful of water, and quickly rinsed the wound on my arm. It wasn't as bad as I thought, a bullet graze, really, but it was the type of wound that bled a lot. So, I then grabbed a fist full of mud and slowly packed it around the injury with hopes that it would help stop the bleeding.

I spent the next 30 minutes or so trudging uphill. It was painfully slow and challenging since my body began to shiver as hypothermia started to set it. Then parts of me went numb as well to include my right elbow still full of cactus thorns. My clothes still weighed heavily, too, and were far from drying out. The only part of my body that felt normal was my feet since I always wore wool socks inside my boots.

Minutes later, in the dark, I came across a small sandstone ledge. I scrambled up to it and found that it recessed far enough back that nobody could see me from below. Then I inched forward and looked around. To the east, I believed I saw the peak of the hill outline itself against the brilliance of stars, which meant I was close to the top. However, down below and toward the ranch, I could not see any of the men. I scanned my route up the hill, but I didn't see any flashlights. Nor did I hear anything except the wind, which had a cold bite to it.

I followed the ledge for a dozen feet and found a small alcove, not unlike many of the tiny caves around the area. I lowered myself down to my hands and knees and started to crawl in, but one of my senses stopped me: smell. I got a complete whiff of the scent of cucumbers. I immediately withdrew from the cave entrance and stood upon the ledge once more.

The cucumber scent served me as a warning since a rattlesnake den emits the same odor. It was something that I experienced personally, along with my wife, Tracy, when we found ourselves on the front porch to a condominium of the vipers. I still don't eat cucumbers to this day.

I decided to move upward still, and eventually, I discovered another sandstone outcropping. Yet, this one was smaller though it lacked any caves or cervices. By then, I was exhausted from the hike, the cactus thorns, the bullet wound, the swim, and from the stun gun. Finally, I sat down, though, in truth, I think I collapsed.

The wind had subsided outside the ledge, but a slight breeze still reminded me that I was wet and freezing. My teeth chattered as I fumbled with the plastic buckle to my fanny pack and then opened its zipper. My hands were too numb to pull out the contents of the small bag carefully, so I dumped everything into my lap.

First, I found my headlamp and turned it on only to dial down the brightness to its dullest setting. Since I had light, I spotted the water-tight container that held matches but decided against the notion of a campfire considering the men would easily spot it. Then, surprisingly, I found hand warmer bags, four of which I forgot were in the bag. I grabbed the first one and tore open the plastic cover with my teeth. Next, I activated the iron, water, and charcoal solution and shook the bag until it began to warm. I repeated the same steps for the remaining three warmers.

I placed a warm bag under each armpit, another I set on the small of my back, and the last one I secured under my navel against the waistband of my pants.

The last thing I found helpful was an emergency blanket. In reality, it was nothing more than a silver-colored, heat-reflecting sheet of plastic. But I also inherently knew that I would retain any heat I generated while under the plastic film.

Then out of the blue, I remembered my cellphone in the top pocket of my shirt. I reached inside my jacket and found the device. However, when I flipped the phone open, the display failed to light up. I pressed and held the power button, though the unit did not turn on when I released my thumb. The water must have damaged the phone's circuits. Disgusted, I closed the phone and placed it back into my shirt pocket.

So, I turned off the headlamp and pulled the edge of the blanket over my head and laid there quietly atop the hill that Christian Mercy had re-named *Hoka-He*. But, to me, at least, it was not a 'good day to die.' No, on the contrary, I knew I had to survive, somehow.

Eventually, though, my teeth stopped chattering.

* * *

32

SMOKEY GAP JUNCTION

WEST OF MIDWEST, WYOMING

11:15 P.M.

Bill Crooks still sat alone in his old 1960 Willys Jeep pickup while patiently waiting for Deputy Cory Jackson to arrive. The trailer behind him ferried twin Kawasaki four-wheel drive all-terrain vehicles, each equipped with hard-cased rifle carriers. In the pickup bed was a generic Army surplus duffle bag filled with tactical supplies.

Crooks took a sip of his coffee and accidentally spilled some of the liquid onto his jacket. Out of habit, he reached his hand up to wipe off the spillage but then realized it didn't matter since he wore dark brown clothing from his hat to his trousers.

By now, he had run through the plan several times in his head. During each recollection, he sought out the plan's pitfalls, and then upon recognizing them, he made slight alterations. However, his former combat experience taught him that no plan, no matter how perfect, will remain intact after the first bullet. This truth is what bothered him most.

Crooks looked up and spotted the headlights of an automobile sweep onto Highway 387 from the exit ramp. He watched pensively as the vehicle emerged from the overpass and veered toward his position. Now he saw that the headlights belonged to a maroon Dodge Ram 1500, and he continued to gaze upon it as the pickup truck parked next to his. The driver then opened his door, which caused the interior dome light to come on, and he instantly recognized the man.

Dressed in a black shirt and matching tactical style pants, CJ walked around his pickup and approached the lowered window of the Jeep.

"Bill."

"CJ." Crooks acknowledged. Then he asked, "did you bring everything on that list?"

The deputy nodded and responded with a subtle, "yep." Then he briefly turned his back and opened the passenger door of the Ram, and when CJ turned around, he held a rifle in his hand.

Crooks leaned out of the window and turned on a small flashlight to inspect the weapon closer. "Nice gun. It is a semi-automatic SR-25 made by Knights Armament complete with a 20-round magazine, a holographic day or nighttime sight, and a suppressor."

CJ nodded again.

Crooks then added, "I bet that thing is chambered in 7.62X51 NATO too."

"I see you know your weaponry, Bill. What are you carrying?"

He shrugged and then turned the focus of his flashlight onto the rifle that leaned on the bench seat next to him.

"Oh, I brought old Bessie along. She's an M1A chambered nearly the same as yours, but mine is in .308 Winchester. The scope is different. This one has an infrared thermal feature plus a laser ranger finder. It is perfect for nighttime work."

Crooks turned and shone the flashlight on the ground in front of the deputy.

"How far can you shoot that thing accurately?" CJ asked.

"I don't know. I mean, I can place a grouping smaller than your fist center mass on a target at 800 yards."

"Why only 800 yards?"

He shrugged again. "It is simple: 800 yards is the longest shooting lane at the Salt Creek shooting range."

CJ laughed and then went back to his pickup. He turned once more and placed a couple of gear bags in the bed of the pickup. Then he locked up his Ram and climbed onto the bench seat in the Willys adjacent to Bill.

He handed the deputy a cup of coffee and instructed, "better fuel up. I don't want either of us to get sleepy tonight."

The deputy grasped the plastic mug carefully and took a quick sip. Crooks then turned the ignition key, and the old pickup engine groaned to life. The only light source inside the cab came from the glow of two out of the four gauges located behind the steering wheel on the dash. The large speedometer in the center of the panel, though, remained dark.

Within seconds, they had crossed over the cattleguard, which began Smokey Gap Road. Then the Willys' headlights shown upon the buckshot blasted County Road 115 sign, and soon, they were over the hill.

"So, what is the plan, Bill? Where do we look for Eddie?" CJ asked abruptly.

Crooks took another sip off his coffee mug but managed to refrain from spilling any liquid this time.

He turned his head slightly and said, "well, we are going to go to the crossroads of Mondale Road and BLM 37. You know that same area where you exited the Gagnon place to the east near Razorback Reservoir."

In the dim glow inside the cab, Crooks watched CJ nod that he understood about the location they headed.

Then Crooks continued, "we will park at the crossroads and take the four-wheelers to the top of the saddle between those two large hills. I will creep along the southern ridge to put eyes on the ranch yard and provide cover. I dunno, maybe I'll spot Eddie's pickup or Eddie himself?"

"What do you mean about the term *cover*? What do you intend for me to do?"

After taking another swig of coffee, Crooks placed the travel mug between his legs. Then he continued, "that is where your youth and athleticism come in."

CJ furrowed his brow, not comprehending Crooks' assertion.

"Come on, CJ, standard reconnaissance procedure. I will provide sniper cover while you sneak your way into the yard to find Eddie."

CJ nodded.

Then Crooks used his right elbow and pushed the small backpack in the middle seat a little closer to CJ.

"I also have another idea. Open this pack and look inside," Crooks instructed.

CJ did as told and unzipped the pack. He reached his hand inside and grasped and retrieved one of the many identical-shaped objects inside. Then CJ examined the small plastic-cased square box.

"What is this?"

Crooks looked at CJ and asked, "have you ever heard of Blue Force Tracking system?"

CJ dipped his head to one side and then replied, "if you are talking about the small GPS transmitters that give headquarters a precise location of troops in the field, then yes, I have heard of it. But they are not deployed yet."

"Yep, well, that one you are holding in your hand is similar to Blue Force. The difference is that these attach to a vehicle like a LoJack system." Crooks paused long enough to reach over and turn the box around. "Do you see the magnet? All you have to do it place it on anything metal. Then the device will synch up with a satellite to track the vehicle."

A jackrabbit ran out in front of the pickup's headlights, which caused Crooks to stop speaking. He watched the animal bound along, and soon it jumped into the sagebrush along the right side of the road.

CJ seized the opportunity and asked, "what do you mean by the word, *we*?"

"Fair question," Crooks acknowledged and then continued, "the word *we* consist of my buddy, Brit, and his cohorts. You see, he is a part of a group that exists within the folds of government to take care of certain national security problems that arise."

"Is your friend a part of the CIA?"

"No, Brit is not CIA, nor is he part of the FBI, Defense Intelligence Agency, the Department of Defense, or even the State Department. But, as I said, Brit's group is special."

"How does that apply to you?"

"I can't tell you everything, but what I can say is that I worked alongside them for a bit."

CJ shook his head, "you all sound like a bunch of mercenaries."

Crooks reached up and rubbed his beard, then answered, "no, they are not mercs; they don't hire themselves out. But, again, they are a part of the government infrastructure that neither you nor any other citizen will ever see."

CJ shrugged. "Then why doesn't your buddy and his group come out here and deal with this situation?"

"It is a simple principle of resource allocation. Brit's group is too far away, and we, meaning you and I, are in a perfect position to do something."

Crooks abruptly stopped talking and turned left onto Mondale Road. The pair rode in silence for a few more minutes. During that time, the deputy peered through the window. It was dark, and the land remained featureless without even a sliver of the moon to provide enough light to gain any sense of the landscape around them. Then he looked out the rear window and saw the full brilliance of the Milky Way blaze across the night sky.

Finally, CJ asked, "what is this all about, Bill?"

Crooks shrugged, "it is not a what but a who." Then, when CJ wasn't following his implication, he continued, "in your service days, did you ever hear about the group of radicals called Early Dawn?"

CJ was puzzled initially at the question. He knew the term sounded familiar, but then his memory recalled the specifics. "If you are talking about that group of fanatics in Asia who called to decrease the world's population by 95%, then, yes, I have heard of them. But I thought we took them out during Operation Victor eight years ago?"

"Were you a part of that mission?"

CJ shook his head. "No, I wasn't, but a friend of mine was involved." A hush in the conversation caused the pickup cab to go silent, except for the thunderous exhaust leak that drowned everything else out. Finally, CJ broke the silence, "are you intimating that Early Dawn is here?"

Crooks nodded. "Yep, that is what I am saying. My buddy's group has followed Early Dawn for a while now, and I found something that confirms their presence. You see, Early Dawn is neither political nor is it religious. Still, the movement thrives on a collective dream of a global reset in the environment, in governments, and human genetics."

"It sounds like Nazism, doesn't it?" CJ asked.

"It does in a way. I suppose since the key to the movements' success is creating a new super race of humans after eradicating the old one."

"What would it take to exterminate the population?"

"Well, Deputy, nuclear weapons could do it, but then there is the fallout to deal with for years. But I suppose a biological event of some type, like a super virus, could do the job while leaving the infrastructure intact and the environment relatively unaffected."

CJ shook his head in disbelief. "A virus attack? Seriously? But wouldn't that make all of the Early Dawn members sick too?"

Crooks looked over to his partner and leaned closer. "No, not if the group members vaccinated themselves before the release of the virus."

They rode in silence for another mile or so. The sheer amount of information and the implications of such were mind-boggling. Finally, CJ interrupted the pause when he asked, "but, why here, Bill? Why would they set up shop out here in the middle of nowhere Wyoming?"

Crooks grinned. "You should ask yourself, why not here? Think about it: it is an isolated location with zero visibility and can easily blend into the local community. Frankly, I am surprised that more groups like this one haven't set up operations in Wyoming where they could virtually hide in plain sight."

CJ nodded and remained silent for a spell. Then an idea flashed across CJ's mind. "I don't know why but I just pictured all of those missing girls in northeast Wyoming. All of them possess similar looks and athletic abilities, so maybe Early Dawn took them? Am I missing something?"

"No, CJ, you are tracking along with my thoughts. But there is also new intelligence that they are moving out soon."

"When?"

Crooks shrugged. "We don't know exactly when, though intelligence indicates it could be today, tomorrow, or even next week. But we have this lone opportunity to do something about the problem. Though I hope we aren't too late."

Bill Crooks released his foot off of the accelerator pedal and slowly veered off the right side of the road. He carefully drove over a wide and flat spot in the grass that demarked the crossroad of Mondale Road and BLM 37. Both Crooks and CJ got out of the pickup and placed a headlamp around their necks. Then the duo made short work of unchaining the ATVs and backing them off of the trailer.

Next, the men silently put their gear bags together that also included: water, Clif Bars, extra ammunition, and a small medical kit. Additional items stowed were a pair of infrared binoculars, paracord, and Crooks' satellite phone since cellphone coverage was sketchy at best. Lastly, he retrieved two tactical helmets, which he gave one of them to CJ.

"Here. This one is yours."

CJ took the helmet and strapped it onto his head. Then Crooks gave him a pair of night vision goggles that anchored itself on the front of the helmet.

"Wow, Bill. Where did you get these?"

Crooks shrugged. "Oh, I picked them up at a surplus store on Yellowstone Highway outside of Casper."

"Do you do this sort of thing often?" CJ joked.

"Very funny. No, I use these things when hunting so I can see my way through the dark when I set up my roost before daybreak."

The men briefly turned away and returned with their rifles, which they secured inside the rifle cases on the front of each ATV.

While doing so, CJ opined, "you know, when you called me tonight, I thought this was just a search and rescue operation to find Eddie. But now, you are asking me to involve myself in something I know nothing about."

Crooks nodded. "Well, if you want to drop out, I understand, but do it now and not when I need you most during mid-mission."

"No, I am not dropping out. There is too much at stake for Eddie and those missing girls. But Eddie comes first and the other stuff second. Got it?"

"I do, CJ. Eddie is one of my best friends, and my focus is on him foremost."

"What do you think happened to him?"

Crooks shrugged. "I figure he came to the ranch, and maybe he stumbled upon something, though considering it is Eddie we are talking about, I use the word *stumble* purposefully." He briefly stretched his back while sliding his pack his shoulders. Then he continued, "ya, I think Eddie is either a captive or is dead. But, if he is alive, I think we can extract him during the group's confusion getting ready to move out. You know, just like those snatch and grab missions our unit used to send us on."

"I see. But how many people are we talking about, Bill?"

"I don't know exactly, but I assume six to eight men?"

"Great, another mission with little intel and a whole lot of uncertainty."

Crooks withheld comment though as he walked over to his ATV and swung a leg over the seat. "We will head up the road a bit, and then we will pull over before the crest of the saddle between the two hills. From there, we will walk in so that we don't alert anyone on the other side."

CJ gave Crooks a thumbs up and turned off his headlamp. Likewise, Crooks dimmed his too and lowered his night vision goggles in front of his face. Only then did they start the engines on the ATVs and drove off down BLM Road 37.

* * *

33

Meanwhile, Adam peered out of his hiding spot near the barn. Earlier, when he left the underground compound, Adam heard a lot of commotion down by the stock pond below the ranch yard. So, Adam circled outside of the light pole and found himself inside the shop where he hoped to locate a vehicle to drive away. When Adam got there, however, the boy could not see any keys. He even checked the two tractors, and neither of them had keys in the ignition either. Adam thought about running away, but he didn't know where to go?

However, the boy had the presence of mind to look at himself in a side mirror of a pickup. Adam looked carefully at the bolt head that secured the band around his neck, but it was a weird apex type of bit. So he turned around and walked to the workbench located along the back wall to search for a tool.

Then the sound of multiple gunshots in fast succession startled him. So, he turned and frantically searched for something to remove the collar. Finally, he found a small kit with at least 20 odd-shaped bits.

Suddenly, the voices of two men outside the shop echoed inside. Adam reacted instinctively by hiding in the dark shadow behind the implements. Seconds later, Cal stepped through the doorway and into the light, Dodd followed behind. Then one of the large overhead doors opened. At the same time, a John Deere Gator started up and moved toward the opening.

Adam waited patiently. Though in the meantime, he managed to unscrew the bolt that held his collar together around his neck. Once off, Adam turned and hung the device on a hook that held engine belts of various sizes. Then, after a few more minutes, Adam slowly left the shadows and snuck around the shop's wall until he reached the small door. Then, with a leap of faith, he stepped through the opening and into the open space of the ranch yard.

Immediately upon leaving the confines of the shop, Adam counted three men who gathered together around the single yard light on a pole. The blue light from above illuminated their faces, and Adam recognized the two men from a few minutes prior, plus the big guy named Burris.

Again, Adam remained in the dark shadows as he crept into the barn. Then he quietly moved to the other side of the building and exited next to a stack of hay bales. Adam then picked up a couple of the bundles to quickly make a blind of sorts, remaining concealed.

From the bits and pieces of the rolling conversation in front of him, Adam realized that the alarm he'd heard earlier was an intruder warning. Burris said, "intruder," very distinctly in the still of the night. The news puzzled Adam since he didn't know whether the "intruder" was someone looking for him or Misty or it was something else. He surmised that whomever that another person was, it sure had the compound on edge.

What Adam hadn't seen until that moment was the light glowing from the inside ranch house through its windows. His eyes went back to the three men to witness what would come next.

Suddenly, Burris looked toward the house, and he immediately stood tall from his normal slouching posture. Adam leaned forward to observe the scene more closely and even managed to create more space between the bales by pushing one of them an inch or so.

The door to the ranch house opened, and from the backlighting, Adam spotted a small man wearing a hood walk off the front step and across the gravel drive. When the man spoke, Adam heard the metallic sound of a synthesized voice instruct the group to "eliminate the threat."

But, before the men dispatched, the small man said in the same metallic voice he heard before, "don't take too long because we are moving out before dawn."

Those words, *moving out,* echoed inside Adam's head. Then Adam formulated a plan, which meant he would stay hidden until Misty emerged. The boy further reasoned that he might have an opportunity to snatch his girlfriend away from the others.

As he looked back through the crack between the bales, the small man looked toward the barn. At first, Adam felt a wave of panic that somehow he was seen, but the man moved his head in a sweeping motion onto the front entrance to the ranch.

As suddenly as the small man appeared, he turned and walked back to the ranch house. In turn, the three men climbed aboard their John Deere Gators and departed down an undisclosed road on the backside of the house. Finally, after the men left, Adam sat down on a hay bale and leaned his back against the outside wall of the barn. He knew his job was simple: he had to wait.

A mile to the east of Adam, I woke up in a panic from a noise. Frankly, I was surprised that I did sleep, considering my predicament. Logically, I deduced that my hypothermic state probably induced my nap. Still, it did little to make me feel any better. As I tried to clear my brain fog, I recalled hearing the sound of a loud truck a while ago, but I told myself that it must have been a dream.

I no longer shivered, but my entire body felt cold and numb. But then I heard a noise again, which sounded like a motorcycle engine. I pulled the top of the blanket away from my head and then slowly rolled over to peer over the sandstone shelf. The plastic sheet made a crinkling noise, and I prayed that it didn't alert someone below me.

At first, it was pitch black down the slope from the outcropping. But as I patiently watched, two or more people were moving around in the distance well below my perch. First, I saw two headlamps moving gently from side to side as the person walked while looking at the ground before them. Then another flashlight turned on to the left of the other two individuals making three people searching for me.

I rolled back over and out of sight from below and contemplated my next move. When I started to sit up, my right arm gripped with pain. I tried again and managed to sit, but my legs wouldn't move. I reached my left hand down to the knee of my ice-cold left leg, and then I felt the right one. Though I could feel my hand on each leg, my legs wouldn't work for some reason.

I laid back down. Then I reached behind the small of my back and removed the hand warmer pack. Then I did the same thing with the one still strapped to my belly. Finally, my hands worked well enough to unzip my pants, and I managed to shove a hand warmer down each pant leg on the inside of my thighs. I hoped that by warming the femoral artery areas, I could regain my lower limbs' function.

But to do so meant to wait.

* * *

Astride their ATVs, Bill Crooks and Deputy Cory Jackson trekked to the top of the pass that separated Grummond Hill from the un-named prominence to the south. The ride was not without problems due to the absence of any light in the dark sky. Their night vision goggles worked to a point, but even those devices require at least a little moon-light to discern anything truly. But Crooks and CJ possessed extensible experience with the equipment and picked their way nonetheless.

Less than a hundred yards from the pass, Crooks turned off the dirt road and into an opening in the sagebrush. CJ deftly followed behind and then stopped alongside Crooks and shut off his machine. The men quickly retrieved their rifles from the protective cases and slung them over their shoulders. But before he turned around, CJ checked the time on his watch.

Then Crooks dug into another pack and handed CJ another piece of equipment.

"Here," Crooks whispered while extending his hand toward CJ. "Take your helmet off and put this on."

"What is it?" CJ asked softly.

"It is a two-way comms piece so we can communicate quietly. These are similar to what you used during your service."

"What is the range, Bill?"

"We should be good as long as we stay within a mile or so from one another."

CJ grasped the small earpiece while also careful not to bend or break the tiny microphone that extended off of it. Then he put his helmet on once again. Meanwhile, Crooks did the same.

Crooks turned his back to his partner and walked ten yards forward. "Check, Whisky, Tango, Hotel. How do you copy? he whispered.

"I copy," the deputy breathed in return. "COMM check, niner, eight, seven, how copy?"

"Loud and clear." Crooks turned his body around to face CJ. "I think we should push over the saddle where we can make our way over the draw and follow the fence to the south. From there, we will perch ourselves atop the ridge where we can see the ranch yard."

"Yep, that sounds like the same place that Christian and I reconnoitered."

"Good," Crooks whispered. "Time to move."

CJ let Crooks lead the way, and he began to admire the older man's strength and stamina. Not only that, but it amazed CJ that Crooks barely made any noise as he adroitly moved around sagebrush and over loose rock. The duo spent little or no time to cross over the drainage and follow the fence line to the ridge behind the ranch.

Both men unslung their packs and carried them in a free hand as they crept up the embankment. Then, at the crest, they laid prone side-by-side and began to scan the breadth of the area below them.

Crooks flipped up his night vision goggles and raised his rifle. While using the pack as a gun rest, he scanned the area. The ranch yard appeared empty, and the yard light burned brightly as a white orb in his optics. Yet they did not note any movement around the shop or the barn.

"The place to keep your eye on is the other end of the ranch house," Crooks instructed.

CJ whispered, "why?"

"Because that side is the access to the bunker. If we don't see anyone topside, then everyone must be underground."

The deputy snapped his head around to look at Crooks. "You seem to know a lot about this place that you aren't telling me. Do you want to fill in some gaps?"

Crooks continued to scan the ranch yard while he explained, "the former owner of this place built an underground fallout shelter in the early '70s. Look over to the space between the greenhouse and the ranch home. Do you see those mushroom-looking things?"

CJ looked in the area Crooks described through his night-vision goggles. "Yep, I see them. I spotted those things the first time I was up here. So, what are they anyway?"

"Those are part of the ventilation system to exchange the air inside the bunker. I assume that Liam Gagnon is now reusing the space as his laboratory."

CJ looked over to Crooks and asked, "how do the Gagnons fit into all of this?"

"Liam Gagnon, though that is not his real name, has worked for various governments worldwide. His employers also include the United States to conduct gain of function tests on various virus specimens."

CJ shook his head. "What does that mean?"

Crooks shrugged. "I don't know, I teach history, but I bet it has something to do with biological warfare."

But before CJ could reply, something moved on the southern end of the ranch house, which caught his attention. He waited patiently, and after a long thirty seconds, CJ saw a shadow move inside of the window.

"Bill, check out the southern window of the house. I saw the shadow of one person inside."

Crooks fixed his scope on the house, and moments later, he too saw a shadow of someone walking inside the home. But as Crooks turned toward CJ to say something, two new small white orbs appeared in his view.

"CJ, look over at two o'clock," Crooks breathed.

As instructed, the deputy panned over to the hill and he then saw the same small white orbs, but they were moving. Then a third orb appeared. But from that distance, it was hard to make out any shapes.

"Yep, I've got three lights on the slope of the hill over there. But I can't see a human, though."

"Hold on," Crooks instructed and then turned and carefully unzipped his backpack and withdrew a pair of binoculars and handed them to CJ.

When CJ saw the specs, he asked, "how am I going to see anything with these? It is too dark."

Crooks snickered softly but replied, "these are infrared. So, if there is anything over there generating a heat source, you will see it."

CJ flipped up his night vision set away from his face and brought the binoculars to his eyes. He immediately picked up three sizeable bi-pedal heat signatures, moving back and forth as if walking a grid pattern. He relayed what he saw to Crooks, who also confirmed.

The way the men moved about reminded Crooks of something familiar, but he couldn't place it. However, the notion soon set into Crooks's brain, and he said so, "Eddie is alive, CJ."

"How can you be so sure?"

"Those men are walking around looking for Eddie's footprints or even a blood trail."

"How can you tell?"

"Because I have gone through the same motions looking for wounded game animals. Yep, Eddie is alive."

"Do you see Eddie?"

"Nope, not yet," Crooks whispered. He followed the movements of the men as they picked their way up the slope of Grummond Hill. Then a different heat signature registered, low to the ground and a little higher on the hill above the searchers.

"I think I have eyes on Eddie."

"Really, where?"

"About three quarters up the slope and below the peak. Again, CJ looked through the binoculars and spotted the lone image.

Crooks suddenly broke the silence, "they see him, and Eddie is getting up."

CJ dropped the binoculars and shouldered his rifle. Astonishingly, he could now make out the dim thermal forms of three men through his optics. Then a rifle shot thundered across the expanse, followed by two more.

"I can take the guy on the right," CJ suggested.

But after a brief pause, Crooks inexplicably said, "no, hold your fire."

"What?"

Crooks pulled the scope away from his face and looked at CJ. "They spooked a cow elk. Look to the far right toward the drainage."

CJ spun his rifle around and, after a few seconds, confirmed Crooks' observation. "Yep, that is an elk, alright."

"That confirms that Eddie is out there somewhere but well hidden."

"Where do you think he holed up?"

Crooks chuckled. "Knowing Eddie, he is probably in a cave." Then he looked back at the ranch yard. When he turned back to CJ, he said, "now is a perfect time for you skinny down the ridge and place those GPS trackers on the vehicles, which I assume are inside in the shop to the far left."

CJ questioned, "are you sure? Shouldn't we stay here and provide cover for Eddie if he shows himself?"

"I can do that and provide you cover at the same time."

"How many yards is it to the shop from here?"

"Let me check." Crooks raised the rifle scope to his eye and reported, "I've got 904 yards to the door." Then he swung the rifle to the right. "It is 883 to the barn and another 789 to this side of the house." Crooks continued his sweep over to the three men who were entirely visible in his scope. "The perps are only 700 yards away across from us. From here, I can hit anything I see."

CJ sighed. "Okay, but I don't like splitting up because bad things always happen when we do."

"You worry too much. We will be fine," Crooks said dryly.

CJ then sat back on his heels with his knees still on the ground and adjusted his pack. "I am going to swing to the far left and approach the shop from that side, copy?"

"Copy. Happy hunting."

"Very funny," CJ quipped as he backed away and strode off to his left.

* * *

35

Bill Crooks routinely followed CJ's progress from atop his perch as the deputy quickly made his way down toward the ranch yard. Then every thirty seconds or so, Crooks swept the infrared scope to the men who continued their search. By the way, the searchers moved; he assumed they still had no idea of my exact location. Crooks envisioned that I must have escaped to the east and had somehow given the aggressors the slip. Perhaps, Crooks thought, I was still moving and had found his pickup by now.

Minutes later, Crooks unexpectedly viewed a small, round-shaped heat signature appear well above the searchers on the slope of Grummond Hill. Crooks focused his eyes even more closely and waited patiently for the new object to move. After a few seconds, another heat source moved from behind some invisible barrier. The unique shape, however, resembled a human arm.

"CJ?" Crooks whispered.

"Ya, Bill," CJ replied, well out of view.

"I think I see, Eddie. He is way above the searchers near the peak."

"Are you sure, Bill?"

"Yep, I am positive it is a man."

"Good. Now do me a favor."

"Sure."

"Scan the yard again because I am about to move from the shadows to the door of the shop. I don't want to stumble upon anyone."

Crooks looked all around the shop and the barn area. The only things projecting a heat source were the cows in their tiny pens and the dull glow of the warm greenhouse. He also looked at the ranch house and confirmed that nobody stood outside of it.

"You are all clear, CJ."

Through his lens, Crooks observed his partner emerge from behind an enormous Cottonwood tree. CJ paused briefly, looked from left to right, and then moved stealthily to the open overhead door of the shop. Then he disappeared through the threshold.

Meanwhile, Crooks looked back to the slope on his right. By now, the three men stood in a small circle like a football huddle to discuss their next move. He darted his view back to the shop and failed to locate CJ, which meant he was still inside. Next, he panned the slope again, and his heart started to race.

"Hurry up, CJ," Crooks warned. Then, after ten seconds of silence, he repeated, "hurry up, I said, because you will soon have company."

Instead of CJ's voice, Crooks heard a blurb of static but could not make out any words. His attention went back to the men who walked single file in the direction of the ranch yard. One of the searchers stopped and dug something out of his pocket. The flash on orange on the infrared indicated that the man had struck a match and lit a cigarette. Then, like the others with him, the man continued the march downhill to their abandoned John Deere Gators.

CJ successfully placed the GPS transmitters on a Chevy Suburban, a Ford Explorer, and the two ranch pickups inside the shop. But, when he approached the door, CJ paused.

"Bill?" he breathed.

"CJ! You have company coming. Get out of there now."

The deputy moved over to the smaller door. As he started to exit the door frame, he heard the front door of the ranch house open. Then a small figure appeared on the threshold. Instead of retracing his steps to his right, where he would expose himself in the light, CJ threw himself to the left into the darkness. He soon crossed over the short distance between the shop and the barn, and when he entered the side door of the latter, he banged his knee into something immovable.

It was the same joint that CJ injured playing football in college, and his vision turned red as pain jolted through his body. He briefly braced himself and tried to put weight on his injured leg. But it was too painful. So instead, he hopped across the building on one foot and stopped just inside of the other side door. Surprisingly, the whole thing transpired without CJ making a single sound.

As the deputy tried to collect himself, he felt a hand grab him on the shoulder from behind. CJ spun around instinctively and knocked the person back a few steps. Then he recognized the man and flipped up his night-vision goggles.

"Bill, we got a problem."

Crooks turned his attention away from the searchers who had made it back to their off-road vehicles. "What problem?"

"I found Adam. He was hiding near the barn."

"What are you doing in the barn? I thought you were circling back to me along the same way you went down there?" Crooks pulled up his scope again and quickly identified two orbs of heat near the side door next to a stack of hay bales. "I see both of you."

"Good," CJ replied.

Adam then motioned silently for CJ to follow him into the blind of sorts inside the haystack. Once there, the boy helped CJ sit down and pointed through the tiny slit between the bundles. When the deputy looked through the opening toward the house, the side door on the north side opened. A tall female stepped outside and looked around. Then she spun around and said something inaudible to someone still inside the doorway. CJ then moved his eyes toward the house and spied two boy-sized figures walking across the yard toward the shop. One of the small men wore a hood over his head.

CJ's earpiece sounded, "what's going on, CJ."

"Not now, I can't talk," he replied in the faintest of a whisper.

When CJ looked back to the tall woman, he counted seven smaller, trim females following her in single file. Each of them wore simple plain colored knee-length dresses. Oddly, to CJ at least, the women seemed rather obedient.

Simultaneously, the yard filled with the unmistakable sound of the Gators returning. Both of them sped around the house and then out of sight to CJ's right, presumably to the shop.

The distraction nearly obscured the commotion behind the column of females who crossed out of sight from CJ's vantage point. Then, the tall woman turned around and approached two other women. However, the noticeably heavier one wearing a dark sweatshirt and blue jeans screamed that she wasn't "going anywhere." Instead, the unnamed accomplice grabbed the obstinate one by the arm and started to pull.

"Let go of her," a voice said that pierced the night.

Adam's head snapped up, and he tapped CJ on the arm. "That's Misty." But before CJ could reply, Adam snuck out of hiding behind him.

Then the deputy saw the small man walk in front of his lair, where he pushed back the hood covering his head. But it wasn't a he. Instead, it was a small woman. In an eerie synthetic-sounding voice, she commanded, "Brenda, just let them go."

The tall woman looked indifferent. "What do you mean, let them go?"

"I don't want the hassle. Besides that bus driver is nothing but a pain in the butt. So let them go. Besides, we will be long gone by the time they can report anything."

Oddly, another voice objected. "But, mom, I want Misty!"

The small woman spun her head around and said, "quiet, Lucas. It was your obsession with her that has placed us in danger. If you and Burris hadn't gone behind my back and snatched her, I could have made enough vials to fulfill the plan. But, because of you, we have to go somewhere else."

From behind them, Burris shouted out, "Doc, grab your son and Brenda. We are all loaded up and ready to go."

The woman Burris called "Doc" then instructed him to get the other men and Lucas to retrieve the *boxes* inside the laboratory.

"What about the boy down there?" Burris asked.

"Leave him in his cell."

CJ remained stoically silent while he watched the three men and Lucas walk across the yard and into the north end of the farmhouse. Meanwhile, "Doc" and the taller woman named Brenda moved in the other direction toward the shop. When the deputy turned his head around again, he caught Adam darting from the shadows and grab Misty's arm. The boy quickly led his girlfriend and the obstinate one back to the safety of the barn.

CJ shook his head. Adam's quick action was utterly foolish. If anything, it was successful too. Minutes later, the four men appeared again. The aluminum-sided cases seemed heavy since it took one man on each end to carry them. However, Lucas struggled mightily carrying the weight. Within seconds, the foursome passed in front of CJ again and disappeared around the corner of the barn.

As three vehicles sped out of the ranch yard, CJ hobbled around the corner of the barn. He noted that Brenda drove the Suburban and had all the seven girls with her. Burris drove the Explorer along with Lucas Gagnon and his mother as passengers. The last to leave was a pickup truck with two men inside.

"Bill."

"Finally, CJ. What is going on?"

"They are on the move, Bill. The Suburban has seven teenaged girls inside it. I repeat, the Suburban has the hostages."

"Noted," Crooks said. "But what about the others."

"Lucas and Hira Gagnon are in the Explorer with the big guy called Burris. Plus, the other guys are in the flatbed Dodge ranch truck trailing behind. But there is something else."

"What's that?"

"They carried out a couple of large cases too. I don't know what is inside them, but it can't be good."

"Did you see which vehicle they loaded the cases into?" Crooks asked.

"No, I did not."

"That is okay. You know, I watched everything from above. But I am curious as to who Adam ran out and grabbed?"

"Well, one of them is Misty Otten, and the other, I assume, is the missing bus driver, Naomi Wright."

"Why don't you get everyone into one of those Gators left behind and make your way back to my truck. I'll meet you there at the saddle where we will go get Eddie."

"Roger."

Crooks pulled his backpack closer, and he removed the satellite phone. When he powered the device up, the green screen came to life. Then, after a minute of waiting for the unit to acquire a satellite signal, Crooks called Brit. As the connection registered, he overheard an ATV roar down the road toward the east.

A few seconds later, the phone rang, and Brit promptly answered. Crooks quickly gave his buddy the vehicles' description and confirmed that the squad could see live positioning feeds from the hidden GPS beacons. Brit confirmed that three transponders were now moving south along 33-Mile road toward Casper. Additionally, Brit reported that his outfit was within the county's airspace. They would intercept the clan within the next five minutes and strike the compound.

Crooks then made another call before he placed the phone back inside his backpack and left. After emerging from the drainage, he lifted his rifle again and looked through the infrared scope. In the saddle of the pass, he spotted two people sitting inside the Gator while two others neared the crest of Grummond Hill. Crooks thought he heard a faint voice call out, but it was hard to differentiate the sound from the wind, which had picked up strength over the last hour. But then, he saw a man stand up carefully. Then, with the assistance of the other two people, he began to descend off the precipice.

About ten minutes later, Crooks walked up to the Gator and spotted me sitting in the front seat. He stopped and removed his backpack, and dug inside it. Then Crooks produced his satellite phone and pressed a button to make a call. After a brief greeting with the other party, Crooks handed me the device.

"I think you need to take this call, Eddie. Your wife has some news for you."

* * *

36

Thursday, January 31, 2013

Eight miles west of Midwest, Wyoming

3:05 p.m.

Hope and I had long since finished our lunch and had said goodbye to my wife, Tracy, at the café in Edgerton. However, once we climbed into my unit, Hope remained silent. We had already traversed Highway 387 back to Midwest, and at the junction, I headed west. I now drove west of Interstate 25 onto Smokey Gap Road. I was impressed with Hope since she hung on every word of the story. However, I hadn't seen her take a single note. Instead, she nodded her head and kept eye contact with me that informed me she understood.

Hope interjected only once after lunch when she inquired about the baby. I informed her that Tracy birthed not one daughter but twins.

I returned to the story and finished my lengthy narrative before crossing the cattle guard to the dirt road. Hope looked up and noted the same bullet-riddled signage for County Road 115 that I described earlier. Then the hood of my department Blazer nosed over the hill, and I came to a stop a hundred or so yards later.

"Is this where it all happened?" Hope asked.

I shook my head. "No, not really. But if you look to your right, you will see the Otten place where Misty lived."

"Her dad is Steve, right? So he and his wife still live there?"

I nodded. "Yep, Steve and Rhonda still reside at the place. Oh, before I forget, Rhonda has not suffered another resurgence of cancer, if you were wondering?"

"I was, thank you."

I put the Blaze transmission into drive resumed heading westward. I pointed out for Hope the red rock rim in the distance and explained that the area was known as Hole in the Wall where Butch Cassidy and the Sundance Kid once hung out. I also pointed to the Big Horn Mountains to the north.

"It is a strangely beautiful country out here, even if it makes you feel so lonely," Hope observed.

I nodded in agreement. "Yep, it is lonely at that. You could drive for three hours due west of here and not hit another town. But, maybe that is why I like out here and living in the Salt Creek community."

Hope furrowed her eyebrows and then asked, "do you have some indelible dislike for others? Is that why you've stayed here so long?"

I shook my head. "No, I enjoy people. I stayed because I belong to something out here that is larger than myself."

Hope nodded that she understood, yet, in the moments that followed, she remained reticent.

Not long afterward, I pulled over to the faint two-track trail I followed eleven years prior. The powerlines no longer remained, though a few remnant wooden poles lined out to the south.

"This is where I found the corsage and the path I followed that evening to the Gagnon place." Then I pointed to the twin sentinels in the distance. "Over there is Grummond Hill where I holed up that night."

Hope nodded silently, but I could tell she mused about something.

"I know you have a question or two, so why don't you ask?" I offered.

Hope let out a small sigh. "I don't know, Eddie. The whole story seems like something out of a Tom Clancy novel. You know the 'secret' paramilitary group and the mysterious happenings at the ranch. I can't fathom something of that nature happening here, and nobody saw it coming. Besides that, I don't recall anything of the kind hitting the news wire?"

I smiled at Hope. "There are plenty of things that our government hides from us civilians daily. We take it for granted that everything the government tells us is the gospel truth, but they lie."

I paused to allow Hope to dwell on my conjecture. Then I added, "I like Clancy's novels, by the way, but I assure you that it all did happen as I retold. Indeed, there was a group of radicals that called themselves Early Dawn."

Hope shook her head in doubt.

I continued. "to answer your question, yes, they were here, but there are others, you know? For instance, in Elberton, Georgia, you can find a collection of runestones erected in the late '70s. Etched onto the monoliths are decrees similar to Early Dawn's mission regarding the depopulation of the Earth. So is Early Dawn connected to the monument somehow? Perhaps, but I don't want to know."

Hope started to ask a question but stopped. However, I could see from her facial expression that there were plenty of additional questions yet to follow.

Finally, she asked, "didn't you and CJ get into trouble for going against the Sheriff's instruction to leave the Gagnon's alone?"

I laughed while I nodded. "We did, initially, of course. But a few days afterward, some Feds showed up to debrief us, and then they talked our former boss, and then our records became expunged of any wrongdoings on our part."

Hope continued to look at me skeptically, but then an idea popped into my head. I took my cowboy hat off and placed it crown down on the dashboard, and then I pulled down my collar.

"Take a look at this scar on my neck," I instructed.

Hope leaned over and looked closely at my skin. She quickly made out twin burn scars that refused to fade. Instead, the marks still held a purple hue to them.

When she sat back, I explained, "that is where they tasered me. But I could show you the bullet scar in my shoulder too?"

Hope shook her head. "No, I believe you." But after a short pause, she asked, "so who were the Gagnon family in reality?"

I drew in a deep breath and exhaled it slowly. "It is a great question. Unfortunately, it turned out that Liam Gagnon died about a year before this incident. However, his wife, Hira, who was also a virologist, continued their work."

"How did he die?"

"Well, when the strike team went into the compound, they found an underground bunker complete with a laboratory. According to the notes left behind, Liam died while experimenting with a virus of some kind. Don't ask me specifics because I don't understand the science behind it all."

Hope nodded. "Don't worry; I won't ask you. But they did get caught, right?"

"Yes, they did. First, a separate response team intercepted the convoy arresting Lucas, his mother, and the three men. Then a few days later, Robbie Lepsis was nabbed too."

"Good." Hope then cracked a small smile. "I think you owe your friend, Bill Crooks, a bunch."

I smiled in return. "Yes, but I added this chapter to a growing list of Bill helping me." Then I thought of something else. "But the whole episode makes me a little wary though when I think about it."

"Why is that, Eddie?"

"I don't know, Hope. Maybe it is just my imagination, but I fear this sort of thing is only the beginning. Considering how easy it was for a group like Early Dawn to tinker with an infectious disease, imagine what a nation-state could do by throwing their full weight behind weaponizing a virus?"

Hope looked at me inquisitively, yet she asked, "do you think something you are describing could happen without tipping off some intelligence agency?"

"I do, and here is why: 9/11 didn't happen out of the blue. The United States government not only knew about Bin Laden's intention of attacking our country, but they failed to share information. If anything over the last twelve years, it seems that county, state, and federal departments are tighter lipped about info sharing than ever before."

"I suppose you intend to change the culture now that you are Sheriff?"

"I do."

Hope turned and looked out her door window once again. I inherently knew that I tend to drag conversations on ad nauseam, so I let the silence alone.

Out of nowhere, Hope asked, "what about the teenage girls? Were they rescued as well?"

I nodded. "Yep. The teens suffered from some brainwashing too. I am sure it took a whole lot of counseling to get those kids squared away."

We sat silently again in the cab for a minute or two. Then, I started the motor to the Blazer again and made a three-point turnaround. As we pulled away, Hope turned her head toward me and asked, "so how is it that neither the three bad guys nor your friend, Bill Crooks, never spotted you up on that hill? I can't figure that one out."

I chuckled. "Ya, that was something. But the ledge I laid on hid me perfectly from below. But I didn't know that the reflective blanket also concealed my body heat from Crooks's infrared scope. So, luckily for me, when I heard that cow elk dart below me, I poked my head out to see what made the noise. That is when my friend saw me."

"I see. But where was your friend, Christian Mercy, during the ordeal?. From the sounds of things, he had connected himself to CJ's hip."

I guffawed. "Well, it was a little odd, I openly admit. But Christian was visiting family members near Riverton at the time."

"Where is Christian now?"

I rubbed my jaw and confessed, "I don't know. About two years ago, Christian ventured into the Northern Mexico mountains to run with the legendary Tarahumara tribe. He did so after receiving an invitation to race an ultramarathon alongside the world's greatest runners. But then, a month later, CJ received a letter stating that Christian intended to stay a while and learn all the people's running secrets."

Hope nodded. "I see. I am sure it is a perfect place for a runner like him."

I nodded in agreement.

When we reached the cattle guard, I turned onto the entrance ramp that took us back to Casper on the interstate. I kept to myself, mostly, because once again, I felt like I talked too much. But then Hope asked the one question follow-up I'd long expected.

"Where are Misty and Adam now, and are they okay?"

I smiled. "I was wondering when you were going to ask. Yes, the kids were physically fine. But both Adam and Misty reported they received injections of an unknown substance during their captivity."

"Did they get checked out by a doctor, I mean?"

"Yes, but without any information about the substance in the shot, their bloodwork nonetheless didn't reveal any foreign material."

I momentarily paused, then I continued. "After graduation, Adam went to Laramie and attended the University of Wyoming. Misty joined him two years later, and then Adam finished his master's degree while Misty attained her bachelor's. They got married five years ago and have a child."

Hope narrowed her eyes. "Where do they live?"

"In Midwest, of course," I said. "We take care of one another in the community, and now, they do their part by teaching at the school."

Hope nodded. "Of course, though I suspected that outcome."

By the time we arrived back at the Sheriff's Department headquarters, I had recalled one of Hope's initial questions earlier that morning. So when I parked the Blazer in my reserved spot, I shut off the engine and turned my body to face Hope.

"You asked me this morning about why I selected CJ as my Undersheriff. Well, CJ is a great friend, and he did go way beyond the call of duty to find me and save those kids out at the Gagnon place."

"Why did you then?"

"It is simple: Cory Jackson is a good man and the best law officer I've ever known. I don't need any other reason to promote him. I think he's done more than enough to deserve it."

Hope thought about my last comment for a while, and then she replied, "maybe the world could use a little more of men like CJ and you who honor one another."

"Thank you for the compliment," I said. Then I pointed toward heaven, "but the glory is never mine. It is His. I only follow God's plan."

After each of us stepped out of the Blazer, we met face-to-face behind the vehicle. Hope pointed to a small BMW parked in one of the many visitor's reserved spaces, and I followed alongside her.

When she reached her car, I stopped Hope, and she turned around.

"I don't know what kind of story you will write, but my prayer is that it puts that fine community I belong to in a good light. After all the ups and downs in the Salt Creek area, I think someone taking note of how they succeed in taking care of one another would do some great good. Don't you think?

Hope nodded. "I think it will as well. Believe it or not, I kind of like the place now that I know more about the people behind the incredible history."

She turned and unlocked her car with her key fob. Then Hope flashed another smile toward me. "I tell you what; I promise to give you the first read of the article, and I will welcome your suggestions. Is that a deal?"

I thrust out my right hand, and Hope grasped it to shake on the arrangement.

"It is a deal. Now, I want you to have a safe trip home and don't become a stranger. You are welcome here anytime you please."

Hope nodded. "Maybe I will come back for Salt Creek Days this August?"

I grinned in return. "Okay, I'll see you then."

THE END

AFTERWARD AND ACKNOWLEDGEMENTS

The primary setting of the story, west of Midwest, Wyoming, is fictional as well. However, the small Wyoming towns of Midwest and Edgerton depicted in this story are real. They are the last townships within the Salt Creek Oil Field that once held the World's Largest Light Oil Producing Field title.

Another truth is that Midwest High School was the first high school in the United States to host and play a nighttime football game under a lighted field. Additionally, the first paved road in Wyoming began in Casper and ended in Midwest.

Salt Creek Days mentioned in this work is an actual community-wide annual event in Midwest and Edgerton scheduled on the second weekend in August.

Lastly, the Salt Creek Oilfield continues to produce millions of barrels of high-grade crude. In many respects, the Salt Creek Oilfield is mainly responsible for the growth of the city of Casper along with the State of Wyoming. Indelibly, the oil from this small region continues to fuel this nation.

Photos: The cover photo portrays the junction of Highways 259 and 387 in Midwest. The oil derrick has long served to remind everyone of the past, even as history dawns into a new future. The photo of the author depicts him sitting on the porch of his childhood home in Midwest.

The author thanks his wife, Nancy, for her continual support while he lives out his dream of writing more novels such as this one.

Finally, the author invites readers to follow his website for news related to upcoming book releases and ordering of published novels. See phillemaitreauhor.com

OTHER BOOKS BY THE AUTHOR
BITING WIND: A Salt Creek Novel
SALT CREEK: A Novel

Phil LeMaitre is a former resident of Midwest, Wyoming, and graduated from Midwest High School in 1986. LeMaitre is a 29-year active-duty veteran of the U.S. Air Force and now serves as a Christian Life Coach. This work is his third novel with *Salt Creek: A Novel* and *Biting Wind: A Salt Creek Novel* preceding it. The author lives in Florida with his wife and their three youngest children.